NEW WORLD
IN THE
MORNING

New World in the Morning

in the Morning

A Novel

STEPHEN BENATAR

Cover design by Gabriela Sahagun

ISBN: 978-1-5040-0804-4

Distributed by Open Road Distribution
345 Hudson Street
New York, NY 10014
www.openroadmedia.com

For John and Pauline Lucas.

New World
in the
Morning

1

My assistant had gone to lunch so I myself was serving. It was a Saturday but there was only one customer. She had been browsing for maybe twenty minutes and I had been watching her for maybe nineteen. At last she brought a fruit bowl to the counter.

"Nine pounds fifty," I said, smiling, peeling off the sticker. She looked as good close to as from a distance.

"This place is rightly named," she said.

"Thank you. To be honest I wasn't sure. I've sometimes wondered if it weren't a bit twee." *Treasure Island*, scoring a narrow victory over *Now Voyager*, which might have been still more challengeable.

"Then you're its proprietor?"

"You look surprised."

She hesitated. "I somehow expect the owners of shops like this to be dusty old gentlemen."

"Why?"

"Because as a child I was always enchanted by junk shops and it seemed that the men who owned them . . . " She broke off. "But perhaps that wasn't tactful?"

"What?"

"Junk shops."

"Why not? What else could you call them?"

"Oh. Many things. A cornucopia. An Aladdin's cave." She spread her hands. "A treasure island."

"A junk shop."

"Right."

We laughed.

"And of course," she said, "one man's junk is another man's joy."

"Unquestionably."

"Surprising, perhaps, I didn't go in for it myself, this line of business. As I say, I spent so much time . . . and so much pocket money . . . We lived in Camden Town. It was a good area for junk shops."

"And dusty old gentlemen."

"Yes."

"Plus an interesting place to grow up generally? Regent's Park and the Zoo. Theatres, cinemas, museums." I added museums mainly to impress her.

She nodded. "How long have you lived here?"

"My whole life."

"This must also have been a good place to grow up in. Country and sea. Enviable to spend your childhood by the sea."

"The grass invariably being greener?"

"Well, maybe. But for instance . . . are you a swimmer? I mean, a proper swimmer?"

"Yes."

"I thought you might be." She sounded wistful.

"Are you a dancer?"

That was a crazy thing to say. But she seemed to release me from my inhibitions.

"A dancer? Why?"

"I don't know exactly. Something to do with the way you move. The kind of aura you give out. The clothes you're wearing."

"Are these the clothes that dancers nowadays wear in Deal?" In fact it was merely a cream silk blouse and a black skirt, very simple and well cut, undoubtedly expensive. Her beads, her low-heeled shoes, her shoulder bag; they too were black. The effect of colour came almost entirely from her hair, lustrous and shoulder-length and tawny, and from her eyes which were a strikingly beautiful green.

"That isn't fair," I said. "Sometimes it's very difficult to pin down an impression. Was I nowhere close?"

"You were exceedingly close."

"Really?"

"I'm an interior decorator."

"Ah, yes. Of course. I can see how exceedingly close."

She smiled. "My mother saw *The Red Shoes* before I was born and because she enjoyed it so much named me after Moira Shearer. Coincidentally, as well, my colouring was similar."

I gravely nodded my approval. I said: "I always wanted life to imitate the movies. Are you successful?"

"I do the work I like, at any rate. The same as you. And yes. Without false modesty I would say I was successful." She handed me a ten-pound note. By now I'd wrapped the bowl in tissue.

"Aren't you going to haggle? People often do."

"Not on this occasion," she said. "The first time I go anywhere I always behave *beautifully*."

I experienced an absurdly quixotic impulse to return the ten pounds and to make her a present of the thing. I really did feel tempted—and afterwards wished I had done it. But, anyhow, I knocked off one-pound-fifty.

"That's very kind," she said. "It's a gift for the friend I'm staying with. She's going to be delighted."

"Then you're only on a visit?"

"Yes. But haven't I picked the right weekend?" She glanced behind her through the window.

I agreed that she had.

"Especially as I hope it's going to be the first of many. I've been seriously thinking of taking one of those small houses in Silver Street."

"Oh, excellent."

"Thank you. I find it a fascinating quarter, down there by the front. Easy to believe it was the thriving haunt of smugglers."

"'Five and twenty ponies trotting through the dark—brandy for the parson, baccy for the clerk . . . '" I laughed. "Never anyone like Kipling."

"No," she said.

It was friendly rather than committed.

"He also," I added, "wrote my all-time favourite piece of poetry."

"Did he? I remember how the camel got his hump and how the—"

"*If*," I said.

"Your all-time favourite? We did that at school. Not much of it has stuck. Oh, *yes*! 'You'll be a man, my son.'"

Again, I didn't mind the hint of mockery. "If pressed, I reckon I could still recite the bulk of it."

"Perhaps next time you'll give me a performance?"

"I'll start rehearsing."

"Well, it's been good to meet you, Mr . . . ?"

"Groves. Sam Groves."

"I'm Moira Sheffield." If the bowl hadn't been cradled in her right arm, I felt we might have shaken hands. "I think I must've rediscovered my natural habitat! I told Liz I'd be away ten minutes!"

When she'd gone I likened her departure to the flight of some rare bird whose sleek, exotic plumage had momentarily lit up the shop. But if this were indeed her natural habitat, and she proposed to buy a house here, wasn't it likely that one of these days she'd come flying back? *Next time*, she had said. I was always chatting to my customers—one of the nice things about a life in secondhand goods—but I couldn't recall a single encounter which had given me more pleasure.

2

After a slack lunchtime we grew busy again. Spring had come. None too soon; April nearly over. People seemed readier to spend. Several times I stood in our doorway and was mesmerized by that glittering expanse at the end of the road. I smelt the tang of seaweed. Gulls were soaring and screaming. I thought the houses above the beach would all be looking white and clean, as if anticipating towels and swimwear hanging from their balconies. A woman went by in a summer dress. This seemed premature but I enjoyed looking at her and could readily sympathize with the urge to cast off winter clothing. A lot of passers-by smiled at me, although I believed there wasn't one of them I knew. I wondered if you ever got this reaction in places where the weather was more settled. Southern California, say? I had frequent dreams of escape to Southern California. California dreaming.

I myself felt happy. It was a sense of well-being which stayed with me all afternoon. Was still there when I arrived home.

As usual, on hearing the gate, Susie ran round from the back, panted and jumped up, wagged her mongrel tail, rolled over and waited to be tickled. Often my response was pretty perfunctory but tonight I squatted down and really fussed her. Asked about her day, told her a bit about my own. And as sometimes happened at such moments her lips parted and she truly appeared to be smiling. We stayed like this for several minutes and I enjoyed the sensation of being close to the moist earth and of smelling its freshness, of being able to squat for so long without strain, of seeing the clean strong line my thighs presented in their newly laundered jeans, of seeing too the way my hands and fingernails looked good against the dog's white fur; noting how the brown leather of my right-hand loafer, despite the time so often spent in attic and in cellar, still had a satisfying gloss. I enjoyed also my awareness of the bottle of Burgundy and the bunch of yellow roses I'd set beside me on the path.

The front door opened. "I was beginning to think I must've been mistaken," said my wife.

"Hello, sweetheart. No. Just a spot of heavy petting."

"I can see. D'you want me to go away?"

"What do *you* say, Susie?"

Following a moment of distraction Susie merely put her head back and went on grinning. Junie said absent-mindedly: "Who loves her master then? I know it isn't ladylike to inquire but are those roses meant for me?"

"Yes. So long as you'll come to have your tummy tickled."

She didn't do that, precisely, but as she gathered up the flowers and wine she exclaimed over both of them. I rose to my full height, then bent again and kissed her.

"I love you, Junie Moon."

Briefly she rested her head against my chest. I couldn't remember now if those five words, for twenty years my catchphrase, were taken from the title of the movie or from some amateur stage revival. Whichever, we hadn't seen it. But even at sixteen she'd been softly rounded and moon-faced and if she wasn't quite so dewy-eyed and misty any more, having herself these days two children who weren't so very far off sixteen, she was still plump and pearly-skinned, with hair which by turning prematurely grey enhanced that opalescent look.

"I love you, Samuel Groves."

The one endearment triggered off the other. Unfailingly.

After a minute we went inside the house—the three of us—into the living room; I settled in my usual chair and Junie poured us both a drink. This was also a part of the ritual. "How's it been today?" she asked.

"It's been good. The sun made such a difference. This morning I finished turning out that house I told you about."

"Any exciting finds?"

"Yes, quite. One or two nice dresses dating back to the twenties. They'd fall apart, though, if you ever tried to clean them. Some fairly good china. A first edition of *The Cruel Sea*."

"What's that?"

"Novel. They made a film of it. Oh, and a pleasant woman came in at lunchtime. Interior decorator from London. About our own age. Plans to buy a second home here."

"In what way pleasant?"

"Easy to talk to, I suppose."

"Married?"

When I shook my head she inquired how I knew.

"No wedding ring."

"My, my! Aren't we becoming observant in our old age!"

"*She* thought I looked young."

"What made her say that?"

"Oh, she said she expected the owner of a junk shop to be venerable and dusty."

"The main thing is: was she a good customer?"

Was that the main thing? In any case, not certain why, I upped the profit on her patronage.

"Thirty pounds?" exclaimed Junie. "Not bad. What did she buy?"

"Several things but principally a bowl. Present for the friend she was staying with."

"Boyfriend?"

"No. Some woman."

"Perhaps she doesn't like men?"

I stared at her. This seemed so totally out of character. It was also distinctly irritating. "Why the hell should you think that?"

"I honestly don't know." She, too, seemed disconcerted.

9

"Just because she's in her mid-thirties, unmarried, and happening to spend a few days with a woman friend of hers ..."

"I agree. I wish I hadn't said it." She stood up. "I must look at the potatoes."

And the ironic thing was that it had been far more my own type of remark. I remembered how Junie had recently surprised me by saying, in the company of friends, "Oh, these men! They think if a woman isn't married by forty she must be either lesbian or ugly! They simply won't believe she might prefer to lead her own life, not be weighted down by her commitments!"

Until then I hadn't realized that Women's Lib had so much as trickled underneath our door. Also, it was the first time I remembered Junie having used the word 'lesbian' or even, whilst employing its new meaning, 'gay'. Mike and Sandra, too, had seemed slightly taken aback. But times were changing and it was inconceivable that even Junie—or Sandra—should remain untouched.

Yet it hadn't become a problem. Thank God. When we'd arrived back at the house I'd asked Junie if *she* ever felt weighted down by her commitments. There'd been scarcely any pause. "Oh, darling, I was talking in the abstract! It was only that Mike was sounding so smug, I just couldn't let it go!"

It had remained a little disconcerting—and I hadn't much enjoyed our evening anyway, might actually have been teetering on the brink of a depression—but unexpectedly, in the end, it had proved to be all right.

And tonight, in any case, I knew well enough that Moira Sheffield wasn't gay. I could recall the way she'd looked at me.

Instinctively, my head turned towards a set of shelves. This was taken up mostly by books and a CD player but I stretched across and pulled out our earliest photograph album. I opened it three pages in, found a double spread commemorating my sporting achievements when I'd been eighteen. That was the year I'd left school; the year before we'd married. There were pictures of Sam Groves, bowler, batsman and wicketkeeper; Sam Groves, centre-forward; Sam Groves on the diving board; Sam Groves in the boxing ring—with arm upraised to show he was a champ. In each of them you saw either a grinning or else a grimly determined fair-haired giant; healthy, handsome, unstoppable. Poised to win cups, set records, defeat the world.

It all seemed such a long time back. Another life. Yet tormentingly close as well: practically within feel, within smell, within earshot. In and out of present-tense immediacy. Eighteen years ago. Midway.

And really I hadn't changed that much. My hair was hardly any thinner; my stomach, thanks to almost daily sit-ups, remained firm. A few laughter lines; light creases on the brow; no apparent middle-age spread. I was a man now, of course, not a stripling. But essentially I hadn't changed.

I was unaware of Junie's return until I realized she was standing beside me. I closed the album with a snap.

She smiled. "You look as if I'd caught you out."

"What nonsense!"

"Would you like another drink?"

She replenished my glass. I said: "But you haven't told me yet about *your* day. And where have the children got to? This house sounds suspiciously quiet."

"Ah. Matt's still sitting in the garden working on his project. Panic stations: it has to be handed in on Monday—*and* before assembly— somebody rang to remind him! And Ella decided to spend the night at Jalna. She went off after lunch."

"And what about their mum?"

"Well, as for me . . . " I got the impression that she sounded nervous.

"Yes?"

"Well, as for me, I began on the spare bedroom!"

"What!"

She nodded. "I got the wallpaper stripped off, sanded down the woodwork, put undercoat on the door and skirting boards. I didn't get so far as the window because it was growing late and I had to start the supper."

"But . . . ?"

"It must've been the sunshine or something. I felt like it. You don't mind, do you? I was hoping you'd be pleased."

Pleased? I was certainly surprised. The decorating had always been my province; not the choosing but the actual work. I'd been planning to embark on that particular bedroom the following Tuesday evening.

Yet on the other hand . . . It wasn't that I lived for colour schemes and renovation.

"Yes, of course I'm pleased." I felt there wasn't enough conviction in my tone. I tried again. "*Very* pleased! Tell me, though. Whatever happened to Baby June?"

There was a ritualistic answer to that one as well.

"Oh, something rather horrible!"

She laughed.

"You know, I really quite enjoyed myself. Sang lots of songs, thought lots of thoughts, listened to the radio a bit. Was almost sorry when it was time to put on the supper, take a lightning-quick bath, and make myself all fresh and gorgeous for my lord and master."

My lord and master: it seemed a long time since I'd last heard that.

"*Indescribably* gorgeous," I said.

"You know I never contradict!"

"I love you, Junie Moon."

"I love you, Samson Groves."

That was a frequent minor variation. Samuel and Samson were fairly interchangeable.

3

Ella not being at supper, Matt was given her share of the wine—which, even when added to his own, still wasn't much. So naturally, if only as a question of form, he lodged his brief complaint.

Matt was our twelve-year-old, large-boned, darkly blond, favouring myself, whereas Ella, at fifteen, took after Junie. In fact, Matt was so like me at the same age the resemblance could sometimes make me wince; and at such moments I often experienced a sharp longing for my mother—adored, adoring mother—who'd died of cancer a few days before my thirteenth birthday. He had my mother's brown eyes, along with the freckles which, again, I myself hadn't inherited.

Now at table he turned on me that soft and trustful look and I knew at once there was something which he wanted.

"Dad?"

"No. Whatever it is, young man . . . no!"

He grinned. "After supper *will* you help me with my project?"

I'd forgotten. Before we sat down I had said *We'll see.* "Oh, you nuisance! Yes, I suppose so. If I can't get out of it."

"Thanks, Pop. You're a good bloke."

"For the moment, perhaps."

"No, no, for ever."

It gave me a warm feeling, being a good bloke for ever, even if he did conspicuously inspect his fingers to let us see that they were crossed.

While his mother and I were having coffee I told him to run to a nearby shop to buy a couple of Aeros and two bags of crisps—for Junie had shaken her head with regard to herself—so that we'd then have something to nibble on as we laboured in his bedroom.

"Can I get a Coke as well?"

"*May* I?" I spun one of the coins I'd been about to hand him. "If it's tails—yes."

It landed on the carpet with the Queen uppermost.

Blithely disregarded.

"Thanks, Dad." He gave my cheek a hasty kiss. "We'll have a sort of midnight feast."

"Just so long as it finishes at least three hours *before* midnight!"

His bedroom was as untidy as ever but definitely appealing: his divan with its row of brightly coloured cushions, the walls covered with travel posters, postcards, magazine cutouts—mainly of sports stars—and with pictures of animals he'd drawn himself. Books and records filled not only his shelves but overflowed onto his desk; also onto the carpet where they mingled, much at risk, with cars and tennis balls and a seaplane in the process of construction. It was a junior, domesticated version of a treasure island, very father-friendly. I sat on the floor, my feet tucked under me, and Matt drew up his comfortable but battered armchair. In his lap a few sheets of loose-leaf rested on a boys' adventure annual, circa 1970.

It was one of my own, which I had relinquished to him some eighteen months before.

"Now then," I prompted. 'The six people whom I'd most like to change places with.' Six seems rather a lot, doesn't it?"

"Well, I suppose we've had a month to do it. Too long really. With only a week, I wouldn't have forgotten."

"Mmm," I said. "Well, maybe."

"In any case, I've done five."

"Who?"

"Greg Rusedski, Alan Shearer, Darren Gough. David Duchovny and Noel Gallagher. But I couldn't think of much to write about Noel Gallagher."

Alan Shearer reminded me of Moira Shearer. We'd hang onto Alan Shearer, even if we dispensed with all the rest.

"It doesn't seem very varied. Three sportsmen. Two bods out of show business."

"Yes, but different branches of sport and different branches of show business. And no one said it needed to be varied."

"But no politicians . . . doctors . . . women . . . "

"What do I know about politicians—or doctors—Miss Martin said she wanted it to come from the heart. And the girls will probably write about the women: odds-on it's Mariah Carey, Demi Moore or the Spice Girls. Yuk!" He gave an imitation of somebody being sick.

"Yes, but if all of you are writing more or less about the same people, isn't it going to be extremely boring for Miss Martin?"

"That's her problem."

"Yours, too, in a way—if you're aiming to rise above the common herd."

"Listen, Dad. I've done those five. They're fine. I don't want to change them, I haven't any time."

I looked at his face and saw how obdurate he was. I decided not to push. "Okay, then. So the sixth has got to be a real humdinger!"

"Gosh! How you keep up with all the modern lingo!"

"Quiet, you." While we searched for candidates we opened our bags of crisps and munched companionably. He offered me his can of Coke; I shook my head. "Do these people have to be alive?"

"Oh, Dad, I'm not going to write about Julius Caesar or Napoleon. Or William Shakespeare. Or Robert Louis Stevenson. Forget it."

"How about Ghandi?"

"No thanks."

"But with all of history to choose from, can't you see your list seems a little . . . Impoverished?"

"She said from the heart."

I had a burst of inspiration.

"How about Superman?"

"What? Oh, for Pete's sake, Dad! Get real!"

"Well, wouldn't you change places with Superman? I would. And I bet she didn't exclude people out of the comic strips and fiction."

He looked at me pityingly. "I wouldn't change places with Superman. Superman is creepy. He's a pain."

"Christ! You're difficult to please."

"Watch it," he said more happily. "I'll tell Mum!"

We settled back into ruminative crunching. I said: "I hate to feel restricted, though."

"Then don't."

"Want to find the really perfect example."

He seemed gratified by the degree of importance I was attaching to it. Held out the Coke again. I accepted. I think we both felt very close.

"Hey, I've got it! A fellow, Matt, that no one else will think of. Do him justice and you're guaranteed to shine."

"Who is it, then? You?"

"Well, that hadn't actually occurred to me."

This time Matt was puzzled by my suggestion rather than outright dismissive.

"Theseus? You mean, the bloke that killed the Minotaur? What makes you think I'd want to be like him?"

"Oh, lots of reasons."

My son looked sceptical.

"Firstly, young Matthias, he rid the world of the greatest evil then hanging over it. He saved hundreds of lives. Thousands. Maybe millions if you bring it up to date . . . the cumulative effect of unborn children . . . "

"Dad, it's a myth! Theseus is a myth! But you certainly do believe in things, don't you—I mean, once you get going?"

He sounded half admiring, half uneasy. I ignored it. I gave him a moment to relate this myth to modern times: to think in terms of nuclear warheads and the like, of tyrants such as Pol Pot and Saddam Hussein. I hoped he would make his own connections.

"Secondly, he delivered people from other kinds of oppression."

I thought Nelson Mandela might come into his mind. Or Martin Luther King. Mother Theresa. Albert Schweitzer. He probably hadn't heard of Dag Hammarskjold or Pope John XXIII.

"You make him sound like Jesus."

I decided to ignore this, too. It was no part of my aim to encourage irony on such a subject.

"Thirdly, he had a marvellously romantic love affair. When he set off to kill the Minotaur, Ariadne held the thread which would later guide him out of the labyrinth, even though by doing so she was betraying her own family."

I paused again, endeavouring to remember all the great twentieth-century love stories in which a woman provided similarly heroic assistance. Surely there had to be a plethora.

But I could come up only with *Spellbound. Pandora and the Flying Dutchman.* And Jean Kent throwing herself in the path of a bullet intended for Stewart Granger.

"Fourthly, it seems to me that right from the moment he started getting ready to go off in search of his father he led an absolutely golden existence. Full of adventure and achievement and a steady sense of purpose!"

"Imagine going off in search of your father!"

"But what do you think of it?"

"Well, I don't know. Just Superman in shorts and sandals . . . tunic and sandals."

My incipient impatience began to increase. "Matt, I simply don't believe you'd choose not to be like him! And why the heck should he be creepy? Oh, forget the movies, can't you?"

Yet he remained indecisive.

"Here," I said, "pass over the paper and the biro!"

That made up his mind. He surrendered them at once. He also handed me the annual.

Then thoughtfully unwrapped his Aero and with a mouth full of chocolate began to cut out the shot-putter from an empty packet of Scott's Porridge Oats—to the detriment, no doubt, of his mum's sharpest pair of scissors.

4

There was still enough light to permit a pleasurable wander in the garden—Junie and I strolled hand in hand across the grass. The air felt gentle and a blackbird singing in the branches of one of our apple trees was answered, counterpointed, by a thrush. We made a tour of the estate: admired the goldfish in the fishpond and the splendour of a clump of daffodils upon a bank; the tiny buds of blossom that were now appearing overhead: we had pear and cherry trees as well as apple. It was a beautiful half-acre, bounded by a high wall of weathered brick. We sat on a wooden bench in a small natural arbour, stretched out our legs, looked back in the declining light at the soft red brick of the house itself.

"You know, I never take this place for granted," said Junie. "Do you? That's one of the things I was thinking about today. How fortunate we are."

"Especially when you consider what's going on in other parts of the world. Genocide, oppression, torture . . . Earthquakes, floods."

I should have been a moralist.

Clearly, already was!

"Yes, but I wasn't meaning that. I meant—without comparison."

She gave my hand a squeeze. "Remember how we so much liked this house that we used to make detours on our way home from school, simply to look at it? It wasn't grand or anything but I just knew any family must be happy here. At peace with themselves. I imagined flag-stones on the kitchen floor, rows of jams and pickles in the larder, breakfast in the garden, flowers on a polished table in the hall. Sun-light filling every room." She paused, in wonderment. "And in some ways it's been even better than that. For instance I hadn't reckoned on that bright red Aga: practically the hub of the whole house . . . "

"You hadn't reckoned on the house at all. Whoever would have thought we'd end up in a rectory?" I smiled, wryly. "And without my having to take holy orders?"

Indeed, the whole thing had seemed extraordinary. (Miraculous, said Junie.) Suddenly we'd heard that a new rectory was being built actually in the church grounds, some half a mile away; this pres-ent one would soon be up for sale. We'd known instantly that it was meant for us. Yet our utter conviction hadn't saved us from anxiety, nor obsession. We'd likened it to being in love. It was in fact more stressful. I'd never experienced such fear of ultimate frustration: there could exist no other house so wholly right for us. It was ridicu-lous how childish we had been. Well, no—not me. Junie. *Now* she had grown placid but that was only because of years of trust in my protection. *Then* she had seemed as mercurial as I myself had been stoical and strong.

Stoical, strong *and* resourceful. We went to Junie's parents; asked for help. I was in the mood to barter: an unacknowledged pact. They'd known me for three years, had all but adopted me. Groomed me, tagged me. They themselves had married young and—they said—been happy as lovebirds. Likewise they'd always claimed I had no need of university. 'Gilding the golden boy,' was what they'd called it. (Golden Boy: my epithet at school.) More honestly they could have called it, 'Risking his faithfulness.' No, they said. Better to settle down in a good job, get married, raise children, stay in Deal. The Fletcher clan was nothing if not familial.

Staunchly so.

The house belonged to the Church Commissioners, who knew

there were other parties interested and had therefore decided, finally, on a sealed bid auction.

We had no idea, of course, what our competitors were offering. We became reckless. Didn't care if we went too high. Didn't care how long it might take to pay back Junie's parents.

Pay them back, that is, the difference between the sum we'd offered and the far smaller sum which a building society had offered *us*. In order to be eligible I had hurriedly applied for a position at Lloyds Bank in the town.

The day we learnt we'd got the house should have been, as Junie said, one of the most exciting of our lives. It was only a pity I suffered from a toothache during most of it—and perhaps, too, a small bit, from reaction.

"But yes," I agreed now, "we have been *very* fortunate."

For a while we appreciated in silence what we had.

Then I prodded the grass with the tip of one shoe. "It'll soon need mowing." I hadn't cut it yet this year. "Isn't it amazing how those daffodils keep hanging on? A week ago—ten days ago—I really thought their time had come. You've got to admire their tenacity."

"Resilient," said Junie.

I laughed. "Are they resilient? All right, you've got to admire that, too."

After a further few minutes I yawned. I withdrew my hand from hers and sensuously stretched out my arms. It was an evening that induced contentment and gave a pleasant preview of approaching summer.

"You wouldn't feel like walking Susie with me?" I asked.

"Oh, that would be nice, darling, but I can't. For one thing I've got some pies in the oven: pies to take tomorrow. And for another it would mean leaving Matt on his own. I know he's quite a big boy now and that we shouldn't be away for long but all the same . . . "

"He is quite a big boy now. Do you realize it's his birthday in under a fortnight?"

"How can I forget? He gives us plenty of reminders."

"If we were Jewish he would then be fully adult." I was aware my feelings were confused.

"It's *my* birthday in about six weeks. I think I'll be fully adult, too. Oh, I'm not so sure. Maybe."

"As you know, he wants some dumbbells. If you like I'll order you the same."

"Why not take him on your walk?"

"He's just got in a bath. To celebrate completion of his project. He's been lent a Stephen King and means to have a wallow."

I called the dog and went out on my own.

5

We walked down to the sea. I found a stick for Susie to chase along the shingle and, during intervals of hurling it, tried to skim flat stones across the waves. Moonlight set a path upon the water and the sky was packed with stars. For a full minute I stood there with my head thrown back. I imagined I was Captain Kirk, commander of the starship Enterprise, now speeding boldly through the galaxies. It was fun to think of him unshakably protecting us.

"Good evening, Mr Groves."

It was Moira Sheffield. I'd been so caught up in space I gave a start.

"I'm sorry," she said. "I feel we interrupted some important metaphysical reverie."

"Yes, I was whizzing through the stars with Captain Kirk."

"Oh, in that case it was important. It's just that seeing you I didn't stop to think." She added: "But it's a small world, isn't it?"

"Not when you're looking up at the stars," smiled her companion. "Good evening," she said to me.

"Mr Groves . . . Mrs Dawlish . . . though I believe you two already know each other."

"No, no," said Mrs Dawlish, who was fortyish and pleasant-looking but, in this half-light at any rate, wholly unfamiliar. "It's only that I've been into the shop once or twice; no reason why you should remember. I'm surprised I don't come in daily—it's by far the most enthralling shop in town."

"Thank you. Yes, of course I remember you." We shook hands. It occurred to me as somewhat strange that I should be shaking hands with *her* when I had never done so with her friend.

"And by the way," she said, "I love the fruit bowl."

Then Susie came bounding back from wherever she'd been and jumped up at all three of us. I called her off sharply—and much to my satisfaction she obeyed.

"Oh, that's all right," said Miss Sheffield, bending to stroke the chastened animal. "But why Susie? I'd have thought you'd call her Patch."

"Susie's short for Black-Eyed Susan."

"Ah."

I was pleased to be discovered not totally predictable.

"Isn't it a heavenly evening!" said Mrs Dawlish. "I feel we hardly had need of our coats."

"Mr Groves is evidently a hardier type."

"Or just more reckless," I said.

"Doesn't your wife," asked Miss Sheffield, "tell you that you ought to wear a coat?"

"How do you know I've got one? A wife, that is. Or come to that—a coat?"

She laughed. "Oh, don't be difficult! I may as well reveal it: you were the subject of a spot of speculation. I said you didn't look as if you could be married. Liz said she was certain that you were."

I had wondered whether they would have spoken of me. And clearly Miss Sheffield's impression had been favourable: *D'you suppose he might be single?* I felt so gratified that—ludicrously—I began to get an erection.

"First . . . why did you think I could be single? Did I come across as queer?"

"Good heavens, no," she smiled. "Not at all. You looked too . . . "

"Young?" I interpolated.

"Let's just say, too unbowed by care and the responsibilities of family life." She, also, was sounding slightly less than serious. "Too boyish—no, that isn't right. Too happy, maybe? I'm not sure what it was; merely a feeling."

"And you, Mrs Dawlish? I must have impressed *you* as appearing to carry the world upon my shoulders?"

"He's playing with us," said Miss Sheffield. "Now that isn't nice. It's not the hallmark of a gentleman. We made ourselves vulnerable and he betrayed our trust."

"Perhaps I'm simply not as cynical as Moira," said Mrs Dawlish.

"Yes, she is cynical, isn't she?" I was aware that I was flirting; almost as blatantly as the woman in question.

"Also I think to myself," went on Mrs Dawlish, "that if a man is in his thirties and interested in women and—well, I may as well say it—as attractive as you are . . . then certainly he's married. There rests my case."

"And I suppose," said Miss Sheffield, "that if into the bargain he has a dog . . . None of it conclusive, mind, but yes I admit that gradually I might be coming round to your way of thinking. I'm going to lose my 20p."

"You had 20p riding on this?"

"And finally—most damning of all, the bit that really clinches it—he won't tell us! Now why should he be cagey?"

"Okay, I'll come clean, then."

"Well?"

"No, I'm not married."

"*Not*?" exclaimed Miss Sheffield.

"No. You win your 20p."

"Living with someone?"

"No."

"Not even that?"

"Not even that."

"Which just demonstrates, doesn't it, the truthfulness of first impressions? One shouldn't lose one's confidence."

"Well, what about *my* first impressions?" asked Mrs Dawlish, reasonably.

She didn't get an answer.

"But Mr Groves. How in heaven's name have you escaped so long?"

"*More* cynicism, Miss Sheffield?"

"Oh, but possibly it's justified. I mean—having once been married myself."

I lost my levity; gave a shrug; said nothing.

"So where does that leave me?" asked Mrs Dawlish. "I still am. Married."

"Plainly it was Mrs Sheffield," I answered, now smiling again, "who was handing out those burdens which make a person bowed! Plainly it's Mrs Sheffield who represents the kind of woman a potential husband must escape from!" Then I recognized how tactless I was being: an actual husband had already done so. I almost apologized but was frightened to compound my gaffe.

"Wrong," said the butt of all that mild disappointment. (Yet why should I feel disappointed?)

"Wrong?"

"Yes. *I* was the one who needed to escape. And, besides, you had it right before—*Miss* Sheffield; I took back my own name." She paused. "But as a way of breaking free from all such confusion—how about Moira?"

"Sam," I said, automatically.

"Yes, I know."

"And Liz," said Mrs Dawlish, "if the fact of my being not merely married, but even fairly contentedly so, doesn't altogether rule me out. At the moment I *am* a grass widow, which ought to count a little in my favour."

"Actually, I—"

"We were just filling our lungs with sea air," said Moira, "before tripping along to *The Lord Nelson* for a quick one. You wouldn't care to join us?" Even in only the moonlight—especially, perhaps, in only the moonlight—her smile was surely as entrancing as any smile of Lady Hamilton's. Her complexion looked flawless. I felt a longing to touch her skin; to brush the back of my fingers slowly up one cheek.

"Well, thank you, yes, I'd enjoy that. I—oh, hell—I haven't any money on me!" I'd given the last of my small change to Matt; had left my wallet in my jacket pocket when I'd swopped the jacket for a jumper.

"I shall treat you," she said. "Out of my winnings."

"And if we have time for any second round," said Liz Dawlish, "I shall treat you, too. But I shall have to do it, unhappily, out of nothing but the simple goodness of my heart."

"And how about you, Susie? What's yours going to be? A refreshing pint of five-star water?"

Susie had been sitting on the pebbles throughout all this. Now, as Moira spoke to her, she cocked her head inquiringly as if desperately anxious to understand, and her long white tail swept rhythmically across the stones. She was being a model dog, perfectly behaved. Moira bent a second time to stroke her.

"Good old Susie," she said, as she straightened up. "I expected you to testify for Liz!" We began to mount towards the promenade, the shingle slipping noisily away beneath our feet.

Here was my opportunity. For the retraction of a lighthearted act of derring-do which I'd performed because I'd wanted to see if I could get away with it—yes, and how it would have felt. My opportunity, after that spontaneous foray into a forbidden world (O brave new world: already having drinks bought for me, unilaterally, by two nice-looking and sophisticated women!) and into that heady kingdom of what might have been. A brief, ten-minute trespass.

But far *too* brief. Impossible to leave so soon.

So why not make it an hour? Playful rascal back to solid citizen by midnight. Contrite but forgiven. And understood. Reassured he hasn't lost his dormant—maybe atrophied—attraction.

"What's this?" I said. "Susie, star witness for the Dawlish camp! Then can't a single man who's lonely be permitted to possess a dog?"

"It truly didn't occur to me he couldn't—not at first. But subconsciously, perhaps, I still think of dogs as belonging to families. Stupid of me. I'm sorry."

"Actually she belongs to our neighbours," I told her. "They're rather elderly and sometimes I walk her for them." Gilding both the lily *and* the golden boy. It all came to me so easily. No trace of guilt; not yet, in any case. Before, it had been fun. Now, it seemed addictive.

"Our?" she repeated. "*Our* neighbours?"

26

That gave me pause. But she misread my hesitation, thought I hadn't understood the question.

"Do you still live at home, then? With your parents?"

"Oh, no, my parents are dead." Gilding be blowed: when hoping to deceive you stick closely to the truth. "My mother died when I was a boy and my father . . . " I hadn't realized I would mention this but suddenly discovered that I could. "Well, my father died just two days afterwards. From then on I was brought up by my gran."

But now I was faced with a choice: should I resurrect Granny and give my life a flavour of nobility and sacrifice—the grateful grandson honouring his debt—or should I tear away completely from the thought of apron strings (implicit, however uncritically, in the surprised tone of the question) and perhaps invent a commune: a way of living which, ideally, had always quite appealed to me . . . especially if located on some sundrenched, far-off island? And of course lodgers were another possibility—although slightly more mundane.

"Your father died just two days afterwards?" The cynical Miss Sheffield was very clearly shaken.

I kept my tone casual. "Well, they talk about people dying of a broken heart. And you never saw a husband who . . . " In fact I couldn't keep it all that casual.

"And people really do die, then, of broken hearts?" she asked after a moment, quietly.

I nodded. "Especially when assisted by the right number of aspirin."

"Oh, dear God!"

Mrs Dawlish also drew in breath.

But in the space of scarcely a minute all this had got too heavy. "Maybe," I suggested, "it wasn't quite as bad as it sounds." Which was unquestionably the biggest lie I had yet told them. "I managed to cope with it. At school. Threw myself into my studies. Into sport, as well. Became a bit of an all-rounder." Well, that was certainly true, although now I'd made it sound, practically, as if I'd *benefitted* from being an orphan.

"And then it was your grandmother who looked after you?"

"Yes. So now I look after my grandmother." There was a pause. Possibly liars, too, abhor a vacuum. "She's eighty-six years old."

She would have been, anyway. And if this were so, I'd still have been looking after her. Well, naturally. As I'd been doing—that is, as Junie and I had been doing—until about seven years earlier.

"Though may I suggest we change the subject?"

"Of course. Forgive me. I didn't mean to stir up painful memories."

Then, for a while, there wasn't much conversation at all; merely the clatter of cascading stones. But we were almost on the front. I re-attached Susie's lead. We were opposite an ice-cream parlour, in which, despite the hour's lateness, business appeared fairly brisk. Liz spoke of the holiday atmosphere. At first all our comments sounded forced but soon the easiness returned. Moira was looking out to sea. "Have we been pardoned for dragging you down from the stars? I still feel it was mean."

"Nonsense. The stars will be there anytime. But you, madam, go back to town tomorrow night."

"That was extremely gallant."

"A bit creepy, actually." I nearly said—so very nearly said—*As my son would undoubtedly be the first to point out.* "But sincere," I added, with a flush.

She smiled. "Oh, by the way, I've definitely decided to go ahead with that cottage in Silver Street."

"I thought you already had decided."

"Not completely. I finally made up my mind over lunch."

In the lamplight her red hair, in conjunction with the green scarf that matched her eyes, was one of the loveliest things I'd seen.

The red hair—the pale skin—even the dusting of freckles which I hitherto hadn't noticed.

"So when do you move in?"

My inner voice said: *Are you ready for such complications?* My inner voice answered itself immediately. *You bet I am!*

"It could be quite soon," she said, "the house being empty." Yet then it seemed she'd thought of something. "Perhaps, Sam, you'd like to take a look at it? I could do with your advice."

"Yes, I'd be pleased to."

"Do you mean that? In which case . . . well, how about a week from tomorrow?"

I had to think quickly; but though my brain often seemed to function only in slow motion, tonight it slid smoothly on castors. "A week from tomorrow would be fine."

"Or on second thoughts—how about tomorrow itself?"

I'd have given almost anything to be able to say yes.

"No, I'm sorry, I can't."

"*Next* Sunday, then."

"Right." I forced myself to play it cool but I suppose I was in the grip of a kind of fever. Practically a madness.

This wasn't the time for a reversion to solid citizenship.

This was my time for living dangerously.

6

When I got home Junie was in bed. "You two must have had a long walk!"

"No, I cheated. We went to the beach and then I felt like a beer. Spent half an hour in *The Lord Nelson*."

"Oh, nice! I'm glad you did that."

"Yes, it was good."

Almost perfect, indeed. The only thing that could have made it any better was my not having to watch Moira first—and then Liz—paying for my drinks. In prospect this had sounded quite appealing but in reality it hadn't seemed right.

No, there was a second thing which I'd initially regretted: Liz reminding Moira that life began at forty and the inference which I had naturally drawn from this. But *so what* I had managed to say to myself, after a while. Four years was nothing. I wasn't a child.

Now I ran downstairs to make our bedtime cup of tea; and sang as I waited for the kettle.

"You sounded very jolly! At first I thought it was the radio."

"I'm sorry."

"What for? It's good to hear you sing. I suppose you couldn't, by any chance, fancy a biscuit?"

"I'll get the tin." But back in the kitchen I realized that the beer had made me hungry. I cut us both a sandwich.

"Oh, what treats! How wicked!"

This was the kind of midnight feast Matt would have approved of. It was fun eating our sandwich and our slice of cake—I'd decided to go the whole hog—sipping our tea and reading our library books. In my case it was *The Shape Of Things To Come*. But I should think I read barely a dozen lines and took in the meaning of about three. I wasn't even aware that Junie had looked up from her own book and was studying me.

"Penny for them!"

"What?"

"You were miles away. I'd love to know what you were thinking."

I held up my novel. From now on I should have to be more careful.

"Merely indulging in a spot of time travel."

"And plainly enjoying yourself. It was mean of me to pull you back."

Oh, the irony! In this case so glaringly obvious but, even if it hadn't been, I had always prided myself on being alive to irony.

"Poor darling," she said. "So pathetic."

"What is?"

"You wandering off into your own little world and me pulling you back with such a bump."

"Simply to remind me of the time, what's more! Then offering me only a penny in recompense!"

But it *was* late. I went to clean my teeth. Whilst doing so I gazed critically at my reflection. I should never have eaten that sandwich, nor that piece of cake, nor those earlier crisps and chocolate. (The pints of beer had been permissible.) Starting tomorrow I must cut down on fats and sugar, say no to any snacking. I could probably lose four or five pounds in a week and four or five pounds would be sufficient.

But then I squared my shoulders and held myself erect. Oh, what the hell. Eating was one of the pleasures of life (except at those periods when I grew compulsive) and anyway I looked all right. To become obsessive over a few odd pounds—and in truth I swiftly grew obsessive over anything, health regimes, language-learning, economy drives—this could be seen as wholly life-denying, childish, negative.

Entirely out of tune with the way I was feeling at the present. And intended to feel for ever.

Carpe momentum!

For even the cleaning of one's teeth could offer you an experience to savour! I thought about toothpaste. I had never given a lot of thought to toothpaste. What was it made of, how was it coaxed inside the tube, when had it been invented? I thought about the rest of mankind cleaning its teeth, in times of peace and in times of war, sharing with me this unhymned facet of being a member of the human race. I felt warm towards the human race. How many thousands, I wondered, were spitting out into the basin at this precise moment, declaring themselves to be my brothers, uniting in the great adventure. It occurred to me I might have garnered some rare new insight, even if I couldn't at once put a name to it.

I felt warm towards the human race; warm towards my wife. When she too had been to the bathroom and switched off her lamp and murmured a drowsy, "Good night, sleep tight," turning her back towards me, I slid across and put my arm about her and nestled up close. Compliant as ever, she turned again and I levered my other arm beneath her.

"Aren't you feeling sleepy?" she asked.

"Not a bit."

"Me, I'm feeling sleepy."

"You won't do in a moment. I'm in a mood to make you sing! Every inch of you."

"That's good," she said. "And I think I know what every inch of me is going to sing."

"What?"

She gave a yawn. "*Let's Put Out The Lights And Go To Sleep.*"

Junie had a sense of humour but she wasn't generally witty. Her sally was so spontaneous and surprising, possibly as much so to herself as to me, that we got the giggles. We rolled about in utter helplessness until it really did begin to hurt, and even after that our laughter kept resurfacing. I was reminded of the lyric from another song: 'You've got a sense of humour . . . and humour is death to romance!' But Mr Berlin had it wrong; or at least in this case he had. Junie was so aroused by our merriment and by the pleasure of her own success, aroused in both its senses, that she sat up and took off her nightdress while I was still wiping away my tears. She slipped down again and I felt her rounded breasts and radiant warmth, both especially glorious on first contact, move in and settle against my chest. I let out a long and well-contented sigh.

"I wish you'd learn to sleep nude."

"It's too cold."

"Not tonight. I think summer's on the way."

"Besides. You know I don't like to be looked at."

"But that's silly. You've got a nice body."

"Podgy."

"No. It feels wonderful."

"I'm glad you think so. You feel good, as well."

In essence, we'd had this conversation often.

"In what way do I feel good?" This was, ostensibly, a new inquiry. "Explain why I feel good."

"You just do."

"But why? I know why you feel good. You're all powdery and soft and comfortable."

"Comfortable!"

"Like a peach, with its warm and fragrant bloom. Ripe deliciousness, juicy perfection. I wanna be a wasp!"

Yet the buzz I made was more like that of a bee; and the lip-smacking little nips were probably like those of no insect or animal on earth.

Junie giggled again and feigned alarm at falling prey to so resolute a sucker. Feigned anxiety, too. "But won't fruit that's ripe and juicy be getting near its sell-by date?"

"Nonsense! Never!"

"That's not the way I look at things when I'm walking round Sainsbury's."

"And not just any fruit!" I insisted. "Weren't you paying attention? I was being specific."

"Yes. I was a lovely, dusted, hothouse peach! I don't mind you being specific."

"Well, then. Specifically . . . " I began to itemize; the lyric poet might here have slipped away a little but every part I singled out received a fondle and a kiss, and Junie murmured happily with each enjoyable stopover. "Was that specific enough? Well, now it's your turn," I said.

"Oh, it's just the overall effect," she replied. "I'm like the person who says *I know what I like* but can't really give you all the reasons."

I didn't need to say that, again, this fell some way short. Miss Martin would *not* have marked it highly.

"All right, let me think now . . . Specific reasons? . . . Because you're exactly like Samson," she began, "all hard and lean and *strong*, with lovely broad shoulders and a lovely broad chest and large biceps . . . and just the right amount of body hair . . . and a beautiful thick cock . . . and, oh Lord, I *am* sorry!" She had struggled, unsuccessfully, to suppress another yawn.

At one time I'd have thought that 'cock' fell into the same category as 'lesbian' or 'gay' but I myself, in the context of bed, talked about 'tits' and 'arse' and 'cunt', and in this regard Junie had insensibly followed my lead—as she had, indeed, in most others—so that these days there was no longer the least surprise on my part . . . nor, naturally, the slightest objection. But, even so, her yawn had warned me that I ought to cut back on the talk and proceed with the action. "Any particular requests?" I asked.

"No. You choose. Anything."

"Like your back massaged?"

"Lovely. But you're doing all the work."

As usual! The thought was involuntary. I felt ashamed.

"I don't mind that. Your turn the next time."

"I can't think where you get the energy."

"Roll over."

She'd always said I had a talent for massage and, as I worked, she stretched beneath the arch formed by my thighs and burrowed down voluptuously into the mattress, sighing deeply. I kneaded and pummelled and felt my sweat breaking out. During a moment's respite I turned the lamp on and she protested only feebly. As I moved slowly down her back I glanced from time to time into the mirror on her dressing table. I derived as much excitement from the sheen of my own body and the taut look of its muscles as I did from the increasing responsiveness of hers. When I reached the base of her spine I gave her bottom a couple of tentative smacks and finding she squirmed pleasurably beneath them gradually increased their power. Eventually I asked her to turn over. I pushed her legs apart and introduced my penis.

And wondered how many millions of my brothers might be keeping me company. I rejoiced in it. Male solidarity. All those bums going up and down in unison with mine.

However, it was disappointing. I'd been inside her for maybe less than a minute—to a count of merely twenty-nine—when I found it impossible to hold back.

"I'm sorry, Junie. I'm out of practice."

"Never mind. So long as you enjoyed it. I did."

"But listen." By now I'd raised myself from the hips up. "It's really wrong—*and* sad—that we haven't made love for at least three weeks."

She smiled at me. She was pink and creamy in the lamplight. "So what are you going to do about it?"

"I don't know, I'll need to cogitate." I grinned. "Cogitation completed!"

"Good. Do you know, leaning back like that, you look all glistening and golden and masterful up there?" She ran her hands across my chest, innocently tweaking dampish curls, then stroked my upper arms and shoulders. I felt myself begin to stir in her again.

"And don't I always?"

"Always," she agreed.

"Shall I tell you the results, then?"

"Of all that careful thinking? Please."

"Gonna fuck you in the morning—fuck you in the evening—fuck you at suppertime . . . Yes, ma'am, kindly take note, ma'am. I hereby file intention of turning into the world's greatest lover."

If she had replied, "But you already are," or, "I think you're practically there," then the stirring might have strengthened into hardness. "Well, sounds all right to me," she murmured.

I withdrew. "I love you, Junie Moon."

"I love you, Samson Groves."

Then I gave her a parting kiss on the cheek and leant over and pulled out a wad of tissues. After we'd mopped up and she'd struggled into her nightdress she switched off the lamp. I turned on my side, away from her, and she snuggled against my back.

"Thank you for that," she said.

"Thank *you*, my love."

"You know what the trouble is, Sam? Most days I get so tired. By bedtime all I can do is lie here like a sackful of flour."

"Nonsense. You're a marvellous lay."

"It's sweet of you to say so, but all the same . . . Well, just wait until the children have left home and then you'll see how different it will be. Not that I'm wanting to wish any of our lives away, obviously . . . " She sighed again and I felt her long release of breath, cool, fanning my shoulder blades.

"You shouldn't have taken on that extra job today. The decorating. You'd better let me finish."

"Oh, but I told you. I find it creative. Relaxing."

"Matt won't be leaving home for six years. Six at the earliest. I'll be forty-two by then."

"What's wrong with that?" She laughed. "And besides. It'll give me plenty of time to lose weight."

"I warn you: I'm not waiting six years until our next fuck. I might just get by—with a lot of self-restraint—until the morning."

"No, you silly, I didn't mean that. I meant, until you chase me naked through the house again . . . "

"Ah . . . Good night, Junie."

"Sleep well, darling."

She turned again, and, retreating to her own side of the bed, soon settled into slumber.

7

I couldn't sleep, though—not for ages. At first I turned restlessly from side to side but then lay mainly on my back, hands beneath my head. Was Moira awake? I pictured her red hair splayed across the pillow; her slim dancer's body sprawled languorously and bare; arms stretching in sudden exuberant abandon, as she, like myself, contemplated the future and felt an irresistible urge to express something wonderful. I felt confident that if she *were* awake she'd be thinking of me—and almost as confident that if she were asleep my shadow would be pressing on her dreams. And her dreams would be in Technicolor.

I was going to be so *good*, so worthy of those dreams. A new man. Dynamic, cheerful, kind. Patient; understanding. Aware. Truly the Rock of Gibraltar that Junie sometimes called me.

Away with gluttony. Meanness. Lack of charity. Away with jealousy and fear; small-mindedness. From now on I'd be living entirely for others. The doorway to life was so blazingly obvious once you'd discovered the key; I could only feel amazed and regretful I hadn't done so sooner. But at least, thank God, it had happened while I was young. With perhaps a second allocation of thirty-six years still to look forward to.

Yet even if there wasn't, even if there was merely one of ten years . . . five, three, two . . . why, even this could prove sufficient. *The Short Happy Life of Samson Groves.*

Yes. Even one year—broken down into segments—could provide abundance.

Of course there'd have to be deception. But purely for the common good. It was through Moira that I was going to grow and blossom and bear golden fruit; through me that Moira was going to encounter love and passion and fulfilment. And Junie would awake to find an incomparably more thoughtful and devoted husband. Ella and Matt would awake to find the best damned father on record. It was as simple as that. I aimed to become the kind of dad I myself had used to dream about.

I remembered not so long after the death of my parents watching a film on television: *Down To The Sea In Ships.* The story concerned a boy of my own age—an orphan like myself—who, by the end, had discovered not simply a friend but a father-substitute. This, in the person of the young Richard Widmark, whom the lonely lad (and I) had slowly come to idealize. And, oh, the envy that I'd felt! An unremitting ache which for days—weeks—had left me with a sense of deprivation not exactly more real but somehow more insistent than the one I'd experienced a month or two earlier . . . and of course was still experiencing. In February, in my pyjamas, I had climbed out of my bedroom window, which overlooked the back garden of my grandmother's house, and stood there on the sill for fully twenty minutes, trying to find the courage to jump off.

It had remained for sometime afterwards: that insistent ache in the pit of my stomach.

I suppose that for a boy of thirteen I was being remarkably immature. I could hardly imagine Matt, who frequently gave the impression of being almost a man (and who, I had noticed only that evening, was already—and disconcertingly—filling out his jeans), I could hardly imagine Matt ever fantasizing that he was the son of Alan Shearer or David Duchovny or . . . who were those others he had chosen? Well anyway, if he did, then all this was going to change—change dramatically. Move over, David Duchovny! Here comes Samson Groves.

I looked at my watch with its illuminated dial.

Two-fifty-three.

Very carefully I got up—went downstairs to the sitting room—did half an hour of vigorous exercising. Then ran a bath. Several times I started to sing in it; had to check my song abruptly. Washed my hair. In fact I'd washed it less than nineteen hours previously but I felt like total immersion. Total cleanliness. Baptism.

Mens sana in corpore sano.

Likewise, although again they scarcely needed it, I trimmed my toenails, looked for any cuticle I should remove, looked for any hair visible in either ear or nostril. Rebrushed my teeth. Was almost going to shave but decided this was maybe overdoing it. Anointed myself in Cool Water.

It was ten-past-four when I went back to bed. This time I knew I'd sleep. Still marvellously happy, of course, but physically and men-tally relaxed. Not that I worried about not sleeping. Sleep didn't seem important. Tiredness was nothing but a state of mind.

And, as if to confirm this, I was awake again by half-past-eight and feeling great. Sunlight buttered the edges of the curtains and I stretched and lay in blissful comfort, thoroughly conscious of my sense of well-being, drinking it in along with a dozen more tangible things: usually unnoticed details of the flowered wallpaper; the repro-duction Pissarro above our mantelpiece, the faience candlesticks, the gilded and becherubbed mirror which I'd also brought home from the shop; my own bunched biceps as I stretched again, the well-shaped contour of my arms when I straightened them once more, the light gold sheen from wrist to elbow. I turned my head and let my right hand fall across the pillow above Junie's hair. She stirred and my fin-gers gently intruded into the short, thick, silvery mass. It was time for her to wake.

"I love you, Junie Moon . . . " I put my arms about her and she burrowed into me, all warm and sleepy. I kissed her eyelids and her nose and cheeks and she made small noises of contentment. When I entered her she still wasn't properly awake but made the same agree-able squeaks, wore the same beatific smile. This time I counted up to three hundred and thirty-eight. By the following Sunday, I determined, the score would have increased to at least a couple of thousand. I felt utterly confident. It had happened before but now the difference was, it would be permanent. And now I wasn't doing it simply for Junie and myself. I had the feeling that Moira would appreciate it more than Junie did—I mean, appreciate it more consistently, more wholeheartedly. Yet in any case . . . one thing was sure . . . both of them would benefit. I'd be doing it for the three of us.

I went and washed, then returned for my bathrobe. "Darling, stay there," I said. "I'll bring you breakfast."

"Really?"

"Got it all planned. One of a thousand small decisions I made during the night. From now on I intend to pamper you."

"But you already do."

"No, I've looked after you, protected you, but I don't believe I've pampered you. You're very precious to me, Junie Moon."

"You, too."

It was a good—it was the right—beginning to a day. Any day.

"What were the other small decisions?" she asked. "All nine hundred and ninety-nine of them."

"Mainly to do with loving you more and taking better care of you."

"All right, then, I approve. But I'm sorry if it means you had a sleepless night."

"Don't be. I'm not."

I fetched *The Observer* from the doormat.

"Better watch out," she said. "You'll make me even more dependent."

"Better watch out, had I?"

Perhaps she didn't realize I was joking. "I only meant . . . you mustn't spoil me too much. What would happen if you ever dropped dead?"

I laughed and went down to the kitchen. Susie uncurled from her basket and stretched and came forward to greet me. I fell to my knees and put my arms about her neck; gave her the sort of fussing she'd received on my return from work. "Did you sleep well, Susie? Did you dream you were chasing bunnies . . . or that you were lapping up beer and wolfing down crisps? If you tell me your dreams I'll interpret them."

She loved being spoken to like that; in my mind I slightly adapted the couplet by John Masefield: "He who gives a dog a treat hears joy bells ring in heaven's street." I wished that Moira could have seen us—briefly pretended she could. The quarry tiles were cold and hard against my knees but such minor discomforts were well worth it for the sake of seeing Susie's expression: subtly different, yet not definably so, from her look of the previous evening. It was a pity, I felt, dogs couldn't purr.

Moira was still strongly with me as I washed my hands and carried out a recce of the fridge and larder. I began to sing. Although over the years, obviously, I had given Junie breakfast in bed on many occasions, I had never before done a cooked breakfast—and I was glad of that: the chance to be doing something for her for the first time. It would be good, in fact, if every day could hold some first-time experience. That or some new thought, insight, item of knowledge. This, then, was a further resolution to add to my list.

And perhaps it should also be committed to paper, that list—expanded on, made tangible. Yes . . . and thinking about it . . . why not a journal? Lists were dry but a diary could be lively and entertaining, creative too, a place in which to formulate and grow, be curious and open-minded. Suddenly I felt I should never have laughed at that man who claimed he'd been utilized to score a melody for Mozart; nor at the woman who said she'd many times met Freddie Mercury . . . but only after his death. There were melodies by Mozart now lining up for me. Meetings with Freddie Mercury. With Audrey Hepburn; Princess Di; Princess Grace. John F Kennedy.

But first I had to concentrate on breakfast.

I prepared two trays, one for Matt as well as Junie; went into the garden, barefoot, to pick a tulip to lay on each. I fried eggs, bacon, mushrooms, tomatoes—poured orange juice—decided to take this main part upstairs before starting on the toast and coffee.

It occurred to me what tune I was humming: an old one from *Annie Get Your Gun*. When we were in our teens I had used to serenade Junie with it.

> "The girl that I marry
> Will have to be

As soft and as pink as a nurseree;
Stead of flittin'
She'll be sittin'
Next to me
And she'll purr like a kittin . . . "

I smiled. I remembered her saying, "Yes, I like the idea of being a doll you can carry!"

And I *had* carried her—all round the house, all round the garden, all round her parents' house. Even, once, out in the town. In retrospect, people had seemed surprisingly indulgent. Is it true, then: all the world loves a lover?

"I'm so glad I have someone I'll always be able to lean on. Lots of girls haven't, you know. You can't think how happy that makes me."

Now I delivered Junie's tray. The intake of her breath, the soaring of her hands, was undoubtedly genuine. "But what are you trying to do?" she cried. "Fatten me up for Christmas?"

"Why not?" I was Spencer Tracy. "What meat there is on you is cherce."

"You're sweet. You're a liar but you're sweet."

"Do you love me?" I asked.

"Ever so. Millions and millions."

Matt, too, was happily surprised. He struggled to sit up and did so with the air of still being in the midst of dreams.

Like me he didn't wear pyjamas. In the light of what I'd noticed yesterday I thought his shoulders were also looking broader. A light shadow spilled across his chest: the possible forerunner to a quantity of blond fuzz. One thing was certain. If he meant to throw himself into his training with the dumbbells, I should clearly have to intensify my own programme of exercises.

Soon, of course, he'd start to take more interest in girls. And vice versa—obviously. Already I could see he was becoming quite a hunk.

"Young Matthias," I said. "I reckon you need building up."

He, as well, had occasionally had breakfast seen to by myself— cereal, toast, a bar of chocolate—but even so . . . "Gosh! Eggs? Mushrooms? Did *you* cook them?"

"Who else?"

"Not bad. Not bad at all. Where's the fried bread?"

"Sorry. Must've forgotten."

"And the sausages?"

"Sorry."

"But thanks, Pop, this is cool. You're a good bloke. Ta."

"No crossed fingers?"

"No crossed fingers. But next time . . . "

"What?"

"Don't forget the fried bread."

Standing in the doorway I lifted two fingers at him; and they weren't crossed, either. He giggled. "I'll tell Mum . . . "

I made the toast and coffee—real coffee. I discovered a jar of honey in the larder; I knew Matt preferred honey to jam or marmalade. Honey on butter! (*Anything* on butter was the kind of extravagance I had generally frowned on; but not this morning. Nor, indeed, ever again.) I even prepared Susie a piece of buttered toast with honey, which I put on the grass near the back door. She guarded it between her front paws and looked at me askance, as though she supposed I might be passing through some form of crisis.

"Have *you* eaten anything yet?" asked Junie.

"No, but it's ready and waiting."

"Well, go and have it, please. Your eggs and bacon will be cold. Mine were delicious. It was all delicious—every mouthful."

I didn't mention that I wouldn't be eating eggs and bacon. Despite my decision of the previous night I'd now resolved to shed those extra pounds. Not wholly for the sake of appearance: asceticism got catered for as well: less self-indulgence in the future, a bit more restraint, a promise of my having reacquired control. (Surely I had once been in control?) Over appetites—digestive juices—destiny.

Therefore I drank only orange juice, no coffee; spread only honey on my crispbread—no butter. Went to collect the trays. But not even Matt took me up on my offer of more toast. And Junie scolded. "You'll wear your legs out running up and down those stairs! You can't guess how grateful I am, though. But your own breakfast wasn't spoilt, was it?"

"Not a bit."

"And did you enjoy it as much as me?"

"No, I enjoyed you more."

"Did you get as much enjoyment out of your breakfast as I did?"

"Yes thank you. I got at least as much enjoyment out of my breakfast as you did."

"No, I'm sorry, I don't believe you." She took my hand. "It's sad. You've stopped being trustworthy. Besides being an idiot."

"I'm glad. Yes, how sharp of you to notice! I have stopped being an idiot, haven't I?"

Answered by nothing but a gently smiling forbearance, I told her she was unique; that most people would have found me quite insufferable.

I stacked the crockery and cutlery and looked out at the garden as the water ran. All that blossom. It was perfect. For a minute I propped myself there, my hands resting on the edge of the sink, and gazed out longingly, trying to take in every detail, imprint it clearly for all time, down to the robin on the branch of one of the cherry trees, the celandines and daisies beneath it, the Solomon's seal with its clusters of white flowers, the neighbours' black cat already basking on our brick wall. Seeing it on a postcard, or on the lid of a chocolate box, you might wonder if it hadn't been retouched.

Then I began the washing up. Even apart from the view, I enjoyed the sensual warmth of the sudsy water—as well as, before long, the recollection, which I often had at times like this (well, chiefly in the bath), of sailing my yacht across a pond in the park, on holiday with my parents in Torquay. Sometimes as I grew older I seemed to miss my mother more—I mean, more at thirty-six than at thirty. But this didn't seriously induce a feeling of melancholy, I simply wished I had more photographs and that I still possessed that little yacht, which, oddly, I could never remember having sailed on any pond in Deal.

My eyes misted, however—which struck me as perverse. Why on earth this morning, why today of all possible days? But after a moment it made me smile.

Sorry, Dad. I haven't forgotten. Big boys don't cry.

When I'd cleared up I shaved and dressed: a short-sleeved shirt today, first of the year. I recalled how yesterday, seeing that woman in her summer frock, I'd considered short sleeves premature. Now I apologized to that woman in her summer frock. Caution was for the timid, the untrusting. Caution wasn't for the treasure seekers.

Then I performed my regular Sunday chore: took a shovel round the garden, a shovel and a stick, collecting Susie's poos. Normally, during those five or ten minutes, my expression might have been one of mild distaste—particularly if the poor thing had been suffering from diarrhoea—even if such distaste was greatly leavened by self-protective humour. This morning I actually sang. Actually executed several dance steps, fairly lively ones, though not, I hasten to add, after the shovel had become well-filled.

Matt was in the garden, feeding the fish, putting out more nuts for the squirrels, replenishing the bird food; fortunately the neighbours' cat was elderly and somnolent.

My son looked at me in some wonder, shook his head and tapped his temple. I would have sung whether he'd been there or not, have gone in for all those silly, clownish antics. But it was good to have an audience.

8

We left the house at half-past-eleven; for some reason later than usual; on Sundays we almost invariably went to Jalna. (Jalna was the only place I knew which had a double-barrelled name: Jalna—the Dovecote: always scrupulously observed on envelopes by close friends and members of the family. Most members of the family.) Sometimes I would moan like hell about having to go. Sunday is my one day off, I would say—or, rather, shout—to Junie and the children; why can't I have the freedom to enjoy it? This is worse than going to church, I'd shout. This is worse than going to prison. (This is exactly the same as going to prison!) I'll join a potholers' association! Ramblers' club! Witches' coven! Anything . . . so long as its meetings unfailingly fall on a Sunday! Exclamation marks appeared to fly thicker than arrows over Agincourt; or over one of Junie's uncorrected letters.

Usually, the kids would either giggle or do their best to suppress their giggles; depending less on me than on their mother. Junie could be bent to my will in nearly anything that hadn't to do with her family but now she'd assume an indulgent smile which was infuriating (relegating me to position of third child, whom she must patiently seek to propitiate) yet which could generally coax me back towards a sheepishly grinning—if residually grumbling—form of acceptance. Until the next time.

Yet occasionally I'd take a real stand: sweep the children off to ride on a steam railway or see some distant castle or visit the Tower of London. To a degree, Junie could sympathize, but would mostly decline to accompany us; and her sympathy was intellectual, not of the heart. Occasionally too (for this was happening over *many* years) I'd insist I needed to get on with the decorating or needed to go to clear the contents of some house. Once, when I was feeling outstandingly bolshie, I'd declared I should like simply to spend the day in bed and take a little holiday, inaugurate a Samuel Groves Day, to be celebrated at least biannually, with fireworks and bacchanalia and a service of thanksgiving. I don't know—being much too grand even to inquire—in what form the message finally got through, but I remember they sent me back a cakebox filled with iced fancies and cheese straws and sausage rolls. (However, I refused to be touched . . . let alone humbled. I gave them to the children.) I thought how marvellous it would be just to pass the day like any normal family, reading the paper, popping out to the pub, watching TV, dispatching the children to Crusaders and spending the afternoon in bed.

Not that you couldn't do all those things at Jalna (the Dovecote) save perhaps the last. And not that I didn't generally have a pretty good time there—a better one than I might well have had at home. It was just its inexorability which I complained of. Its claustrophobia.

Its in-breeding.

And yet, before Junie and I had got engaged, it was precisely this close-knit quality which had most appealed to me; one of the factors, even, which may have influenced my hesitant proposal. I'd no longer had a family of my own, except for my grandmother, and had always longed for a sibling—ideally, for several. Junie was the youngest of five sisters; and the others, despite being married, still lived in the locality. I suddenly found myself drawn into a mainly young, charming, good-looking group whose members were full of fun, mutually devoted, and around whom existed an aura of almost storybook enchantment, of *Bright Day* exclusiveness. I had of course met Junie's parents on countless occasions—and all of their daughters and their daughters' husbands at least once—but although Mr and Mrs Fletcher were ostensibly the most hospitable couple I had ever known, and were obviously fond of me, even hopeful of me, their hospitality didn't truly extend beyond their own children and their own children's families; for whom Sundays were kept sacrosanct and unadulterated. Only following my engagement to Junie did the sabbath walls of Jalna finally fall before me. The outsider put away his trumpet and belonged.

But after a few years, when most of the initial glamour had worn off, though not without leaving a pool of variable affection, I'd once asked Junie if there weren't some unpublished list (or maybe even published—why not?) outlining the requisites for the perfect Fletcher son-in-law: a willingness, say, to remain forever within easy reach of Deal; to subscribe seventy-five percent of his Sundays, Christmases and other bank holidays (subject, of course, to rotas: only one family missing at a time) along with an equal percentage of his annual vacation . . . naturally to be subsumed into the Fletcher summer booking on the Continent? I'd acknowledged that Saturdays, at present, might be optional, but had ventured that all birthdays and wedding anniversaries were inalienably the property of Jalna. Junie had laughed and admitted, in a tone of faintly clannish pride, that I maybe hadn't got it all that wrong. I'd suggested with a degree of self-congratulation and mordant black humour that the son-in-law who really wished to make it big should have disposed of both his parents.

But today I neither moaned nor meant to wax satirical. Instead, as we drove towards Jalna, I thought about the diary I was going to keep. I must have been to Junie's childhood home nearly a thousand times but I decided I would try to look upon this as my very first visit—or else, on the theory that you should live each day as though you would be dead tomorrow, as my very last—and attempt to catch it through the viewfinder of my opening entry. "What's the date?" I asked.

Junie wasn't sure; and Matt said nothing.

"April the twenty-seventh . . . or possibly the twenty-eighth," I repeated slowly, taking my hand off the steering wheel and laying it briefly on my wife's. "Nineteen hundred and ninety-seven or ninety-eight or thereabouts?"

"You didn't know it, either. There's really no call to mock."

"In any case, a day to conjure with. Momentous. Uniquely historic."

"Why?"

"Simply because it is."

"Oh, Mum," cautioned Matt, wearily, from the back seat. "He's going to say that this particular day will never come again—not ever—ever. That's why we've got to savour it. He's going to inform us that history is being made today . . . just like on any other day which we can read about with bated breath. Dad's in one of his *improving* moods. Can't you tell? Don't you know your husband yet?"

"Ah . . . Does anyone ever know anyone?" I inquired—improvingly.

But that was purely to point up a general truth. I certainly knew his mother. I knew his mother probably as well as I knew myself.

"He'll now go on to mention that today marks the very beginning of the rest of our lives," said Matt, in the same tone of quietly tolerant resignation.

"Newborn like the spring," I added.

"Newborn like the spring," he explained.

"Well, I can't help it. You blasé wretch. I *feel* newborn."

"Yeah. May you lead a long and happy life."

"Thank you, Matthias—my precious sweet love. I really do intend to."

"I give you till about lunchtime."

"As long as that?"

"Going on past experience."

"Ah, but today's different," I assured him.

"Yeah, yeah."

"*Today* is different, *I* am different."

"How different?"

"As different as possibly can be. You'll find out."

"All right, then. Let's put it to the test. Please, Dad, will you make me a present of five pounds?"

I chuckled . . . and pulled the car over. "What are you doing?" Junie asked.

"Looking to see how much money I've brought." In fact I knew perfectly well. I'd again left my wallet in the bedroom but had neatly folded a couple of notes and placed them in a pocket of my jeans. Now

I fished one out. "Yes, you're in luck," I said. "Except we'll have to make it ten."

"Darling, you're crazy!" And although Junie was smiling she honestly did sound a bit appalled. "I think you may have gone out of your little mind."

"Well, *I* think I may have just come into it." I started up the car.

"Come on, Dad. You'd better take it back." Matt prodded me on the shoulder. The folded note was in his hand.

"No, Mattie, it's yours."

"D'you mean that?"

"Yes, I do. It's for your being so intuitive and clever and mature. For expressing yourself so well. For remembering all my tiny pearls of wisdom."

"If it goes on like this," he said, "I may start writing them down and learning them for homework."

"Wise fellow. Just tell me, though. Who's the spiffiest father in the whole wide world?"

Matt had pocketed his ten pounds.

"Ask me again in another week."

I laughed. So did Junie.

"But I've got to admit it, Pop. Since last night you do appear different. Somehow." (I didn't say so but I found this tribute the most gratifying he could have made.) "Is it going to be okay, Mum, d'you think . . . for me to keep this loot?"

"Why ask me? It's your father's money. I've got nothing to do with it."

Yet Matt still seemed unbelieving.

"Dad, I'll get it changed at some point and give you back your five. That would be fair, wouldn't it? After all, I only asked for five."

"Perhaps, then, this will have taught you not to set your sights too low? Not to ask too little out of life? In any case, my darling, I want you to hold onto it."

I added: "And let me say that I admire you for your integrity; for your reluctance to exploit the situation."

He leant forward and kissed the back of my neck.

Already, I thought. Already three small items for the diary. *Cooked*

NEW WORLD IN THE MORNING

breakfasts. Ten-pound note. Demonstrative affection. I smiled at him in the mirror.

And a fourth one: *acknowledgement of difference.*

Unsolicited, to boot.

We turned into the drive, drew up by the front door. There were two other cars parked along the verge and a further two behind those—first-comers always left space for later brethren. Jalna was in a quiet and tree-lined cul-de-sac; a fifteen-minute drive from us, from Cowper Road. It was a fairly attractive house, Tudor style, built during the nineteen-thirties. Relatively imposing . . . but in no way as beautiful as ours. I'd never have considered swopping.

Ella came to meet us. She'd been sitting on the swing in the front garden, awaiting our arrival. "You're late!" she announced, moodily.

"Hello, darling," cried Junie, through the open window. "Have you been having a good time?"

"Hello, Mum. Oh, not bad, I suppose. Hello, Dad. Hello, Susie."

"Hello, Matt," said Matt.

I walked round the car, lifted my daughter and gave her a big hug. She seemed to have grown heavier since the last time I had done this. Nothing daunted—indeed, responding to the challenge—I then hoist her well above my head and swung myself around a couple of times, laughing up at her. "Hey, why so physical?" she asked, when I had set her down.

"Because you're my little girl and because you always used to like my doing that. I remember when you couldn't get enough of it. *Again,* you'd say, *again!*"

Susie jumped up at her as though the two of them had been apart for weeks and while Ella stroked and patted her, and Junie was taking her fruit pies out of the boot and handing three of them to me, Matt said to his sister: "He's acting pretty weird today. If only I cared for you a bit more I'd pass on a tip which could definitely prove useful."

"Like what?"

"Like, for instance, see what happens if you ask him for a piggyback or something."

"You must be nuts. Why should I want a piggyback?"

"Or *something*," he repeated, almost spitting out the word. "Anything."

"I don't get you," she said.

"You're so thick," Matt told her, dispassionately.

Though neither of my own children wanted piggybacks or to ride upon my shoulders, or to be whirled around like aeroplanes—as Ella had so lately been—there were plenty of other children who did; and some of them not a whole lot younger. "Oh, *poor* Uncle Sam," was a cry heard many times during the course of the afternoon, "now, won't you please take pity on him, you monsters?" But this wasn't only because of piggybacks and the like. For who was it who, while the rest of the fathers dozed in their deckchairs, organized a crude treasure hunt around the garden and, after that, a game of hide-and-seek in some nearby woods (with Susie proving so much of a liability, poor excited thing, she had to be shut away inside the house; I would somehow make it up to her) and, after *that*, played several bouts of tag—even having to throw off his shirt and wipe himself down with it? "Well, truly, doesn't that put you four sluggards to shame?" asked Octavia, whose husband was pasty-faced and stolid and looked fifty although he wasn't yet forty-five.

"Oh, he's only making up for lost time," he answered good-humouredly; Raymond's glamour might have gone but not his geniality. "He's feeling bad he didn't get here soon enough to help mark out the tennis court. We've got to be nice to him."

(And here, with an early diary entry in view, *I Capture the Dovecot*, I was already thinking that, for the sake of avoiding complexity—always an aspiration—I should have to make these characters pipe up in turn.)

"Yes, indeed," agreed Ted, who also wouldn't have looked any great shakes these days without his shirt. "The least we can do is give him this chance to salve his conscience. Life doesn't always provide us with a second opportunity. We urge you to go for it, Sam. Just go for it!"

Unlike these other two, who were businessmen, Robert was a librarian. The poor chap suffered from anaemia and ought by rights to have found each Sunday's get-together more wearing than anybody; but either he drew strength from togetherness or else was seriously well trained.

"Sammy, I get scared," he said, "so painfully worried that you might simply burn yourself out—too much, too soon, too fast! *Then* who's going to creosote the fence and paint the greenhouse and build the rockery and attend to all the other little things that no doubt Mimsy and Pim have already lined up to keep us entertained throughout the summer?" He shook his head, sadly.

"Listen," said Jake, who was the most intellectual of my brothers-in-law and actually had a thick book of poetry open on his lap. "Why are you standing there as though you had nothing better to do—just blocking out the sun? You can take the children on a long hike or something." He added graciously, "That way you can atone for the disturbance you created a short while ago, with all that screaming and running about in the wood."

I said: "You're like a bloody barbershop quartet. You're like a troupe of performing seals. Hasn't anyone ever told you?"

"Yes, they're a thoroughly smirky lot," Yvonne confirmed, with grudging laughter. She was next up in line from Junie and like all the Fletcher girls was short and bouncy and big-chested. "Well, I wouldn't take it. You're larger than they are, Sam. For my part I give you full leave to grab Ted and teach him a good lesson."

Rose and April also granted me permission to educate—respectively—Jake and Robert. Octavia chipped in, as well.

"But I thought they were my friends," I opined piteously, hanging my head.

"Well, of course we are," crooned Raymond. "Now, if we weren't, we'd hardly be putting you forward for Uncle of the Year. Would we, guys?"

"Uncle of the Year! Would you *really* do that for me?"

"You have our word on it."

"Oh, shucks! I don't know what to say."

"You don't have to say anything, Samuel. Just run along now. Perhaps to Sandwich and back. No—forget about *and back*. Jake will get the kids lined up in pairs."

"Oh, yes? Let him but try!" Rose, who'd objected to my using my shirt as a towel, was now shaking it out forgivingly, about to bear it off to a clotheshorse or to an ironing board, despite Junie's halfhearted remonstrances that I shouldn't be so pandered to. Or mothered. (In a way, surprisingly, I liked the notion of being mothered.) But Rose had become my champion; roused, she twirled my shirt about her husband's head as a baton of subdual. She was like the Devil Girl from Mars; Drum Majorette from Hell. I timidly expressed the hope this mightn't be allowed to interfere with the placing of those nominations.

Soon, though, it was teatime. My dieting plans had gone awry—not so badly during lunch but I needed now to preserve my energy. "Today I want the biggest piece of everything to go to Sam," proclaimed Myrtle Fletcher, raising plump and dimpled forearms. "And the smallest piece of everything to go to Robert. I heard what he said about creosoting fences, etc. So did Pim. He won't get much of a glass of sherry, either."

"You on the other hand, Sam," said my father-in-law, "will have a tumbler if that's what you'd like." He was a small man, rosy-cheeked, bald-pated, amiable. Always synchronized his viewpoint with his wife's—at any rate, in public; "I need to," he would say, "the old girl's got a longer reach than mine!" He'd been kind to me and I was fond of him, wasn't proud of the fact that I had grown increasingly to feel contempt: subservience in a husband troubled me. Either I couldn't have been so fully aware of such meekness at the start or it had become more pronounced over time.

"Oh, Lordy, Lordy," said Robert. "Even the walls have ears."

"And the kitchen has open windows, too, where Pim and I discovered, to our disappointment, that it was for *ingrates* we were making tea! I'm sorry to have to inform you of something else. Your own two daughters were amongst those of us who heard."

We stayed in the garden. The children, whose ages ranged from seven to sixteen, either sat on the grass, on rugs or cushions, or roamed at will, eating their scone, sandwich or piece of carrot cake. My own deckchair was positioned next to Jake's. "The Brain and the Brawn," he suggested. I slightly resented this—well, as much as I could have resented anything in my current frame of mind and on such a sunny afternoon. Or as much as I could have resented anything that part of me found flattering.

He was certainly the scrawniest of the sons-in-law; sharp-nosed, long-chinned, rope-veined. But he always seemed straightforward. Receptive to new ideas. Was likely to be popular, I thought, amongst his pupils.

He had been preparing a lesson for the following day.

I protested.

"Just because you have the Oxford Book of Something-or-Other to use as a tea tray! That doesn't mean you're the only one around here who likes poetry!"

"Oh, sure," he remarked. "'If you can keep your head, when all about you . . . are losing theirs and blaming it on you, if you can trust yourself when all men doubt you, but make allowance for their doubting too . . .'"

During even so brief a recitation, I had been thinking about Moira. As though I had ever—quite—not been thinking about Moira.

"Here," I said, "you mustn't knock Kipling!"

"I don't," he replied. "But I bet you couldn't recite me four lines of anything a little more weighty. Excluding Shakespeare."

"Is that so? How about Dryden?"

"Four lines of Dryden?"

"Would that impress you?"

"Well could."

"All right, then. Listen to this . . .

'I strongly wish for what I faintly hope:
Like the daydreams of melancholy men,
I think and think on things impossible,
Yet love to wander in that golden maze . . .'

Word perfect, I assure you."

"Yes," he said, slowly. "I can believe it. I'm not actually familiar with that passage—"

"*Rival Ladies*," I told him. "But my point is: not all of us are total dunderheads."

"After nearly twenty years, Sam, do you imagine I don't know that? And, after nearly twenty years, can't *you* imagine I might ever so slightly be pulling your leg?"

But my education had always been a touchy subject. I'd never been to university, had nothing in the way of what *I* considered a genuine qualification: some tangible proof in writing. One of these days I hoped to set this right. Go up to Oxbridge preferably—get to be a rowing blue.

Well, anyway. You gotta have a dream.

"How much more of it can you recite?" He laughed. "Old Memorybags!"

"Of the Dryden? None. But you asked for only four lines. What about two from Alexander Pope? Also impressive?"

"Possibly."

"'Know then thyself, presume not God to scan; the proper study of mankind is man.'"

"Oh, anyone can recite that! With the exception, I mean, of anyone in this garden."

"And lastly I can offer you the whole of *The Whiffenpoof Song*. But, sadly, not its etymology."

I sighed. Stood up and went to pass a plate of macaroons. Also one of flapjacks.

As it happened, a few hours later I did in fact give voice to those little black sheep who had lost their way—baa, baa, baa! (And wouldn't get home till the Judgment Day—baa, baa, baa!) But not as a solo. We'd built a bonfire and after a light supper we ate buns and drank hot chocolate around it; some of the children would later place foil-wrapped potatoes in the embers. Ted told a ghost story; not a very scary one, although most of the adults simulated terror. Then we had a spelling bee and played 'I Spy'. Everyone seemed smiley and relaxed . . . increasingly so as the night grew darker. Cosy, too—we all had woollen jumpers. Beside me lay Susie, well-fed and content and interested: eyes constantly on the move, snout resting on her paws. (How could all those other households honestly prefer cats?) Young Gary sat with thumb in mouth and head against his mother's breast, and Rose absently stroked the hair back from his brow. I wondered if Jake ever suffered from claustrophobia. He or any of the others. Impossible to tell. I seldom did while I was actually there. I smiled at Junie and my daughter, both sitting straight across from me. People said there was no such thing as a perfect day, and of course there probably wasn't—I supposed—yet I really didn't see how this one could have been improved on. Our initially lusty singsong was now petering out but as I looked at all those friendly faces in the firelight, faces so familiar I usually didn't think much about my fondness for the people attached to them, I suddenly felt regretful that next Sunday mine wouldn't be among them. Although I knew this was merely sentimental and would certainly be fleeting it wasn't easy to shake off. What's more, it happened even before somebody, I believe it was Octavia, led the rest into something I hadn't heard for ages: "Here's a happy tune, you'll love to croon, they call it . . . Sam's song." Lots of nods and smiles in my direction and cries from some of the children—"This one's about Uncle Sam! This is about Uncle Sam!"

What was ironic was that it was immediately followed by another that could easily have provoked a few nods in my direction . . . although, obviously, not with the smiles.

Don't Fence Me In.

9

We returned home at roughly ten. At roughly eleven I took Susie on her evening walk. "Is it necessary?" asked Junie. "She's been charging around so much I would have thought she was exhausted."

"But, darling, she was shut up for over an hour this afternoon, and, hearing all the screams and laughter, must have thought, *What on earth have I done?* And, anyway, just look at her!"

Susie had gone to the front door and was gazing back with soulful trustingness in the integrity of man—and with a tail that wagged in tentative anticipation.

Added to which, I myself was fancying a stroll: a short time in which to ponder without interruption, to plan, to dream, take stock . . . or simply be. I often meant to do all this in bed but either fell asleep or was distracted by Junie's frequent resettlings or—sometimes—gentle snoring.

"Ah, Suze," I said. "*I* know your evening walk is one of the few simple pleasures you can really count on. How could your mistress be so rotten as to want to deprive you of it?"

"Oh, Susie. Is that what I was wanting? To deprive you of one of the few simple pleasures you can really count on? Then isn't it a good thing *somebody* here has a heart?" To me she said: "But you won't be going far?"

"No, only round the block. Won't even take the lead."

In fact I'd been considering returning to the beach, to sanctify my day with a tranquil half-hour listening to the ebb and flow of the ocean. But the beach was too far. So now I chose to wander through the back streets. At this time on a Sunday these were wholly deserted, their houses all in darkness. But at least I could smell the sea. And I loved that smell. I'd always been a son of Neptune, even before I'd been a son of Richard Widmark. The sea had made the setting for some of my greatest exploits, both actual and imaginary, but sometimes I'd felt I should simply like to swim out as far as I could, mile after mile after mile—sun-dappled and serene—until either my strength gave out or else I finally walked ashore, all glorious and shining, with muscles now pleasantly tired, onto some lush tropical island with silvery sands, exotic fruits and Gauguin's available maidens. The sea was purifying; it was a transmuter of base metals. It seemed eminently right that beside the sea, and underneath the stars, I should have been brought face-to-face again with love.

The car came quickly and it didn't stop.

For a second I couldn't adjust. One moment I was attending some glamorous cocktail function with Moira, being introduced to many of her sophisticated friends, arousing wonderment and envy. The next, I was staring down at Susie's bloody and broken body. Separating the two had been the heart-stopping thud of impact . . . and then the bastard's tail lights were already burning into the distance.

Yet she was still alive. The whimpering and the slavering and the frenzied breathing, the bared teeth and the smell of panic, all testified to that. I knelt beside her and laid my hand on her head and spoke her name softly and repeatedly, whilst trying to work out what I should do. And she gradually gave over snarling and attempting to struggle up.

I knew that the vet lived on the seafront, in a flat over his surgery. We were halfway there and I thought it would be better to carry Susie straight to Mr Dodd than carry her back to the house—also quicker and less frustrating than my trying to get a lift. No lights had been switched on; no windows had been thrown open. Everything remained as silent as before . . . almost . . . the only difference being a crying baby and a whimpering dog. Nobody had come to his front door.

I would have come to my front door.

So would Junie, Ella, Matt and nearly everyone I knew. They would all have come to their front door.

I felt an urge to stand there and throw back my head and howl. Howl until the incident was marked, its inhumanity acknowledged, in some way shared in.

But that wasn't going to happen.

"Okay, Suze. Easy does it, you mustn't be afraid! You're going to be all right."

Okay, Suze, easy does it, you're going to be all right. For the next ten minutes this was the refrain running through everything I said. I felt it mattered she should hear my voice. "You're going to be all right, Suze. Mr Dodd will take away your pain. You're going to be all right. As good as new! Oh, dear God! Dear God!"

Yet that was dishonest. I had nothing but scorn for anyone who, at moments of stress, turned to a god he otherwise disregarded. God played no part in my own world. I didn't need him. I wasn't the type to lean; I was the type to be leant upon. "You—are—going—to—be—all—right—Susie. Do you hear me?"

She was still conscious but a dead weight and my arms were aching long before we reached the vet's. She smelled dreadful. She was dribbling copiously onto one of my cable-stitch sleeves and there was blood and heaven knew what else across my chest and stomach. I saw scarcely anyone. I passed the ice-cream parlour we had passed the night before but now it gave the impression of still being shut for winter. It was odd to think that only a little over twenty-four hours ago we'd all been drinking inside *The Lord Nelson*—Susie making up to Moira and Liz, rather than bothering with myself.

To my relief there was a light in one of the windows above the surgery; it showed pinkly through thin curtains. Not that it would have made any difference if there hadn't been.

Mr Dodd looked like a young man out of an American soap. He had striking if somewhat vacuous good looks and thick blond hair combed back into a peak. But then you noticed the skin at his throat: not baggy so much as crumpled and crisscrossed and crêpey: and later on you learned he was a grandfather and you set him down as one of the creepiest people you had ever met.

(Superman, I can assure you, Matt, could never hold a candle to Mr Dodd!)

But when he came to the door he instantly took in the situation and opened up without the least sign of reluctance. While I held Susie down and did my best to look away from everything the harsh surgery light was so cruelly exposing he conducted a lengthy examination, having first administered a pain-dulling injection.

In an attempt to distract myself, I wondered why Mr Dodd, if you saw him about during the milder months, invariably wore an open-neck shirt, with nothing visible beneath, when possibly—with a skil-fully arranged cravat or some high rolled-over collar—he could have gone on looking thirty-five forever. It was perplexing. Did he suffer, then, from a blind spot . . . or was it more from that self-destructive urge we're all supposed to have, but which, speaking for myself, I could never properly recognize? 'O wad some Pow'r the giftie gie us To see coursels as others see us! It wad frae mony a blunder free us, And fool-ish notion.' (Another four lines I could have quoted happily to Jake, and might well have done, had Mr Dodd been present.)

Yet the poor man was always thoroughly agreeable; besides being a first-class vet. And at present my mind couldn't dwell for long on quirks of personality or appearance.

"I'm afraid she's very badly hurt," he announced at last.

"Well, I can see that!" I said. "But she'll be all right, won't she? She *is* going to pull through?"

"It's not these gashes on the body we need worry about. It's the damage to her head."

"Concussion—right? But concussion heals with time."

"Unfortunately, it's more than that, Mr Groves. I'm sad to have to say it—"

"No," I cut in.

"But I truly feel—"

"No," I repeated, "*I am not going to have my dog put down!*"

"But I don't believe she can make a full recovery. I am sorry. I appreciate what you're going through—"

"No!" I said.

The sound of my tone. The set of my features. Obdurate like Matt.

"Very well, then." Without a shrug he still conveyed the impression of one. "In that case, I'll now give her something to help her sleep until morning."

"Don't you see? We love her. My wife . . . my children . . . It wouldn't be like home without her."

"Of course. I understand that. Yet I still think that when you've had a chance to reconsider . . . I know none of you would wish to condemn her to a life of—a life of—"

"But how can you be sure? *Can* you be so sure . . . ?"

"Short of a miracle," he answered. "Yes."

I paused.

"All right, if that's the way it is," I told him, heavily, "then there's nothing else for it, is there? We'll just have to hope for a miracle."

He drove us home; assured me with an air of concern that he would come to look at Susie in the morning.

Burrowed in the pocket of my jeans, opened the front door for me. Then departed.

"Samuel—is that you? Do you realize you've been gone an hour? Over an hour? I've been getting so worried. So cross. You said ten minutes! I'm almost coming to believe I can't trust you any longer."

I called back up the stairs. In other circumstances I'd have found it satisfying, my being able to vindicate myself so fully. Even now there was a sneaking sense of righteousness. Junie was still pulling on her dressing gown as she came running after me into the kitchen. Her hand was on my shoulder, squeezing in mute apology, while I settled Susie into her basket. At the same time I added all the salient details. "I think I may sit up with her," I said.

"But, darling, there's no point. Not if Mr Dodd's sedated her and told you it'll last all night."

I allowed her finally to lead me up to bed.

"We mustn't let her die," I said, in a voice that seemed treacherously to quaver. "It wouldn't be right, she's had barely half her life . . ." I was aware how inadequate this sounded but I was now having actually to hold back tears and I had a strong feeling that if after so many years of hard-won self-respect I were suddenly to start blubbering I might not find it easy to stop. That would scarcely be helpful right now; and, more to the point, could insidiously spoil something we had all come to value. Once there had been a first time of showing weakness, who could say there wouldn't be a second?

"I promise you," answered Junie, "we'll do our very best to save her. But, love, do try to keep your voice down! It's far better the children shouldn't hear us." She smiled ruefully. "I suppose it's a minor miracle that *I* didn't wake them!"

There! That word again! It struck me as auspicious. And at the top of the stairs there was a horseshoe hanging on the wall. I brushed my hand against it as we passed.

Come on, I thought. *Be positive! Broad-shouldered! Unbeatable!* This was the sort of thing I always said to myself when going through a depression; or, anyhow, beginning to come out of one. And there were plenty of other situations in which it was equally apposite. Of course there were. I turned and gave her a ferocious hug.

"Darling, it's going to be all right, don't worry," I said. "Yes, all of it! I love you, Junie Moon."

10

And I slept well. I awoke at half-past-six feeling refreshed and practically as optimistic as on the day before. Drew back the curtains to discover another bright sky, then immediately ran downstairs to take a look at Susie. She appeared inert but her breathing was less laboured. She really was on the road to recovery. I squatted and stroked and spoke to her as normal because although I naturally expected no reaction it would have seemed like betraying a trust if I hadn't, and of course I hoped some emanation from my words and actions might be reaching her. I carried on our conversation as I filled the kettle. I doused my face in cold water. Then, buoyantly impulsive, I walked into the garden and had a long pee on the grass. It was the first time I'd ever done this and it made me feel romantically close to nature, standing there erect and naked in the early morning sun and watching my urine arch like a fountain from some Greek or Roman statue, shoot up prismatically before it frothed among the daisies; and if anyone in either of the next-door houses had happened to be looking from an upper window . . . well, just too bad. Or just too good: let them, for once, set eyes upon a real man. Waiting for the kettle to whistle I meandered round the garden; savouring the dew beneath my feet and the air between my loins. I did a few physical jerks, defiantly facing those same neighbouring windows: toe-touching, running on the spot, swivelling at the waist—with legs apart and arms in line with shoulders. I'd have done more but then the whistling came. I made the tea, put a couple of Petit Beurre on each of our saucers, was careful not to slop as I returned upstairs, and, having wiped my soles on the carpet, got exuberantly back into bed. I hadn't bothered to take anything to the children; it wasn't yet seven. As usual, Junie only properly came to whilst drinking her tea but even so she'd instantly asked about Susie and been relieved by what I'd told her. I fetched us both refills, despite not really wanting mine nor drinking more than half, made love to her ("What, first thing on a Monday morning!" she'd exclaimed, laughing)—and to a count of eight hundred and seventeen—then went to shave and have my bath. A perfect start to a second, potentially, perfect day . . . although, obviously, blocking out that bloody motorist and the effect of his swift uncaring passage through our lives. I wondered if he were feeling any remorse.

Yes, it had to be a 'he'. I found it impossible to believe that a woman wouldn't have stopped.

Reclining in my bath I thought about the possible openings to today's entry. *This morning I peed naked in the back garden and frightened the horseflies . . . ?* No. Perhaps not.

I arrived at the shop a minute before nine. Mavis didn't work on Mondays. Until high season she came in only on Thursdays, Fridays and Saturdays. But at five-past-nine I rang her. Knowing she'd be up. Knowing she'd be worrying about her empty bank account. Basically, she was *always* worrying about her empty bank account. Or, more exactly, about the doleful insecurity of a probably loveless future.

"You're saying," she repeated, "the whole week? Five days? *Already?*" She had a breathy voice. Her emissions fairly aspirated down the line.

"Six, if you like."

"But, Mr G, you can't afford it—not fulltime—you know you can't! Not as early as this!"

"Here," I said. "You let me go bananas over *my* finances and I'll let *you* go bananas over yours! Wouldn't it be useful?"

"Breathlessly." This didn't seem totally the right word but I felt glad to hear her say it. "And apart from the money you know how much I enjoy just being around."

"Great. Then when will you start? This morning?"

"You really mean it?"

"Of course I do."

"Then I can be with you in thirty minutes! Or twenty, if you're planning to go somewhere . . . ?"

"No, no, take your time. Why not come in after lunch and we'll count it as a full day?"

It occurred to me afterwards that I could simply have doubled her wages. But she might have viewed this as blatant charity and, besides, it gave her pleasure to be here—hadn't she just said so? Got her out of the house. Provided escape from a querulous, demanding mum.

And she'd have been coming in fulltime from the beginning of July, anyway. So if her wages became a problem *then*, rather than now, what difference did it make?

Moreover, it had seemed the proper thing to do . . . and doubtless we'd survive. Live every day as though your last. Commit yourself, unreservedly.

It was like when you'd been the captain of a team and your eleven or fifteen players had all relied completely on your judgment. Now I had a crew of only four: Junie, Ella, Matt and Mavis. A tiny ship but for all hands, hopefully, a happy and secure one; responsibly navigated.

Four people and a dog.

Partly thinking about this, I walked slowly up and down our central aisle, renewing my acquaintance with the stock, picking up several objects at random, speculating on their history; studying a daguerreotype taken at the Great Exhibition; experiencing, as usual, pleasurably mixed feelings, an awareness of the transience of life but also a strong sense of sharing and connection.

And this morning, too, for the second time, a boy's catapult suddenly bore me back to childhood: to the remembered sunlight and long country days—to the big adventures and subconscious knowledge of my always being protected—to a stream where I'd gone fishing, the warm smell of a bakery long since closed.

This morning, in addition, I saw the shop through someone else's eyes. Moira had been here. Her feet had trodden this drugget, her eyes had seen these pictures—these paintings not only suspended from the walls but stacked against the skirting boards—seen the books, clothes, records, furniture; the glass-topped cases displaying jewellery, medals, coins; the various tables strewn with all the clutter of forgotten lives. Between the tables ran a network of passageways. Moira had traversed them all. Now I threaded them myself and imagined that this—consolidated by my present line of empathy—drew me closer to her.

Of course, I was drawing closer in another sense. Only five days before she'd be coming back to Deal!

Only?

At half-past-twelve I rang home. Wanting to know what Mr Dodd had said.

"In fact, he sounded rather hopeful. Susie's drunk a little milk and eaten a few scraps of meat and she knew the garden was the right place to do her business. And she remembers where it is, too—I mean, on the other side of the back door. Also it's obvious she can recognize her name. Mr Dodd seemed really pleased."

Oh, hadn't I said! Hadn't I said! I swivelled on my office chair and—free of the table on which the telephone rested—held my legs out straight and clicked my heels in celebration. "Where is she now?"

"Back in her basket. She's still a bit whiffy, though. Will you be able to bath her?"

"You bet! There's a meeting of the Players tonight but I can bath her before supper."

"Did you like your sandwiches?"

"I'm sure they'll be wonderful."

I always said Junie's sandwiches were as varied, inventive and well-filled as the finest New York deli's . . . although I often wished I'd been in a position actually to check. Neither she nor I had ever travelled further than Europe. Europe in the company of the clan.

"Ambrosia on wholemeal," I added now, conservatively. I used an American accent.

"I've started on the wallpapering."

I still found that incredible: both oddly discomfiting and oddly reassuring. "Great," I said. "I look forward to seeing it."

"Just don't expect too much. I'm only a beginner."

"I'm only a little lamb, sir." *Tales of Toytown* . . . passed on to me by my parents.

"Well, I suppose I'd better let you go. I think I'll stop and have some lunch, as well. You mustn't worry about Susie."

Mavis came in soon afterwards. She was a large unwieldy type of woman who affected a girlish manner but had a genuinely sweet expression which declared her both eager and easy to please. Yet she had absolutely no dress sense and more than a smattering of facial hair. She was only in her forties—I didn't understand how anyone could be so careless. I suspected she was lesbian. I had taken her over with the shop some twelve years previously, when—with the aid of a loan from Lloyds, where up till then I'd still been working—I had managed to buy the business.

Now, mercifully, that loan had been repaid.

"Mr G," she said, "you are the best boss ever! Did you know that? I shall write to the papers to suggest a nationwide survey: Boss of the Year Award! Presentation dinner at the Dorchester." (And to keep me going until then, bless her heart, she had brought me a large bar of Cadbury's Fruit-and-Nut.)

Well!

Yesterday, Uncle of the Year.

Today, Boss.

Tomorrow? Husband, Father or—hey, now!—how about the relevant body trying *this* one on for size? Lover?

Or should I settle all-inclusively—perhaps a shade more modestly—for Man? Who cared about specifics?

Anyhow, as a foretaste of this greater glory Mavis had also brought me a rum baba, to eat with my sandwiches. (She liked to dole out her surprises one at a time: something I could well appreciate, since I often did the same, both at home and in the shop.) She was ebullient and this fact alone, even more than the chocolate or the baba or the Dorchester award—no, actually we had decided on the Ritz—provided ample justification for what had been, after all, a mainly impetuous phone call.

But I had learned from experience about the danger of not acting when the spirit moved. The road from Deal, I'd used to claim, would be paved with good intentions. Such a copout. As far as *I* was concerned, the road from Deal would now be paved with nothing but ordinary asphalt—and the road from Deal could like it! No future tense permissible.

With this in mind, I made out two cheques during the afternoon, one for the homeless and one for disease-prone children in Africa. When later I popped out to the post office, I left the shop hard on the heels of three old ladies who had paused to rearrange their headgear and didn't realize I was right behind. "What a delightful young man! My dears, don't you wish there were a few more like *him* in this world?" I ducked back through the door and was sure they hadn't noticed. But I think I must have blushed.

Returning from the post office, driven by impulse, I made a detour into the small old-time stationer's around the corner. That journal. At home I'd found a book which—though it dated back to school—hadn't ever been used and was moderately substantial. But, unsurprisingly, it was a bit scruffy. It seemed to me now that perhaps this brand-new project deserved as much respect as this brand-new fellow who aimed to make it so reflectively his own.

And almost at once I saw something in Ramsey & Whittaker's that my heart could leap up and respond to.

It was a tooled leather book in green, thick enough to contain an average-sized novel—say, *Catcher in the Rye* or *For Whom the Bell Tolls*—the tops of its pages gloriously gilt-edged. And it was shockingly expensive. But an *objet d'art*, I told myself, which might either end up as an heirloom or else as a channel for communicating truths to strangers; in both cases making it possible that the best of me, the zest of me, would survive. Something compact, something a person could easily hold in one hand, something which in years to come—whether in two or two hundred—would tell the world that I had once been here and what my being here had meant to me. A unique record. Unique testimony. If it were ever to be published, it might ensure that I could still make friends, share my experience of this otherwise impermanent existence, give my life importance, long after I was dead.

Besides. Whereas on the one hand I could always have it near me, even on my deathbed, this precious distillation, this gilt-edged memorial—on the other, if I suppressed my current instinct, I'd soon lose track of the money I had saved, might even end my days regretting it, such a very *small* form of saving. Clichéd but true: with us ordinary individuals it was the things we didn't do which had the greater power to nag.

So I took a breath and clutched the book and bore it to the counter.

When I got home that evening (with an attractively chunky bracelet for Ella, since, whether or not Matt had spoken of his ten pounds, one obviously had to do one's best to equalize), when I got home that evening I was fervently hoping that Susie would come ambling—at least *ambling*—around the side of the house to greet me. But, no, as I walked into the kitchen she remained leaden in her basket, awake but not raising her head. She had eaten her supper, however, and had apparently spent a good part of her day in the garden, though often only blundering across the flowerbeds and even crashing through the shrubs to stand there with her muzzle pressed against the wall—just staring at the brickwork until such time as she was turned around and so could lumber off mechanically towards the subsequent obstruction.

I stroked her now for several minutes without obtaining much response.

"Perhaps Mr Dodd was right," said Junie, as I stood propped against the Aga with my ritual glass of Martini, "when he thought in the first place it might be kinder just to have her put to sleep."

"No. He wasn't right. Nothing about it would have been right."

"Oh, Mum, we can't," cried Ella. "We can't!"

"In any case," I said, "it's still very early days. We've got to give her a fair chance."

I went to look at Junie's wallpapering; called from the landing with unfeigned admiration; then stripped down to my shorts and returning to the kitchen carried Susie to her bath, which I'd already prepared. Normally, knowing all too well what lay ahead, she put up a good deal of resistance, but this evening she let herself be borne upstairs without even a token splaying of her legs. After that, she simply stood in the warm water and neither made any attempt to escape nor raised any objection to the shower attachment. As I applied the shampoo, I sang to her, songs like *I'm gonna wash that man right outa my hair*, which perhaps didn't seem incredibly appropriate unless the driver of the car were the man being referred to, and *How much is that doggie in the window?* which I hurried to point out didn't mean we were looking for her replacement, merely harked back to a time when *she* had been that doggie in the window, all huge black patch and fluffy white fur, climbing over and tumbling around her much less frolicsome companions. Now she stood there in rigid acceptance (trembling as usual and as usual disconcertingly whippet-like beneath the rinsed, still dripping hair) but what was more normal, and therefore greatly reassuring, she afterwards ate with every appearance of enjoyment the handful of sweet biscuits that was always her reward for enduring bathtime, and also settled on the rug before the Aga to complete the drying-off process with an air at least of comprehension if not of actual contentment.

I asked Matt to clean and disinfect the bath, a process which took nearly as long as the bathing itself, for at eight o'clock I needed to be at Ruth Minton's. Tonight the Dover and District Players were to be reading and casting *The Deep Blue Sea*.

In recent years I'd played in two other Rattigans: a small part in *Separate Tables* and a far larger one in *The Browning Version*. Indeed, my roles were getting better all the time and I'd found so much satisfaction in performing them that, until early on Sunday morning, this belated discovery of a real vocation had been turning into a probably very silly but certainly very serious regret.

Yet now (it had suddenly come to me again while I was washing Susie) I didn't believe any longer in belatedness, nor in the harbouring of regrets, either silly *or* serious.

"Supposing I were to apply to RADA?" I asked Junie at supper. "It's a dream, I know—madness even to mention it—but overlooking all of that, don't you consider I possess the talent? I mean—just maybe. And the looks?"

"Ha!" said Matt.

"Pipe down. I'm talking to your mother."

"The looks for the Hunchback of Notre Dame?" he suggested.

Ella, though, was more encouraging. "Don't listen to him, Daddy. I think that's a pretty cool idea."

"Children, your father's only joking," announced my wife, wearily.

71

"Half joking," I amended. "Remember, every joke contains an element of truth." I smiled at Ella, gave her a fond wink. I liked it when she called me Daddy, when she forgot to be acerbic. It was my handling of her which must so frequently have been misguided—tonight, she'd been delighted with the bracelet, touchingly pleased it hadn't just come out of stock but had been chosen with great care at a jeweller's in the High Street. (All right, this was a fabrication but one which had given an immense amount of pleasure; whatever I did, I must on no account forget to mention it to Mavis.) And I resolved to cultivate Ella's friendship more assiduously than I feared had often been the case.

"So how precisely would we live?" asked Junie.

"Why, very much as we do now. You yourself could run the shop." I was talking wholly impromptu but growing more and more convinced as I did so. "I don't know why we've never thought of that before."

"Well, I do. I do! You've always told me you don't approve of working wives. You've always said it's the man who ought to earn the living."

"Just like I've always said it's the man who ought to decorate the house."

"Exactly."

"Then maybe I've been wrong. My God! Haven't I just been shown some pretty overwhelming evidence?"

"What! Can I quote you on that?" asked my son.

"*May* I quote you on that? My young Matthias, I hope I never mind admitting if I've been at fault. Old-fashioned—anachronistic—whatever. I'm not always that bright. I make mistakes. I know I'm superficial. But people change. People do change. You've got to give me that."

He was pretending to write it down; using his tablemat as a reporter's notepad. "What came after 'not always that bright'? What came before 'not always that bright'? I need to do you justice."

"You need to be a lot less cheeky. This is a meaningful discussion."

"Sam, are you really serious about this?" Junie was staring at me as though I was someone who'd just wandered in off the street and helped himself to vegetables.

"Yes, indeed I am. About what, precisely?"

She spread her hands, a little helplessly. "Well, about wanting to go on the stage."

"Cross my heart and hope to die."

There was a pause. I said: "I realize that I may have been sounding a tad frivolous but even so—"

"Oh! In a minute he's going to tell us he was only joking," interrupted Matt, sadly. "I mean, about 'superficial' and the rest of it."

I raised an eyebrow at him. He'd clearly forgotten yesterday's kiss on the back of my neck and what had given rise to it. Well, only to be expected. Thoroughly normal. Perhaps tomorrow he'd remember it. Or ten years from tomorrow. Or fifty.

"But even so," I continued, "you'd hardly have wanted me to get all intense and heavy about it, would you?"

"Daddy, I think you've been sounding fine."

"Thank you, darling. I appreciate that."

Junie began to giggle.

The giggling went on. She had to wipe her eyes. The children joined in—me, as well—puzzled though we all were.

"Mimsy and Pim!" she said. "Mimsy and Pim would have a fit. Only remember how they reacted when you decided to leave the bank!"

"Is that why you're laughing?"

She nodded.

"Your mother and father," I observed gently, "have no say whatever in the way we live our lives."

In spite of her own implied criticism, there followed a slightly uncomfortable silence. I had often wished—in one respect, anyhow— that the loan they'd made us when we bought the house hadn't been converted into a gift as soon as I could have begun to pay them back.

"It's none of Mimsy's business!" declared Matt, hotly, apparently deciding, after all, that perhaps I did have the looks and unconsciously relegating his grandfather to the subordinate position which indeed he held.

"Now, stop it, that isn't respectful," said Junie. "And all this is getting out of hand! To be honest, Sam, I'd probably quite enjoy managing the shop but I thought you were perfectly happy with the way things were. It never occurred to me—"

"I am," I answered. "I am." I'd finished my meal and now I went round behind her to kiss the top of her head. "I'm as happy as anybody ever could be. I have an excellent wife and two excellent children. What more could a man ask for? It's just that occasionally one likes to dream. To dream of doing something a little more colourful. To dream of . . . " I hesitated.

"What?"

"Oh, I don't know." I became self-mockingly grandiloquent. "Of sailing into unmapped waters, of spreading one's wings like a wandering albatross—or a sunbird—or a roc. Of realizing perhaps a larger bit of one's potential."

"Trust our dad! Who else would ever spread his wings like a rock? Who else would even think of it?"

"R-o-c," I smiled. "As you very well appreciate, little monster." Matt had been all but weaned on the adventures of Sinbad.

"Yet getting back to the subject in hand . . . ?" prompted Junie.

I gave a shrug. "Oh—as I said—I'm probably being adolescent. Stargazing. After all . . . out of every thousand expiring actors how many d'you suppose ever really get there?"

"Possibly," said Matt, "aspiring ones might stand a *fractionally* better chance."

"Why? What did I say? Nonsense," after he'd explained, "you're imagining things! I'll go to make the coffee."

Junie called after me. "But you could if you truly wanted. If you thought there'd be the slightest possibility. I wouldn't try to stop you."

"Yes, go on, Dad, why don't you?" shouted Matt. "You old expiring actor, you! And anyway what's so wrong, I'd like to know, about being adolescent?"

"Bet you could, Daddy," added Ella. "You're by far the hunkiest dad in Deal."

I put my head back through the doorway.

"You're very sweet, all of you! We'll have to see. No promises, mind. I certainly don't mean to rush into anything. I plan to be incredibly circumspect."

Head withdrawn. Head put back again.

"And, Matt, there is absolutely nothing wrong with being an adolescent! Nothing! Don't you think it for an instant."

Junie followed me out into the kitchen. "Oh, by the way, Mimsy and Pim were heartbroken to hear about Susie. But they're keeping their fingers crossed. And if there's anything they can do . . . "

"That's very kind," I murmured.

"And they thought you were totally wonderful yesterday. But they told me not to tell you."

I laughed. Junie went back to fetch more things off the table—or possibly to encourage the children to do so. For the moment, I forgot about making coffee. Supposing I *could* get into RADA? It wasn't feasible, of course . . . but just supposing? Not simply would it be a means of expanding my horizons: of maybe one day actually travelling a bit, of getting *really* overseas: to New York perhaps (to check out the delis), San Francisco, Hollywood. It would also mean that, sooner than this, at least during RADA's term-time, I'd be able to stay partly in London: an end to any problem over being with Moira. (And indeed wouldn't that alone represent an expansion to my horizons!) It seemed too good to be true, a readymade solution when as yet I'd hardly been on the lookout for one: thinking no further than that little house in Silver Street, which I now saw would have been hopelessly impractical. But this changed everything. Moira in the week; Junie and the children at weekends. The ingredients for paradise.

For paradise . . . Capten, art tha listenin' there below?

And—who knew—into the bargain I might even make a reputation?

The possibilities seemed endless.

In the end I didn't even go to Ruth Minton's. The deep blue sea still beckoned but this was a deeper, bluer, wider, warmer, infinitely more inviting ocean than any that had ever lapped upon the shores of Dover or of Deal.

And to expand a little on that Rattigan metaphor . . . the sleeping prince had finally—finally!—awoken.

Later, he wrote a lengthy letter to RADA, this newly arisen prince; addressed it simply to The Secretary, Royal Academy of Dramatic Art, London. If it was meant to get there, then it *would* get there . . . and I knew for certain that it was. I asked for information regarding grants, scholarships, auditions. I listed the plays I'd been in and let them have a recent photograph I liked—it had been taken on the beach and made me look all of twenty-eight—together with five hundred words on why I thought I should be suitable. I knew full well I had to sell myself.

I enclosed a stamped addressed envelope, and copies of cuttings from the *East Kent Mercury*.

The mouths of pillar boxes were too small, so for the second time that day I walked to the post office. At such an hour it seemed odd to be doing this without Susie, practically disloyal—and, naturally, there wouldn't be any collection before morning—yet at the same time it was comforting to suppose that my fate was now stamped, sealed, very nearly official, and would soon be winging its way into the hands of arbiters. Or at least—not to get *too* metaphoric or highflown or roc-like about it—to suppose the envelope was.

(Though for Junie's sake—no, for all our sakes—I certainly wanted to remain rocklike. As rocklike as ever.)

That night the count was up to almost a thousand . . .

Yow-w-w-w!

11

The following morning partial sanity returned—although, thankfully, only partial. For the first moment, I felt alarmed by what I'd done, but then I laughed and shrugged and thought oh what the hell. Cast your bread upon the waters . . . nothing ventured, nothing gained! All my life, I now believed, I'd played things far too safe. I was thirty-six. In another four years . . . ! Thank God I'd woken up in time.

Ungrudging endorsement: the phone at the shop rang merely a few minutes after I had walked in.

"Sam? Good morning. This is Moira Sheffield."

I'd recognized her voice on the first syllable. Although my heart at once reacted it hadn't had time to monkey with either my pitch or my phrasing. "Sweet heaven," I declared. "I was just thinking of you."

"Really? What were you thinking?"

"Only the worst."

"What a relief! How are you?"

"Fantastic. You?"

"Also pretty well. But listen, Sam. I've decided I shan't be coming back to Deal next weekend, I—"

"Oh, *no!*"

I shouldn't have said that, obviously I shouldn't, at least not with such emphasis. The words had been shocked from me. I felt cold with disappointment.

"But wait," she said, "let me tell you why. I've been offered two tickets for that new American musical, the one at present getting so much hype, and frankly I hadn't the chutzpah to turn them down. And then the title seemed to clinch it. *Half a Farthing, Sam Sparrow?* Oh, what relevance! They're for next Saturday evening. I wondered if you'd like to come."

"My God."

She laughed. "Is that a yes?"

"Exact translation: I should *love* to come. There's nothing that could possibly give me any greater pleasure . . . " Yet I was speaking with deliberation. My brain was trying frantically to get to grips. In my own mind the sentence wasn't finished but she didn't realize this.

"I'm so glad. I think that—despite the hype—the show should turn out to be fun."

"I haven't really caught the hype, just the hit tune, which is as catchy as all get-out." (Strange lyric, though: 'You feel that you're on trial, and so you're in denial, you want to cry and run a mile, but still you lie and still you smile, and smile and smile and smile . . . ' Rather dopey.)

"Yes, hard to get it out of your mind, once it's there; no doubt we'll drive each other crazy! Now what I also thought was this: is there any chance of your making a full weekend out of it—coming here on Friday night—getting your assistant (Liz tells me she feels sure you have one) to be in charge on Saturday? There's plenty of room at the flat and I've already made some plans for interesting things we could do together— you said the other day you don't know London awfully well . . . " But then she faltered. "Or do you think I'm being presumptuous?"

"Presumptuous? Good heavens, no. It all sounds out of this world, but . . . "

"Is it your grandmother? I was worried it mightn't be as easy as I hoped."

"Yes. May I ring you back? Say—in an hour? Will you be home?"

She gave me her number. "See what you can manage, then." I promised that I would. We ended, a bit bathetically, talking about transport.

Forty minutes later I rang Junie.

"Darling, guess what! Guess whom I've just heard from!"

"RADA. They've offered you a place."

"Not yet," I said, "although I admit they're being a little slow."

"Then I give up," she said. "Who?"

"John Caterham."

"John Caterham! Good gracious! You mean the John Caterham who was in our class at school?"

"As opposed to all the other John Caterhams we know?"

"But how—why—where? I wouldn't have thought he'd even got your number! Or knew what the shop was called! Where was he phoning from? Or do you mean it was a letter?"

"No, I spoke to him. He asked after you, of course. Sent his love. Couldn't believe our children are now old enough to be at the County High or that old Hinchcliff *still* hasn't retired."

"But what about his own children? Aren't they—?"

"Remember he married later than we did. Well, come to that, I imagine *everyone* married later than we did."

"How many has he?"

"Three. But listen, Junie, let me tell you why he phoned. He's still living in that place near Lincoln and they've got some important cricket fixture next Sunday, but one of their best players has broken his leg and John's desperate for a good replacement. He asked if I could go up for the whole weekend and I said yes because, although it's actually a bit of a bind, it does sound as if they're in a fix and I was really quite flattered. Mavis will look after the shop on Saturday but I said you might pop in and relieve her at lunchtime. Naturally John would have asked you and the kids but his wife's away at the moment—her mother isn't well—and they've got the workmen in and anyway what with its being Ted and Yvonne's anniversary celebration on Sunday . . . "

The gabble was to let her understand it was all a *fait accompli*. I had no fears she'd stand in my way but I hoped she wouldn't sound reproachful.

Which she didn't. Not at all. I should have known better.

"Darling, obviously you've got to go! It's like you're answering a Mayday signal and although we're going to miss you—of course we are—you could scarcely have refused. But just imagine! John Caterham! After all these years!"

So then I phoned the station: as Moira owned a car we'd both considered it unnecessary for me to drive—and anyway I wouldn't have wanted to leave Junie and the children dependent upon lifts. I was just finishing the call when Mavis arrived. It was lucky we'd agreed she needn't begin until ten—because even in the midst of tidying or cleaning she was apt to thrust her head around the door to share a thought or put a question and I could hardly, suddenly, have requested her not to. Besides that, there were certain areas of the shop from which a phone call could be heard . . . especially when the radio wasn't on . . . and I wouldn't have wanted to be asked (she was fully capable of it) why had I been speaking so softly and what guilty secret did I have to hide. Therefore, to guarantee myself a good five minutes of privacy, I sent Mavis out to buy rum babas before I rang back Moira.

And found the line engaged!

I counted, in a determinedly disciplined fashion, up to fifty. Then rang again.

Walked round the shop and made myself breathe deeply; this time counted up to sixty. My pulse rate had gone mad and even my bowels threatened treachery. My bladder, too. The patisserie was only down the road and what if on my third attempt the line continued busy . . . ?

It didn't.

Benevolent heaven. In reality, the delay couldn't have lasted longer than three minutes. I relaxed.

Well, up to a point I did. I still needed to impress. And to hurry things a bit.

I said: "If I leave here mid-afternoon on Friday I should get to Victoria at six-forty-eight. Precisely. Which means, of course, I'll have a pretty long wait at Dover Priory. I hope you appreciate that."

"Oh, I do! I shall be at Victoria at six-forty-seven-and-a-half in a strenuous attempt to compensate!"

"Thank you. To strike a more serious note, however, you don't have to come to meet me. I used to be a boy scout; could probably still find my compass."

"I'm glad to hear it. To strike an even *more* serious note, however, I should *like* to come to meet you."

"And to strike the most serious note of all, however, I was simply being polite—haven't any wish whatever to reject a sympathetic guide. No, on the contrary, I'll carry a white stick and tap my way along the platform like blind Pew."

"You're better-looking than he was."

"That's a weight off my mind. I can't believe I've only met you twice."

"It's going to be fun. I'm looking forward to it. Oh—and while I think of it—will you bring your dinner jacket?"

"I . . . Yes, of course."

"We'll do this thing in style."

"You bet we will." I heard the bell above the shop door. "Oh, damn, I'm afraid I've got to go! Customers."

"It's all right, Mr G, only yours truly!" called out Mavis, over the partition.

"Be seeing you Friday, then. Ciao!"

"Ciao!" answered Moira. I cursed the interruption, even while I sensed it was a blessing. Left to myself I might have gone on talking for an hour. That would have been lovely, but . . . but I wanted to play it cool. I was totally without experience of intrigue, yet knew I had her interest and also knew, according to received wisdom, that at this stage it would be safer to retain a little mystery, keep her guessing, separate my heart from my sleeve.

"You are an idiot, Mr G—it was only yours truly," Mavis repeated. She'd now opened the office door. "Sorry about that."

I tilted back my chair and hitched both thumbs into my trouser pockets. I was magnanimous. "Nay, lass, think nowt on't."

She giggled, held up the paper bag, took my change out of her purse. "I had to get meringues. They hadn't got babas."

"No sweat," I said. With Mavis I could play it cool.

Yet even with Mavis it was partly touch-and-go. I felt I could have let out a whoop. Felt I could have run a mile. (Literally.) Could have jumped into the sea with all my clothes on. Jumped into the sea without a stitch. Kicked a football (we had one), hurled a cricket ball (we had one), watched them either disappear above a rooftop or else re-descend to make the perfect header, present the perfect catch. I could have rung the bell on one of those things which test your strength at fairgrounds—felt I could have broken the machine.

But I merely sat there at my desk, with the most active thing about me being my brain. "Too soon to make the coffee?" asked Mavis.

"What?"

"Coffee?"

"Coffee? If you like. Up to you." Yes—sure. There were times when I could be remarkably chilled out. "Hey, Mavis. I want you to tell me something. And I want you to be perfectly candid."

"Oh, Lord! I hate it when anybody says that."

"Does my hair need cutting?"

"Is that it?"

"What?"

"The thing I've got to be perfectly candid about."

"You mustn't ever underestimate," I said, "the importance of wear-ing your hair the proper length."

"Mine or yours?" she asked, playfully. I had grown as used to the unruliness of her hair as to the exuberance of her breathing. I had to ride out my lack of tact; hope she either hadn't noticed it or hadn't been offended.

"And next weekend, you see, I aim to cut a dash."

She gazed at me—her head held slightly to one side. At rare moments Mavis seemed to lose her little girlishness. "A rugged dash or a sophisticated one?" she inquired.

"Both." I told her about what Junie had described as a Mayday sig-nal and she was suitably impressed.

"In cricket togs I'd be inclined to go for the more rugged kind. I like you with long hair."

"In white flannels, yes. But what about evening dress?"

That perhaps was indiscreet. Yet all she said was: "My word, is there going to be a dance? Well, Mr G—life is a compromise. You'd better play the match, then run off to the barber's as soon as stumps are drawn."

"I don't believe in compromise."

"Ah . . . I always said you must've led a magical existence!"

"You did?"

"No, not really." She shook her head in apology.

"But how right you would have been! A *very* magical existence."

Abruptly, I stood up. "I'm going out for twenty minutes. You, my girl, can eat the two meringues. Make up for a lifetime of half measures."

While I was in the mood I went into the bank and by chance was able to get an interview with the manager. (No, not by chance: by charm: by the irresistible persuasiveness of someone convinced that life, let alone bank managers, could deny him nothing. From now on, I reminded myself, I should never *not* be in the mood!) Hal Smart had been a schoolfriend. Because we'd regularly had our arms around each other in the rugger scrum and larked together in the shower it meant I never felt trepidation about asking for a loan; Hal knew better than to condescend. (In fact if either of us felt superior, it could well have been me: although he'd once been slim and muscular, in the last ten or fifteen years he'd put on a lot of weight and lost a lot of hair; no stranger would have considered us the same age.) This morning he readily agreed to my request; understood about the upkeep of old houses—owning one himself. We asked after each other's families and said, as we always did, that we must all get together sometime. Then he walked me to the main door and slapped my back by way of farewell; an attention not every overdrawn client was likely to receive from his bank manager. "All the very best, Sam!" I wanted to tell him I'd already got it. I strode away jauntily, with my shoulders squared and my hands in my trouser pockets, like a man who'd just staged an eminently successful holdup and knew in these enlightened times that the censors were going to let him get away with it; enjoy the fruits of his inventiveness and daring.

From the bank to the hairdresser's . . . but only for the merest trim. (Okay, Mavis, I admit—a compromise!) I also had a manicure. It was good to have a svelte and pretty blonde hold your hand and relate to you the latest chapter in the saga of her search for Mr Wonderful. I offered her some worldly-wise advice.

Then finally, or almost finally, the men's outfitters: the snazziest in town. A dinner jacket. With more warning I could have had it made;

the one I settled on, however, looked extremely dashing, even without the proper shirt or tie or shoes—and I was assured that without fail the alterations could be carried out by Friday. I turned this way and that and was far more impressed than I revealed to the probably gay assistant. Why on earth had I ever waited so long? I was a toff. I was a man-about-town. I was the model off the cover of a Harrods catalogue.

I wrote the cheque in the same happy fashion that I'd handed out tips at the hairdressers. With something of a flourish. I needn't have, not until Friday.

Equally, I could have waited for the trim and manicure till then, merely have booked an appointment. But why? If you were going to live each day as though your last, didn't it behove you, on each last day, to look, and therefore feel, as fine as you possibly could?

But I'd been absent from *Treasure Island* for over two hours. On occasion it was almost unbelievable how quickly time could pass.

"Mavis, what do you think of my hair?"

"Have you had it done?"

Well, that was absolutely as it should be.

"No wonder you've been gone so long! I must be mad. I thought you told me twenty minutes."

"You are mad. Twenty minutes! What an extremely *odd* idea! But I'm sorry—have I made you late for lunch?"

"It doesn't matter. I did eat both meringues. And telephoned to warn my ma."

"Oh, that reminds me, I've a present for your ma. Wondered if a bottle of wine might cheer her up a bit. Encourage her to shimmy like her sister Kate."

"Or maybe shimmer like her uncle Sam. Bless you," said Mavis. "You are good!"

12

"I've been thinking," I said. It was the same evening, while we sipped our Martinis. Poor Susie sat beside my chair, with her head on my lap, and we told ourselves she was improving. After all, it hadn't yet been forty-eight hours. I scratched behind her ears and she seemed to be enjoying it, for she had closed her eyes. But the old vitality was missing—for the moment—and although there were many things which she plainly remembered, far too often we would still find her with her nose against a wall or against some other large blank area, like the back of a settee or the front of a bookcase, merely standing and staring and placidly waiting. This obviously was worrying and Mr Dodd had said we should see how she was doing in another week. "That old defeatist," I'd declared. "He doesn't reckon for the power of love. You've got to be positive, haven't you, Suze? It's love that's going to pull you through."

"Hurray for love!" said Junie. I don't know why that should have sounded slightly out of character.

Not unlike her reply—a short while later—to that opening gambit of mine. *I've been thinking.*

"Well done," she said.

Though she was smiling.

I stared into my drink. It had been the lead-in to something quite important. "How are things?" I asked. "You seem a little tired."

"I am—a little. Not wholly unexpected. It's probably because my period's due."

"Oh, hell. Already?"

"I don't mind, really. The sooner it comes the sooner I get it over with."

"Yes, of course." I did my best to adjust to this. "You poor old thing, it isn't right; you have a lot to put up with, don't you?"

"Mmm, it's unusual. Not many women get periods. Why me, I ask myself. Why me?"

I laughed. If she were acting a trifle strangely I reflected that (a) it was good to have a wife who could still surprise one after seventeen years and (b) that it was principally her period talking. (Which shouldn't have begun until the following weekend—blast it! Ah, the best laid schemes o' mice an' men an' o' potential Casanovas . . .)

But I had always hoped that at times of small reversals like this I would remember Count Basie's basic philosophy. 'Life is a bitch and if it's not one damn thing then it's going to be something else.' I topped up our drinks: *Martini—for the beautiful people.* And when we sat down to supper I almost immediately got up to fetch four wineglasses and a bottle of Sauternes from the sideboard. (On the way I tousled Ella's hair. "Oh, *Dad!*" she said—and jerked away her head. "Oh, *Dad!*" I said, with the old familiar sense of disappointment.) "What's that for?" asked Junie, surprised, indicating the bottle.

"Mum, don't stop him!" cried the children, in rare harmony.

"I'm going to put it in the fridge so that we can have it with our puds."

"Fine," she answered. "Good idea. I simply wondered why."

"In celebration," I called.

"What of?"

"Just of things generally. Of life. Of the fact you're all so nice."

"That's very sweet," said Junie, once I had returned.

"Oh, Pop," said Matt, "I got my project back today."

"So soon?" I asked.

He lowered his head, gave a shamefaced smile. "I know I let you think the deadline would be yesterday but I suppose I misled you: most people handed in their work about two weeks ago. Sorry."

"And that call you had reminding you?"

"Peter Bale—to warn me Miss Martin was finally losing her rag."

"Well, anyway. Thank you for coming clean about it. I think that's what really counts."

"Though perhaps it would have been even better," said my wife, "not to tell such a fib in the first place." Junie had this awful reverence for truth.

"At all events, Matthias . . . What was the verdict?"

"Miss Martin seemed pleased with it." His look of penitence had quickly faded. "Especially—you were right—with that thing I did on Theseus. That thing *you* did on Theseus. But she said I left out the ending. Said he wasn't someone I should really wish to emulate."

"Why not?"

"Because of Ariadne."

"What about Ariadne?"

"Well, you sort of gave the impression they got married, lived happily-ever-after, all *that* kind of guff. One of the great love stories, I think you said. She told me he turned out to be a louse. That he deserted her."

"She accused Theseus of deserting Ariadne?"

"Yes."

"Called him a louse? I can't believe that. I'm sure you must have got it wrong."

"Dad! How can you dream up louse? Dream up desertion?"

"Then—I'm sorry—*she* must have got it wrong! You'll have to tell her."

"Well, I suppose it's not so world-shakingly important." He shrugged.

"Of course it's important!"

"Then you tell her! *I* shan't."

"And don't think I won't. Next parents' evening? When's that?"

"You don't mean you'll actually be coming?"

"Try and stop me."

"There's one on . . . I think it's a fortnight Thursday."

"Then make me an appointment!"

We all laughed, myself as much as anyone. "Action Man," observed Matt. "Three cheers for Miss Martin!" said his mother.

Action Man . . . I savoured this for several seconds. On one of the tables in the shop there was an Action Man stripped down to his black briefs. I often saluted him as I went past—or set him back on his feet if vibrations had caused him to topple: despite his magnificent physique he wasn't that well-balanced. "Glad you've noticed the resemblance," I said.

"Why don't you just phone her, Dad?" asked Ella.

"No, you shut up," said Matt. "He's coming to the parents' evening. They both are. Aren't you, Pop?"

"Course I am."

"Promise?"

"Only the grave could stop me now. Honest!"

"Honest Sam Groves," said Junie. "My husband the bookmaker."

"Funny you should say that." Though I hoped she didn't have in mind a fairly recent but far from funny incident.

"Why? Is that what you're thinking of setting up as?"

"Well, no. Not necessarily. But you remember how I said earlier that there's something I've been thinking about?" Yes, this was as good a time as any; the children could be in on it, too. In on it right from the beginning. "It's this. That RADA business last night. I don't believe it's going to come to anything. I don't see how it can, one's got to be realistic. One's got to be—"

"But, oh, Daddy," Ella exclaimed, "you're not giving up the idea of being an actor?"

"Darling, you really shouldn't interrupt," admonished Junie.

"If RADA auditioned me and decided to take me on, that would be fantastic, Ella. But what I'm saying is—it isn't very likely. Yet supposing it was? We'd been talking about Mum being the one to look after the shop, hadn't we, getting out a bit, meeting people, discovering—?"

"Well, I can't say I'm all that disappointed," Junie cut in. "You don't have to worry that you might be letting me down."

"You said you'd quite enjoy it."

"That's true but—"

"Junie, hold on. I went to see Hal Smart today."

"Hal? You mean, on business?"

"What other reason would I go for?"

I paused. It had suddenly occurred to me how sad was that remark. Hal and I had once been very close. I'd actually had a crush on him. For practically the whole of my fifteenth year, during what had turned into an unexpectedly curative, even an almost carefree time, the two of us had been inseparable. 'They'll never prise apart young Groves and Smart,' some budding versifier had once scrawled across the blackboard, 'they're like apple with cloves, young Smart and Groves,' and I recalled how I'd secretly felt immensely proud to form half of such a brilliant couplet, a couplet which had seemed to me quite as inspired as any in the *Golden Treasury*, of which my grandmother had given me a copy. But now . . . some twenty-two years later . . .

"Yes, of course on business," I said. No wonder I should be such an expert on the matter of life's little ironies. Seeing Hal now could sometimes make me shiver in disbelief. And also in embarrassment: we had once embraced while in the shower.

"And . . . ?" Junie queried.

I looked at her.

"Darling, what were you leading up to?"

"Oh, yes. Sorry. I got sidetracked." Remembering a rider the nasty Evan Saunders had later added to that couplet—though only verbally, thank God, it was never taken up. 'Apple with cloves, young Smart and Groves. The tastier tart—young Groves or Smart?' In some ways I'd minded it less at the time than I did today. Or, at any rate, it hadn't tarnished my then pride in the original.

I hastily reassembled my thoughts.

"Woolgathering," I smiled. "It's just that . . . Well, you know I never worry you about these things, Junie—not normally—but the shop isn't doing all that well at present. It's probably nothing serious, of course: the usual pre-summer lull: and I suppose I should never have thought of taking Mavis on fulltime . . . " Junie didn't know I'd taken Mavis on fulltime; this seemed a good moment to reveal it. But, even in spite of that, I hated having to appear so negative. It required a great deal of determination and like Matt last Saturday I kept my fingers crossed—

although *un*like him I didn't parade the fact. This helped a little: feeling like my son. Gilded youth! Gilded youth, I thought, but really not so many years divided us, merely twenty-three, less than a generation, I oughtn't to forget that. My own golden future gleamed every bit as bright.

"Oh, *Sam* . . . !" Junie got up. She came and did to me what I had done to her the previous evening: stood behind my chair and put her arms about my neck and kissed the top of my head. "I knew you'd been behaving a little too cheerfully these past few days! Darling, I should have realized what it meant. I think you're *very* brave but I also think you're *very* foolish . . . " She bent and put her cheek against my own.

Unsurprisingly, all this solicitude made my eyes moisten. No less predictably, it brought a mocking reaction from our children. ("Oh, no, not again! And see that, Cinders? Action Man is having to dash away a tear!") Junie resumed her seat while I reprimanded my offspring, although with a tolerance roughly matching their own, for being so silly and immature—and was unsporting enough to remind them that they hadn't yet received their wine.

I turned my attention back to Junie. "Sweetheart, it's truly not so tragic as it sounds." And now I hammed up the eye-dabbing. "Especially since I've had a bit of a brainwave—and it's all due to this thing about RADA; I mightn't have thought of it otherwise. Now, we have a real need to supplement our income, right? And the job opportunities in Deal at the moment—like in any other small town in this country— are virtually non-existent and—"

"I could maybe get a job at Marks & Spencer's," said Junie, "or British Home Stores or somewhere. Sam, you should have *told* me if we were getting into difficulties."

"No. That isn't your department. Nor is it for *you* to try to get us out of them. It's very sweet of you, darling, but . . . "

I gave a shrug.

"But what?"

"But I could earn a far better wage in London than you could ever hope to earn down here, where if there's anything at all, it's most likely only part-time and poorly paid. Besides, darling, you know me: I've never liked the idea of my wife going out to work."

"What would I be doing at the shop then? Getting a suntan?"

"That's different."

"How?"

"You'd be the owner. The wife of the owner. It's somehow not the same."

"Mr Spock would never understand," declared Matt, mournfully, shaking his head.

"Captain Kirk would."

"Well, I'm not too sure about this," said Junie. "I don't think I go for it. We're a family. When would we ever see you?"

"At weekends. I'd be home every Friday night; wouldn't leave again until Monday. You'd hardly notice I was gone."

"Is that what you honestly believe?"

"Obviously it's an arrangement that none of us really wants. But if we look at it positively there may be *some* advantages. I mean—apart from all the extra money and the higher standard of living and the holidays abroad."

"We already have holidays abroad."

"Yes, but that's only because your parents pay so much towards them—and naturally have the major say in where we go. And that's nearly always to some part of France. But this way we could occasionally branch out: Italy, Greece, maybe even California. Just think of it, how good that would be for the children's education . . . "

Ella and Matt were instantly in favour of extra money, a higher standard of living and holidays abroad. Even Junie herself was invariably influenced by any question of the children's education.

"Also," I said, "think how special the weekends would be. A father coming home brings presents and a husband coming home takes his wife out to expensive restaurants on a Saturday night."

"That's not fair," said Matt, immediately.

"And his children."

"Okay, it's getting fairer." Then he said: "So long as it can be relied on, absolutely." His tone was now lugubrious again.

"Hey!" I said. "Matthias! What do you take me for? A welsher?"

"What's that? No. An expiring actor."

This showed signs of developing into a running gag between us. I laughed and hoped to foster it.

"Oh, but you're being crazy," protested Junie. "Presents! Expensive restaurants! You'll have two homes to run. Meals. Train fares. It will be enough of a problem just breaking even."

"What do you mean, two homes to run?"

"What do you think I mean, two homes to run?"

I recollected myself, spread my hands and gave a smile. "But, Junie, you don't understand. My needs are simple. A cheap bedsitter with a gas ring. I don't care about the area, I shall always have my home to come home to." I laughed. "Darling, it almost sounds as though you doubt my potential earning capacity. As though you doubt my real worth."

"The only thing I doubt," she answered, "is the ability of others to recognize your real worth . . . though since when has a person's earning capacity been the measure of a person's worth?"

Then she added: "And you know I don't mean to be brutal but what precisely would you say you're qualified for?"

"Pop, only imagine what she could do if she did mean to be brutal!"

"Here, kids, I think you've got to help me out. What *am* I qualified for?"

"Oh, we'd like to help you out. But the trouble is—poor Cinders hasn't any imagination and you told me not to lie."

"No, no, it was your mother who told you that. You know my credo. Anything that I can hope to get away with!"

We had a jolly time. Between the four of us (though, to be honest, the women advanced far fewer suggestions than either Matt or me, whether sensible or silly—of the latter, "Join the army!" was a fairly typical example) . . . between the four of us we came up with at least a dozen serious possibilities. However, Junie laid down two conditions which she said were non-negotiable.

Firstly, she wouldn't have me going into security work and, secondly, insisted I must hold onto my Saturdays. Beyond that, she didn't think that most of the other jobs, even in London, would pay particularly good salaries; but on the other hand she didn't really mind (she supposed) how much I might choose to demean myself—none of them did—provided it only happened at a reasonable distance from Deal.

"Yes, what do dustmen get?" asked Ella.

"And roadsweepers?" speculated Matt. "Or window cleaners? Lavatory attendants? Milkmen? Posties? Gravediggers—*alas, poor Yorick!*—with recitations on the side?"

"Oh, there must be literally hundreds of things that Daddy could do!"

I wasn't too comfortable with the idea of perfectly honest livelihoods being thought of as demeaning, but at least there weren't likely to be that many roadsweepers, gravediggers or dustmen passing through our hall right now and it didn't seem the proper time to get pompous.

"Of course, you *could* always sell your body," suggested Matt. "Though, I'm not sure, do you think you'd find any takers?"

So we drank our wine and altogether had considerably more fun than if nothing had changed and I had spent this evening as, until last Saturday, I had fully intended to. In stripping wallpaper and in sanding down paintwork.

And we talked about my project, off and on, for the next two hours or more—with the children, without the children—managing to find a few fresh arguments, yes, but in the main basically repeating ourselves.

"Well," Junie said at last, "we might as well give it a try. If it doesn't work, it doesn't work. And I suppose we really haven't very much to lose."

"No, not a thing," I replied; my sombreness of tone hardly attesting to my gaiety of heart.

13

Wednesday and Thursday represented in one sense quite the longest two days I could remember, even though, simultaneously, there was a part of me that didn't hope for them to hurry. Matt would have laughed at me and felt impatient but I kept saying to myself: this time is special—unrepeatable—don't wish it over. So I passed the hours in a kind of sun-shot haze and imagined myself about to leave the quayside, the impatient traveller anxious to be properly under way but the home-loving man still appreciating his view from the ship's rail. All the people waiting on the dock, waiting to see me off, appeared at their very nicest, whether they were relatives, acquaintances or total strangers, and I felt that every word I called back ought to be wise or humorous or in some way worth the uttering. Is it true, is it kind, is it necessary? Even when I spoke only to Susie, or to the rubber plant in the hall, or to the yucca at the bend of the stairs, I aimed to choose my sentences with care. With careful spontaneity. That seemed to be the order of the day.

And here's a small example of how everything works out if you're steering a true course and thinking principally of others: Junie's period didn't come—not on the Tuesday, nor the Wednesday, nor yet the Thursday. And even though I couldn't help myself at odd moments thinking about Moira (calamitous, I'd discovered, on one occasion earlier in the week)—even though on the Thursday morning, running late, I scarcely tried to discipline myself at all—the count shot up amazingly: well over two thousand, which represented a solid thirty-five minutes, possibly more. No one could feel hard-done-by at thirty-five minutes, or *not* hard-done-by at thirty-five minutes, even if it might occasionally provoke a stifled yawn. (Yet poor Junie, you couldn't blame her: a pair of demanding children in the house made up an enervating package.)

But then—would you believe?—on Friday, when I'd decided I wanted in any case to begin this tremendous day in a state of chastity, Junie informed me that her period had arrived during the night! It was practically sufficient to give you faith in the existence of a god—that is, if you were a little weaker and more malleable than you ought to have been.

Unfortunately, though, I didn't sleep well on the Thursday night. As a precautionary measure I'd wondered whether to ask the doctor for some Nitrazepam; but although I'd lain awake for a long time during the small hours of Sunday morning (and been extremely happy to do so), since then, surely due to all that unaccustomed sexual activity, I'd had no trouble whatsoever over sleeping . . . no, not even following the heady excitement of that RADA episode. Indeed, in recent years there had been other, equally heady excitements—my playing of Lord Goring, for instance, and of Frank Hunter, and my annual participation in the local tennis tournament—but none of these had ever seriously affected my sleep.

But that Thursday night felt endless and instead of relaxing I worried about it: I wouldn't look my best, my reactions would suffer—my conversation, my sexual performance, everything. I'd be unable to get through the next day with any degree of alertness, let alone of vibrancy. I'd be a tedious, lifeless, disappointing lump.

Maybe the only thing that prevented a full-scale panic—i.e., deciding to postpone the whole weekend on the grounds of someone's illness (whose? not my grandmother's, we'd then have Moira rushing down to help look after her)—was the thought that I might at least manage to doze on leaving Dover.

The reassurance in this idea . . . together with a mug of hot milk and several digestive biscuits which, clearly, I should have taken earlier . . . these finally did the trick; but by then it was half-past-five. And all part of the same irony: we had gone to bed—for once—a little before ten, had probably turned out our lights before Matt and Ella had. Fools that we were; or rather, of course—fool that I was!

Yet anyhow, although I overslept again (therefore we all did) and awoke still feeling tired, this was nonetheless an improvement on the way I had felt at half-past-five. I had to rush my bath and skimp my breakfast but I'd seen to the bulk of my packing the night before. I had also given my shoes a shine and had even tried on my whites—this, naturally, at the behest of Junie, who was cross with herself for not having thought about it earlier.

Skimping breakfast, though—I imagine it was that—meant my bowels didn't function properly for the first morning in I don't know how many, including Sunday, when I had actually *chosen* to skimp. Had I been a little weaker and more malleable than I ought to have been, I might well have thrown my spurious faith right down the bowl and had at least *something* of note to flush away.

Because, you see, if I didn't have a satisfactory movement after breakfast I seldom compensated for it later on and the whole day could be one of bloated, if largely psychological, discomfort. And merely the thought of railway lavatories, whether on the stations or the trains themselves, was almost enough to make me feel tarnished—unclean.

However, despite all the rushing and skimping, I did find time to say goodbye to Susie.

"I shan't be seeing you, old thing, until Monday. Monday night! Four whole days . . . how shall we survive?"

Since for the moment she didn't appear able to roll herself over or hadn't got back to appreciating the whys and wherefores, I had to do it for her, in order to tickle her tummy. This wasn't easy but what made me persevere was the impression of enjoyment that she still conveyed—although more from the way in which her legs stretched out than from any soppily abandoned grin. And the effort seemed worth it.

"But here's your list of instructions, Suze. You must go outside a lot, because you need to get some roses in your cheeks. And you must take your medicine like a good girl. 'I am really getting better!' you will say. 'I shall soon, once more, be barking my head off at every cat in the neighbourhood and soon, once more, be sticking my nose down every rabbit hole on the common! I am really getting better!' All weekend, please, you will repeat those final words without letup. Understood?"

I rolled her back into her previous position and gave her a final pat. She struggled up to follow me, lumberingly, as far as the closed gate.

The leave-taking from my children hadn't been half so affecting. While I was still upstairs Ella—probably reminded by her mother— had called from the front door, "Have a lovely time, Dad, see you Monday," but I'd barely had an instant to call back before I'd heard her running down the path; while Matt, who had gone off a few minutes later with the classmate who invariably collected him, had forgotten to say goodbye at all. This was completely usual but today I'd hoped he might remember. I had shouted down at what I thought was the last possible moment—and had marginally misjudged it.

I didn't say any proper goodbye to Junie because at some point she was going to come into *Treasure Island*. Having baked a fruit cake for the Caterhams, she had belatedly decided she ought to marzipan and ice it. It had struck her that with John's wife away looking after a sick mother—an act of kindness which had probably left three young children badly in need of cheering up—the cake could do with all the decoration available.

I myself reached the shop fewer than ten minutes after my normal time . . . although it was only my ingrained sense of punctuality that had pushed me on; and when Mavis arrived I suddenly wondered why I hadn't eaten my usual decent breakfast, driven over with the keys— then driven home again and bathed and dressed at leisure. That should have been the obvious solution.

Yet because I hadn't thought of it, and now attributed such stupidity to the fact of my having felt so tired, I instantly felt *more* tired. And instead of this weekend shaping up as the most wonderful in my experience, I had premonitions it was going to rank among the most disastrous; possibly *be* the most disastrous.

Again I thought of telephoning Moira, this time to tell her I myself was ill: some sort of stomach bug, nothing too serious, merely incapacitating. *And* infectious—I ought to tell her that. Or was there some other minor ailment which might sound more romantic?

In any case I couldn't do it. Couldn't jeopardize this opportunity for happiness . . . no matter how doomed it might be coming to appear.

I had to go back to the outfitter's after twelve. I'd resolved, half-heartedly, that if by any chance the evening suit *wasn't* ready—or the alterations just weren't right—then I would definitely ring Moira. But not only was everything in order: when I put on the suit it looked terrific; my lack of sleep hadn't in any way damaged my appearance! From that moment the whole downward trend of the day—hitherto irreversible—splendidly reversed itself.

I collected my patent leather pumps. I'd bought them at a nearby shop on Wednesday but had decided not to pick them up until today. These completed my wardrobe. My new dress shirt and cufflinks and black tie were in the bag with the dinner jacket.

Yes, wardrobe completed . . . even down to the white walking stick I'd thought it might be fun to borrow; hadn't I spoken to Moira of tapping my way along the platform, as helpless as blind Pew? (Not that, of course, up to the moment of his fall, he had been helpless, not remotely so—I hoped this made the simile a bit more apt. Disregard his villainy, think about his valour.) I wondered if my knowing we had a white stick amongst our other canes and umbrellas had precipitated that particular piece of foolishness.

When I returned to the shop I found that Junie had already been . . . with the cake for the Caterham family tied securely in a cardboard carton previously used by Tesco's to transport jars of salad cream, but now thoughtfully provided with a good strong loop by my wife. "And also," added Mavis, "she left a message—*two* messages! The first: you've got to score a century and not bother coming home unless you do. And the second: she's decided to drive into Canterbury to try to find a suitable anniversary present for your sister-in-law. We spoke about how hard it is, wanting to buy something nice for the person who has everything."

Junie and I had been speaking about that all week—though admittedly in between one or two other things.

"She said there didn't seem much point in her waiting," Mavis continued, "since I hadn't any idea how long you'd be and she only wanted to wish you a safe journey and a wonderful weekend."

In one respect, of course, it was as well she hadn't waited: I had come strutting back into the shop with no attempt to hide my purchases; and the bags themselves looked glossily expensive, not the kind in which I normally collected jumble. (Plainly another instance of my not having been thinking too clearly but not one that saddened me again; I would simply have said I hadn't mentioned the dance because of the worrying expense of hiring clothes for it.) Yet I was sorry to have missed her. It meant that we hadn't said goodbye as we should have. And although I heard in this the murmurings of superstition I felt it was somehow wrong to be going off at such a time without both giving and receiving a hug—a kiss—a blessing: some brief restatement of our love. I tried to phone her; wondered if with any luck she might have gone home before carrying on to Canterbury. But the telephone just rang and rang, bleakly, in the empty hall.

With only Susie to know about it.

"No good?" asked Mavis. "I didn't suppose it would be. But when I see her tomorrow I'll mention how you tried."

Even so, after an interval of several minutes, I gave it a further shot. She might have been in the garden or on the loo and the ring wasn't a loud one.

"No," I said. "Damn. Well, never mind."

"You're certainly a most devoted husband!"

"Thank you, Mavis. And since that's entirely to Junie's credit I shan't refute it."

"Well, it makes a nice change, Mr G, it really does. We should hang you up as an example."

"Hold me up is what I hope you mean."

She laughed, and for a moment sounded even more husky than usual. "Not that I imagine you'll ever need much holding up!" she said. "You're surely not the sort who'll suddenly begin to sag!" I wasn't sure whether or not that contained a *double entendre*. But—either way— the sentiment was pleasing.

At first, staring at that small yet solid carton, I wondered if perhaps I couldn't leave it. I already had my holdall, plus two carrier bags, plus a white walking stick. But hiding it would have been haz-ardous. Customers often asked for things which you felt you might have seen *somewhere* and supposing Mavis should good-naturedly set off on a wholesale rummage? Or what was equally unlikely—yet at the same time equally possible—supposing Junie herself, during the hour or so when she'd be filling in, should venture forth upon some voyage of discovery! I might be living dangerously but—oh, my God!—I liked to think I wasn't actually going out of my way to *plant* clues.

Also, to leave Junie's cake would have seemed both callous and disloyal; not the right way to be embarking on a big adventure—and especially not so, in conjunction with the fact that we hadn't said goodbye as I'd have chosen. It would almost have seemed I was leaving behind a part of *her*.

I tried to phone again at three-fifteen but she had probably stopped in Canterbury for lunch.

I gave up after that. My train was at three-forty-five. And I wanted to take my time over walking to the station.

Indeed, I wanted to take my time over every aspect of these next three days. *See and appreciate. See and appreciate.* I should have had this inscribed (yes, seriously, I mean)—tattooed—across the under-side of my left wrist.

"I really hope," I said, "that you and . . . Wendy? . . . have a great time at . . . at Herne Bay, is it?" No. Mavis and her friend were spend-ing the bank holiday at Broadstairs—or, at any rate, what would be left of the bank holiday. It hadn't occurred to me: I should have suggested we shut the shop for three days, not just two. Oh, damn! How selfish could a person get? Yet maybe it wasn't too late—"Why don't we put a notice on the door?" But she swiftly salved my conscience.

"No, Mr G." With a vehement shake of the head. "Wend couldn't have got away until after lunch tomorrow. And Mum as well . . . I couldn't have left Mum for *three* whole nights! She's in enough of a hu-ha as it is. But she's not an invalid—that's what I say—and while I can, I've got myself to think of. Haven't I? I tell her it will do her good."

"You're right, Mavis. Occasionally everyone has themselves to think of."

"But you make sure you have a really great time, too. Knock 'em all for six! I mean—both on the cricket field *and* on the dance floor."

"Naturally," I said. "Oh, but, Mavis—by the way—did you happen to mention the dance-floor bit to Junie?"

"You're not trying to tell me she doesn't know!"

I paused, in the face of her astonishment. "If it's deception," I said, "it's only deception on a very small scale. I just don't want to run the risk of making her feel . . . oh, I'm not even sure what the word is."

"Jealous?"

"No—left out."

"Okay, then. Well, I think it's lucky you warned me."

"It wouldn't have mattered."

"You know something?" she said. "I sometimes feel you're almost too good to be true."

"Yes, so do I. And surely we can't both be wrong?"

But talking of warnings . . . I now remembered Ella's bracelet. Dear Lord, three days in which I'd failed to allude to it! Certainly I'd had other matters on my mind but that was no excuse. Not when I was juggling with my daughter's happiness. Her development. Already she appeared cynical enough. Both my children did. (Strange: they could scarcely have been raised by parents any *less* so!) If she found out I'd lied about the bracelet, that might seem the ultimate betrayal.

And apropos of looking after my family, there was something else I had been thinking about—though this time not at all for the attention of Mavis. In fact I had been wondering whether I ought to contact John Caterham—or, indeed, his wife. (Whenever I remembered her I had to remind myself that, no, she wasn't visiting her sick mother; at least, it would have been amazing if she were.) But the odds against Junie trying to reach me in Lincolnshire were so great I really didn't want to beg that kind of favour. John would instantly suppose our marriage was in trouble and I would care about that. I had no wish for any wrong ideas to call up either sadness or self-congratulation in someone who'd once used to play for us, repeatedly, an old seventy-eight of his mother's: 'They tried to tell us we're too young . . . ' (That, maybe more than any other, had always been *our* tune, Junie's and mine.)

Yes, I believed in covering my tracks, of course, but why on earth should Junie ever seek to reach me? In the event of an emergency she had her whole family living practically within earshot.

No. There were risks and risks. You didn't want to get obsessive. Obsession wasn't cool.

"Why on earth are you wanting that old thing?" asked Mavis, as she held the door open. I had the stick lying along the top of the holdall.

"Oh. To play a joke on someone."

"That sounds hilarious. Boys together. Have fun."

I gave a comical nod at the quantity of stuff I was needing to carry. "Be a bit of a waste if I didn't!"

"More than a bit," she said. "It would be tragic."

14

But I abandoned all idea of tapping my way towards our meeting. It wasn't so much I lost my nerve as that it came to seem quite juvenile. *That sounds hilarious* . . . a faintly teasing echo? At any rate I left the stick on the train. It would probably end up in some lost property office and people would wonder what had happened to the poor blind soul who'd had to stagger on without it.

And besides. What if Moira hadn't remembered the reference to Pew? Or hadn't made the connection?

Or if she'd got there late? Imagine! Everyone stepping out of my way, maybe feeling that they ought to offer help.

But she wasn't late.

Even though, to begin with, I scarcely recognized her.

It was crazy. I'd been expecting somebody taller. And her hair was still red—of course it was—but somehow not the shade that I remembered. She wore less makeup perhaps, didn't appear quite so . . . well, so glowing or dynamic. So Technicolored. Was this, then, the woman I'd been walking with, waltzing with—been up in heaven with, while dancing cheek to cheek?

Yet then I saw the reason for my doubt. It was simply the people cutting in between us, thrusting across my line of vision, causing disturbance. I'd forgotten how unceremonious London could be. As soon as I actually reached her—and she smiled—the image instantly grew strong again, clear-cut and distinctive.

Evidently she'd had something of the same problem. "How absurd! I didn't see you—despite your height! I'm getting too shortsighted."

It was ridiculous: the things that could flash across your mind at moments of maximum tension. *Too* shortsighted, I thought. Shortsighted itself was already too shortsighted.

But I merely set down my baggage and extended my hand. She unhurriedly shook it . . . laid her other hand across it . . . then we both leant forward to kiss lightly on the lips.

I had many times asked myself how it would be during these first few moments. Now I had my answer. Apart from the *very* first of them, that one brief second or two, it had been wholly spontaneous and natural and right.

"I was feeling a bit jittery," she laughed.

"*You*?"

"Well, weren't you, then—just a trifle?"

"Oh, possibly. But only the smallest sort of trifle."

And I definitely wasn't going to let on that the closer we'd come to Victoria, then the more time I'd spent in simply wondering whether, first, I could bear to use the lavatory or, second, I could even be said to have any choice in the matter. It's purely nerves, I had told myself, stop panicking, it's purely nerves. But then I'd remembered that perhaps it wasn't; from the minute I had tried on my dinner jacket I had forgotten about my earlier constipation. So now it *could* be a question, I'd realized, either of inevitable contamination aboard the train or of having to make straight for the men's cloakroom on reaching the station. ("Moira, just look after these an instant; gotta run; talk to you when I get back!") Either way, not the most propitious lead-in to a love affair. I shouldn't even have been thinking about such things. Moonlight, champagne and roses would have made a better mix. And that was the period, too, during which I'd decided to dispense with the walking stick. Hadn't felt I could achieve the right insouciance.

But then the Fates had been kind again. With a good twenty minutes still to go, the old man who'd been sitting beside me all the way from Folkestone, yet without addressing a single word to anybody, now began to fuss about the train being late: he had a very tight connection to make out of Liverpool Street. Suddenly he seemed even more agitated than I was—in my efforts to reassure him, my own agitation imperceptibly fell back. He appeared so soothed by what I said that I was then able to start a simple conversation, with the object of distracting him.

He told me he was going to stay with a married son near Cambridge; but that he'd never got on so well with *him* as with his other boy, who was living in Vancouver and for the past seven years had been busily saving up to get him over. Seven years! That struck me as pathetic, since it didn't appear this older son could really be going at it all that hard. But then, fair enough—judge not—I didn't know the situation.

What I did know, however, a surprisingly short time later, was what the old man called the greatest mistake of his life: thirty years earlier his wife had been unfaithful and at the time he'd been unable to forgive it; had walked out and been too proud ever to return. When eventually he'd overcome that pride, and had been on the brink of asking whether she might take him back, he'd learned that she had fallen asleep with a cigarette in her hand. And if he'd been with her, he said, such a thing could never have happened.

But even before her death—oh, for years and years before it—he'd been the loneliest and most miserable man in all existence. Now the only thing he waited for, apart from a month or two in Canada, was to be able to rejoin her and try to make amends. He had often contemplated suicide but wasn't sure if this might not scupper their reunion rather than hasten it.

He was a simple man, and obviously misguided, but I felt sorry for him and casually inquired his name and whether he lived in Folkestone: I thought that one day Junie, the children and I might all drive over to take him on a picnic or out to tea or something. The name was Jack Bradley but he didn't have time to say where his home was, for at this point we'd started crossing the Thames and he exclaimed that he must hurry off to the front of the train. I wanted to help but he had only the one suitcase, which he'd kept the whole time on the table in front of us, so he was away, very agitated again, even before I could slide across the seat and manage to stand up, let alone collect together my own things. Anyhow, I had his name, so it shouldn't be too difficult to track him down and arrange that outing; and I watched his beetling progress through the compartment with something that was already a bit like solid paternal affection. Or maybe filial. I hoped his journey to Liverpool Street would be an easy one.

And then I realized that we'd arrived and I was feeling fairly calm. Well . . . hallelujah!

"Oh, possibly. But only the smallest sort of trifle." I stooped to pick up my belongings.

"What shall *I* carry?"

"How about this? You'll never guess what's in it—not in ten thousand years!"

"I think you've baked me a cake."

I stared at her. Am even prepared to believe I may have gaped.

"What's the matter?" she asked.

"I gave you ten thousand years. It took you all of half a second."

"It isn't *really* a cake?"

"Cross my heart and hope to die."

"How extraordinary!"

"Talk about kindred spirits. Do you think we're telepathic?"

"Clearly no other explanation."

Though it immediately occurred to me that this might have its downside. "Semi-telepathic?" I amended.

"All right," she agreed, "that *could* be another explanation." We laughed—why had I ever felt a second's worry? It was all going to be phenomenal from beginning to end. Good old Junie and her splendid cake! "It's certainly quite heavy," she added, weighing it consideringly in both hands, rather than holding it by the loop. "I hope I haven't said the wrong thing. I hope it's not a jam sponge."

I shook my head. "Not quite. But are you good at riddles?"

"I don't know. Try me."

"When would something that isn't quite a jam sponge—yet has strong affiliations—be likeliest to come between us?"

She pursed her lips in reflection; her pupils moved from side to side. "I'll tell you one thing. I may be telepathic but I'm not much good at riddles."

"You give up?"

"I think I have to."

I illustrated by reaching over and giving her another light kiss on the lips, while the carton remained at roughly waist-level between us. Then I said: "When would something that isn't quite a jam sponge be likeliest to come between us? Why, when it's like the filling in a Victoria sandwich!" Momentarily, I wished a second's worry *had* given me pause before I'd plunged headfirst into that one.

But the sheer and utter awfulness of the solution made us start to giggle; exactly like my children when in facetious mood. Indeed, Ella had recently told me I sometimes behaved like a retarded ten-year-old, which was a pretty cutting thing to say, as well as a sad one, because all she meant, apparently, was that I often exclaimed *Isn't this fun* if we walked along the seafront licking an ice cream, or had races barefoot on wet sand, or even just set off together to the hairdresser's, her and me and Matt. I answered that I extracted pleasure from the simple things and in this lay half the art of living. Cripes, she'd said, but since she couldn't come up with anything more articulate I hoped I might have made my point. Further to emphasize it—and also to annoy her—I took Matt's hand and we skipped side-by-side along the pavement, laughing hysterically and showing off like mad, despite what seemed a bumper crop of passers-by. 'The art of living', in fact, was one of those pet phrases I repeated to myself from time to time as a reminder that life was fleeting and we passed this way but once. By and large I considered I knew more than most about the art of living. Sometimes I'd asked various people if on the whole they were happy, only to be told in effect, "Yes, I suppose so . . . never really thought about it . . . "

Cripes!

Matt, however, had proved gratifyingly receptive. "You said *half* the art of living. What's the other half?"

"Staying positive in times of trouble."

Now, though, in spite of all our laughter, Moira expressed a hope that, over the weekend, the level of our repartee might rise a little. I told her it appeared to have no option.

"I'm still not altogether sure I can believe you've baked a cake for us."

"No?"

"No. So, now. In all truthfulness. We're making a fresh start," she cautioned. "Right?"

"Right."

"Is this a cake?"

"Yes."

"In all truthfulness, mind. You're not allowed to cheat."

"As though I would!"

"All right. Is it a cake, then, which you've made yourself?"

"Do you mean—for myself?"

"No, I do not mean that. Stop being so devious. I mean is it a cake which you yourself have made?"

"Oh. I see. Still in all truthfulness?"

She nodded. Intractable. Unrelenting.

"Then in that case," I said, "I can't honestly claim that it is."

"Ah! At last. Now maybe we're getting to the nub of it." She fitted her finger through the loop and I thought of the little Dutch boy trying manfully to stem the flood. "In other words you're telling me you've bought it."

"Really? I wasn't aware of that. I'm sorry. I didn't set out with the intention to deceive."

"In a moment I am going to scream!" she said.

Instead, she simply smiled—quite broadly—and in the process looked enchanting.

"All I'm asking . . . please Sammy, dear Sammy, kind Sammy . . . "

"Ah, I understand. What makes Sammy run?"

"No. I swear it. Nothing half so complex or so tangled. Purely— *who was it who baked the cake you say that I am holding*?"

It was a fair question and it needed to be answered. But 'in all truthfulness' would have to come later. And come it would— unquestionably. During the week I'd given a lot of thought to this. Whatever else I might be I wasn't a simpleton. For the next seventy-two hours or so, while we really got to know one another, I could carry on with the game: the fun and the frivolity. Or, rather, those were the accoutrements, the colouring on the box, the eye-catching picture on the lid; the game itself was deadly serious. But until the final part of the weekend or, anyway, what I considered the best moment for the raising of it . . . until then the lid must stay firmly in position. Only the cellophane could be removed.

"My grandmother."

We continued to form a totally unheeding island, around which swirled the inconvenienced sea of tourists and commuters.

"Well, that's incredible," said Moira. "What a fantastic person she must be."

"Like grandmother, like grandson," I admitted.

"Hmm. At least I'm willing to believe her influence could only have been beneficial."

"And after all. Who was the one who had to carry it? Spirit it over mountaintop and lug it down through vale and valley?"

"Through vale *and* valley? My, how you make light of it! But was it her idea or was it yours?"

"I cannot tell a lie. I can't, I can't! It was hers. To her alone belongs the credit."

She leant forward again, reached up and treated me to yet another kiss. Unfortunately I was still carrying the holdall and the two bags, so I couldn't put my arms about her. "What was that for?"

"For being a good boy—finally—and telling me the truth."

"Oh gosh—oh gee—oh golly, Miss. I'm going to tell a lot more truth from now on."

"Then I'm very pleased with you, Sammy."

"So can I have another of those nice things to show me that you are?" I heard myself saying to my son: "*May?*"

She did as I asked. This time I dropped the baggage and held her very close.

After some fifteen or twenty seconds she pulled away. "I can see," she said, "that in future I shall need to be a lot more firm. There are those who would even describe *that* little manoeuvre as being chock-full of guile."

I looked chastened.

"So pick up your things, please. Then follow behind and do your utmost to behave."

"I can't."

She must have realized I was now in earnest.

"Why? What's wrong?"

"I'm afraid you may have to wait a moment."

Suddenly she understood my predicament and started to laugh. More practically she bent down and herself handed me the three items. But she didn't comment on the situation. Plainly felt it would be better-bred to run with something safer.

"I simply can't wait," she said, "to open up this tempting box!" One expression of amusement immediately gave place to another. "Oh, good heavens. Just listen to me! I sound like Pandora."

The last time I had heard that name I myself had been the one to use it—to Matt, whilst attempting to list the great modern love stories—and that had been a mere couple of hours before encountering Moira on the beach. Could one honestly ascribe such things only to coincidence?

But if not, what?—and all I said was: "Then it's lucky, isn't it, that I have so much faith in you? You're the one who *gives* life, not destroys it."

She nodded and looked pleased. "Well, at any rate I'll try to leave you with a scraping of hope," she promised.

With which gracious assurance we started at last—but rather slowly—towards the main exit.

15

Her car was parked in a side street close to the Army & Navy. Someone had left a Morgan nearby and I exclaimed excitedly. (Ella would have called this a further symptom of arrested development.) "Oh, may we just have a quick look?"

"Why not?"

"You know," I said, "when I was a young man—that is, an even younger man—the thing I wanted more than absolutely anything was a two-seater identical to this. I used to dream about owning one. Sometimes, I mean, really dream."

"But you still can't have wanted it enough."

I shook my head. "Believe me, it wasn't that. I may have been a dreamer but I had my practical side as well. And a Morgan simply wouldn't have been the right size for a fam— ." I stopped short; saw her look at me; felt I was about to blush. "For a family outing, each weekend, with my grandparents."

I couldn't remember now what I had told her about my grandfather—who had died when I was three—or, indeed, if I had told her anything about him. Neither could she, apparently. She looked back at the car.

"You really are the sweetest person."

I honestly didn't wish to hoodwink her; to win her liking under false pretences.

"If I may let you into a little secret," I said, modestly, "I was only wishing to impress you! I have this awful compulsion to present myself in the best possible light."

"No. You were all confused. I could see it slipped out unawares. You even went a little red." She paused, then indicated the Morgan. "Well, have you now feasted your eyes sufficiently?"

"Fraid not. I could never feast my eyes sufficiently. But life is hard. Force me, please, to tear myself away."

"Why?"

"Why what?"

"Why don't you just take this and then get in?" She was holding out a key ring.

It had never occurred to me to ask what kind of car she had. Apart from Morgans themselves and certain other snappy sports models—and old crocks too, of course—I wasn't much interested in things like that. Nor was Matt.

She said: "Validation of proverb? Everything comes to him who waits. Synchronicity."

"This car is *yours*?"

She nodded. "Though for the moment why not say it's yours?"

To facilitate my inspection I'd deposited my luggage by a railing. Now I actually picked her up and did a pirouette upon the pavement. It reminded me of last Sunday morning: *Hey, why so physical? . . . He's acting pretty weird today.* I saw her face above me, laughingly responsive, with her red hair swinging and her slim arms wrapped about my shoulders; and she felt weightless—or extremely light. It must have been a full half-minute before, reluctantly, I set her down.

"Gracious!" she said.

"Your own fault, you shouldn't give me these surprises. You see, it was either that or flinging my ten-gallon hat in the air and swinging my lasso and firing my repeater. Yee-hee-ee-e-e! May I actually drive it?"

She now handed me the key ring. "It's quite a miracle you didn't lose it! What if it had flown from my fingers and gone skimming through a grating: your dream of a lifetime?"

"I should've sat down and cried."

"Then it's a good job I was holding on."

"My saviour. Will you marry me?"

It was a joke, of course, and she was joking too when she replied, but it gave me an instant of faint queasiness amidst my giddy exultation.

"No. Don't think so. I'd rather go on liking you."

"Oh, very well. The right decision! Lets me off the hook."

Three minutes later I had stowed the luggage—though with some difficulty, there being so little room—and handed her into the passenger seat. I settled myself at the steering wheel but felt in no hurry to start up. I ran my hands over the instrument panel. "If my friends could see me now . . . !"

"Sammy, get serious. Are they *ever* looking at any of the right moments? Say yes and you're deluding yourself."

"Oh, you know something?" I exclaimed. "We *are* kindred spirits!"

"I think it's possible."

"Yes! I knew it from the very minute you walked into the shop! Almost the very second!" I paused, savouring my intensity of happiness, holding the steering wheel like an eighteen-year-old who's just obtained his licence and is about to drive his first car out of the showroom: a gift from either the gods or from every kid's vision of the perfect daddy. "Didn't you know it, too?"

"Well, let's simply say, I liked the look of you."

"Why? Why did you?"

"You looked strong."

I sat there in a kind of virile silence.

"But at the same time vulnerable." This was uttered in a tone of near-apology. "An endearingly lost and boyish air. No, not lost, perhaps. Questing. Innocent."

"Oh, that's all right. I don't object to lost." Now I did at last turn the key and start carefully to manoeuvre my way out. I had to let up a little on the virility bit. "Perhaps you ought to be doing this? How could I live with myself if I were to scrape or damage something?" But she expressed full confidence and soon I felt as much at home behind this steering wheel as I ever did behind my own. More at home maybe: it was my natural, dreamt-of, place: and presently all my instinctive caution had obediently done a bunk. "Thank God it isn't raining! A Morgan wouldn't be a Morgan without its roof drawn back. Do you think those clouds look threatening?"

"Yes."

"They wouldn't dare, though, would they?"

"In fact, the forecast didn't sound too bad," she said.

I glanced back at the sky. "Just listen to her, please!"

Then she did the directing. Her flat was in West Hampstead, in a converted house off Mill Lane, and though she had decided that we ought to go via Camden Town ("Land of the Dusty Old Gentlemen!") she informed me there were several other ways of getting there.

"Like to Rome?" I asked. "And also heaven?" This struck me as quite apposite.

"Well, I wouldn't say that *all* roads lead to West End Green. I don't know about heaven."

I braked for a pedestrian-crossing, although no one had as yet reached the kerb.

"That may be one thing we haven't got in common," she said.

"What?"

"A belief in the hereafter."

It was plain she'd taken me more seriously than I'd intended. I was about to set her straight when she continued. "That was a further impression I received in the shop: I mean, about your being religious."

"Why on earth?"

"I'm not sure. Or perhaps it was that evening. Some little thing you must have said . . . "

"But in fact—"

"And paradoxically that was another part of the attraction you held for me. I envy those who can believe in God: their optimism, their basic serenity. When not crossed with bigotry, of course. Or with hypocrisy."

We were driving on again but I was hardly aware of it.

"And that's the trouble, isn't it, Sammy? It's so often a case of 'Do as

I say, not as I do.'" She paused. "But you appear to be the real thing. I'd say you're one of the best commercials on the market."

I'd reverted to my virile silence; being at a complete loss about what otherwise to do.

Finally I murmured, "Yet haven't you faced the possibility I could be sailing under false colours?"

Oh but what the heck? Lighten up, Samuel. We were then driving round Trafalgar Square and I gave a familiar wave to Nelson and his lions. "I feel like a king," I announced. "And I bet everybody's envying me. You—and the car—and the music . . . " I sang those final words.

"Do you want some music? You could certainly have some."

"No. I shall continue to supply my own. '*If* they made me a king I'd still be a slave to you . . . '"

"King? Well, I don't know about that. But you're definitely a nutter. Albeit a nutter with a nice voice."

"Just one thing missing," I said.

"What?"

"I ought to be wearing my dinner jacket. Hey! Shall I hop out and get changed? Then they *would* call me a swell and no mistake."

"*And* an exhibitionist, no doubt, if you did it on the pavement. But would a swell outweigh a king?"

"A royal swell. A swell royal. Whichever way you look at it . . . not to be sniffed at . . . and putting one in a position to do real good and make a difference to the world. And for what more could any man ask?" An idea occurred to me. "Hey! Let's not wait until tomorrow! Let's deck ourselves out—resplendently—tonight."

"Hey!" she said, mockingly. "Okay, then. All right."

"Don't laugh at me. Can't help being happy. Gotta sing, gotta dance!"

"I'm glad. I'm really not laughing *at* you."

"All this. It's funny to think that one day we're going to die. And no one will remember we were ever here, celebrating the start of a bank holiday, having a good time. And when we're dead Trafalgar Square will still be every bit as busy and people will still be having a good time. It won't make one jot of difference. There was a sad old fellow on the train this afternoon." I didn't know what had reminded me of him.

"Has anyone ever mentioned you have a mind like a butterfly?"

"Oh, yes, Junie for . . . Junie for one."

"And besides. What makes you think everybody's always having a good time? Sentimental old songster! Who's Junie?"

"A girl I used to know at school."

"Girl*friend*?"

"Yes."

"All right. I won't be inquisitive. Well, whoever she is, she was spot on. Do you still see her?"

"Sometimes."

"She still lives in Deal?"

"Yes. Married now. With two kids."

"I see." She smiled. "And along with your butterfly mind, did she ever mention a marked strain of melancholy which pervades even your happiness?"

"No. She never did mention that."

"Because I truly don't think you have to worry too much, not for a day or two, I mean, about your lying there dead while the world goes on without you."

"But even so. I think everyone should hold it at the back of their minds, that notion of mortality."

"Not a touch morbid, maybe, such a point of view?"

"I can't think why. All it does is heighten the pleasure of being alive. Makes you more aware, makes you more grateful."

"Ah, but there you are, you see. *I've* nobody to feel grateful to."

"That's sad," I said—and for a moment I honestly meant it. *What!* Was I already so immersed in that role she had assigned me? Surely Ruth Minton didn't appreciate what a find I was, what a shining addition I made to the Dover and District Players. Even without my attending last Monday's meeting, that part of the shallow charmer in *The Deep Blue Sea* should so obviously have been cast in my direction. Perhaps it had been. *In absentia.* I should know next week.

"Nobody, right now, but you," she added.

The glow which, naturally, I'd already been experiencing now strengthened and spread. "Me? But why should you feel grateful to me?"

"Oh, I don't know. Maybe for bringing back a few *hey!*'s into my stale and staid existence; together with the prospect of some rather awful songs—"

"Madam, they are *not* awful songs! Beware! If you spurn the song you spurn the singer. 'If I were a carpenter and you were a lady, would you marry me anyway, would you have my baby . . . ?"

"No, not awful, then. Let's merely say—a mite dated?"

"But things which are good don't date, they reflect their time. Besides, it only shows that my tastes are wide-ranging; I like modern songs as well. 'You feel that you're on trial—and so you're in denial—you want to cry and run a mile—but still you lie and still you smile—and smile and smile and smile . . . ' QED. Ancient *and* modern."

She laughed. "Not altogether unsuitable, I suppose, for the proprietor of a junk—. For the proprietor of *Treasure Island*."

"Oh dear. Isn't that where we came in?"

"Yes. Why do some people never learn? But anyway . . . you know how I feel about junk shops. And their proprietors."

At any rate I knew how she could give me pleasure. Cause me literally to expand with the pleasure that she gave.

We were now driving up Tottenham Court Road. Hundreds of people were milling on either pavement and I could practically have sworn most of them seemed to be having a good time. But it was wrong to suggest I wasn't a realist. I knew only too well there were bound to be those who were in some way similar to Mavis's poor mum—not to mention all the dispossessed; the junkies and the alcoholics; the mentally unstable. If I were indeed a royal swell, or a swell royal, the first thing I'd do would be to eradicate homelessness. I'd at least make certain of that.

And while my thoughts were heading off in this direction, Moira was wrong about something else. I wasn't worried about the world going on without me; simply couldn't quite believe it, that was all.

But wrong or not she was wonderful. And how could I even say wrong, when these were probably not views she would have stood by under oath? How could I even say wrong when she had provided a racing-green Morgan, a golden, auburn-haired presence and a setting for my own enhanced vitality, which I secretly knew was attracting a good deal of attention? I was well aware I had never welcomed red lights with such a winning air of ruefulness and acceptance. I felt like a film star: a self-effacing, stunningly approachable film star.

"*The Short Happy Life of Francis Macomber*," I said—to me this wasn't a non sequitur. "I'm sure they filmed it in the forties. Naturally, my own will be a very *long* and happy life but at present, I suppose, they'd still refer to it as being short. It started around noon last Saturday. I'm barely a week old. But I think that tomorrow, at twelve, champagne corks should pop, Big Ben strike, cannon go off in Green Park. Something small to notify the masses. To commemorate our meeting; record my radiant—my radical—renaissance."

"I feel that you expect too much," she warned. "*I'd* be thrilled if just Big Ben remembered."

I affected a sneer. (Hoped my loving public didn't misinterpret.)

"Like hearing your name on the radio, you mean?"

"Yes. Exactly. Ariadne Scrumpenhouser."

Had we not been stationary at that moment, I might well have swerved or stalled, if nothing yet more shameful. Pandora and Ariadne within the same half-hour! The very same half-hour!

Could it be coincidence? Something so incredible? There were even those who claimed there wasn't any such thing as coincidence. I couldn't think how they managed it but I had certainly heard they tried.

Yet I decided not to comment for the time being. I didn't want to risk its extraordinariness, risk making it sound nearly commonplace. It was good enough for *The X Files* but even David Duchovny (to whom recently I'd warmed) would simply have to show a little patience.

I observed instead, hearing my own words as if from a distance, "Yes, you're right. Of course you are. A tribute from Big Ben would make a fine endorsement. It would also sound impressive in my diary, might be as much worth recording as . . . well, as driving an open-topped Morgan with a princess by my side. I shall now entitle this journal *The Long and Happy Life of Samson Groves*. Hemingway will eat his heart out. Or turn in his grave. Whichever comes to him the more naturally. Any views on such a subject, Miss Scrumpenhouser . . . ?"

"The lights have turned to green and we're being hooted at. If you're not very careful, Mr Groves, they'll have changed again and you will *not* be popular." Her hand was on my arm and perhaps already she had given me a nudge.

But I was still taken up with the results of my amazement.

"Or," I continued humbly, "would you do me the honour—the very great honour—of allowing me to call you Ariadne?"

16

Her apartment was splendid . . . what else would you expect? Yet I could see why at times she'd want to get away from it. I was sure there were advantages to having the upper storey but it was the lower floor which—although in all likelihood equally cramped—had the use of a garden; or, rather, of a strip of concreted back yard, for the house was a mid-terraced one. However, I suppressed comparisons with our own former rectory in Deal and admired it, Moira's flat, with all the sincerity which I could muster.

"If you're not already at the top of your profession you damned well ought to be."

"Roughly halfway up, I'd say, but getting there." She looked about her. "It's deceptive, isn't it? From the outside you'd never believe there could be all this room."

"No. No, you wouldn't." My sincerity took a nose dive.

She laughed. "You don't agree, though, do you?"

I faltered. "Am I that hopeless a liar?"

"But thank you for trying. And I can see your point. You in your ten-gallon hat! In Kent you've evidently more space to swing that lasso."

"Yes. Don't fence me in. Et cetera. You know, sometimes I feel I wouldn't have minded being a cowboy. To sit tall in the saddle and gallop off into the sunset. The stranger who passes through and leaves things far better than he found them."

"What an incurable romantic!"

"Yup, ma'am. Sure is a lonely trail."

Though *realistically*, I thought, it was possibly a fairly crowded trail: the Shane character irresistibly drawn to pastures new but always hoping he'd be lovingly remembered as someone who had made a difference. The wayfarer. The good Samaritan. Almost the Christ figure. The fellow who had left his mark.

"Trial, maybe, as much as trail," smiled Moira. "However . . . Let's have a look at your granny's cake." She was about to wield her kitchen scissors but I stopped her just in time. It didn't take a moment to unknot the string.

The cake was a beauty. Standing on a silver board and encircled by a wide and frilly band it was decorated with literally scores of Smarties which had bled slightly and looked like the picture on a packet of mixed seeds—except that white icing maybe formed an unexpected base for cottage garden flowers; it produced an impression of snow arriving in the midst of summer.

"I'm going to phone her!" declared Moira.

But luckily I had foreseen that. "She's a little hard of hearing. She'd much prefer a letter."

"It looks like a picture out of *Good Housekeeping*."

"And as though it were meant to keep us going for a lifetime!" I realized that my gaze was full of pride; my voice, as well.

There was more. When I'd torn at the carton sides—I'd had to, because the cake board fitted so well it would have been virtually impossible to prise out—we found wedged beneath it a container of (formerly) frozen pea soup, two jars of homemade jam, and a meat pie wrapped in foil; all very neatly and even prettily labelled. Thank God, while Moira was exclaiming over and examining the first of these finds, I spied a dove-grey envelope which I rapidly palmed, crumpled and pushed up my sleeve: the scratchiest handkerchief ever. With this done, I flushed cold at the narrowness of my escape.

But my relief did nothing to neutralize the prickings of guilt which had followed my pride. (And why should it have?) I now had to remind myself, repeatedly, that the Caterham children were *not* motherless, not even temporarily, and were no doubt regularly nourished on home cooking.

It didn't help a lot.

Yet my own conscience, it seemed, wasn't the only one creating trouble.

"All these things," said Moira, "and I hadn't even planned to be feeding you at home! Apart from breakfast, that is, when I might have stirred myself sufficiently to rustle up some warm croissants and coffee . . . "

I had to make an effort. I peered into the broken box still lying on the table. "Wot! No cornflakes?"

"You see, I thought it might be more fun to eat out. Though I hope it doesn't need to be said we'd be going Dutch."

"Fine. Except rid yourself of that second bit."

"No," she said. "When times are good I think I probably earn more than you do. Or is that tactless?"

"Yes, it's tactless. You are *invariably* tactless."

"And times are good."

"Well, there at least I'm in complete agreement. Times were never better."

"Then let's have a glass of something. *Times were never better!* We'll drink to that. Before leaving."

"Where are we off to? Paris?"

"There's a place by the Heath. I've reserved a table. Hoped you wouldn't think that was a liberty."

"Well, I don't know. It all depends. Shall I be allowed to foot the bill?"

"I really can't see why you should."

"Because I'd like to, Miss Scrumpenhouser—isn't that good enough? Besides. You're giving me a roof over my head; not to mention the use of a magnificent car . . . the fulfilment of a dream! And live each day as though your last, I always say. I came prepared to splurge."

"The roof and the car," she persisted, "are just thrown in. I used the word 'liberty'. I also believe in equality and fraternity."

"I don't."

She laughed. "You're so bull-headed, aren't you?" (I nodded; Junie often said the same.) "All right, I may give in tonight but only on condition you won't be living tomorrow as though your last. Nor Sunday, come to that. Nor Monday."

"It's difficult."

"Why?"

"Live each bank holiday as though your last. That's something else I always say. You can't demolish all my sayings at one go."

"Good grief," she exclaimed.

"Meaning?"

"Perhaps only now am I beginning to realize what I've taken on."

I didn't tell her but I liked the sound of that. I rather cared for the idea of being taken on.

"And by the way," I suggested, "let's put off the glad rags till tomorrow. You see, I don't like everything to come at once. And anyhow I have a grey suit in my holdall. Such a waste of effort not to wear it!"

"You mean, all that effort of having spirited it over mountaintops, then lugged it down through vale and valley?"

"Exactly."

"But what occurs to me now—shouldn't the lugging have been *up*, not down?"

I briefly considered this. "Are you implying that I get things muddled? Back-to-front? Askew?"

She laughed. "No, I'm merely implying you ought to unpack your grey suit . . . and anything else that might be getting creased."

"Including my cricket whites?"

"Oh, most definitely including your cricket whites! Furthermore, I suggest you might want to give it a quick press. I've got a steam iron."

I hoped my expression didn't register my slight degree of shock. Junie would never have suggested that. She would simply have gone for the ironing board and asked me to bring her the suit. At home we had a steam iron too; I wasn't even certain how the damn thing worked.

"No," I said. "Just point me in the direction of a clothes hanger—before you point me in the direction of that drink."

While I hung up the dinner jacket, as well as the lounge suit, I experienced, first, a surely-to-be-expected interest in Moira's bed but then—less foreseeably—something that took me out of the bedroom altogether: an almost nostalgic wave of warmth, of gratitude, even of . . . well, yes, homesickness. Five-past-eight. I wondered if they'd finished supper yet. I thought that in all probability they had. Right now I saw her standing at the kitchen sink, listening to *Friday Night Is Music Night* while she did the washing up.

The telephone rang. It made me start.

Thank heaven. That was what I needed; I was being ridiculous. There may well have been occasions when Monsieur Gauguin had thought extremely fondly of Madame Gauguin after he'd upped and flitted to the South Seas, in quest of freedom and fulfilment. But that was an escapade which had lasted him a lifetime, not merely one weekend.

On the other hand, of course, I hoped mine was going to last a lifetime too—even if only a lifetime of Mondays to Fridays. So in someone taking his first steps into totally uncharted territory, aiming to set free, as he did so, both himself and those he was pledged always to look after, a qualm or two was not perhaps unnatural. Even Theseus had shed a manly tear on first being parted from his mother.

I heard Moira's laughter in the sitting room.

I hadn't been intending to open Junie's letter. Correspondence meant for someone else—even a picture postcard—ought to be inviolable.

But there were mitigating factors. If I'd been present at the time of writing I'd not only have been shown the letter, I'd have been requested to correct it. Or, at any rate, to pass it as okay.

Also, she might have been asking questions of John Caterham to which she really wanted answers; have made little jokes she might expect our friend to comment on; everybody's interests demanded I should know.

I took it to the bathroom when I went to change.

Dear John,

What ages since we met, isn't life full of surprises! Sam says that's what makes it worth living but I'm not always so sure. But *this* one is so nice!

Now you must come and stay with us, now you're back in touch! We have plenty of room. It will be good to meet your wife and little ones. I'm sorry, I must have forgotten her name, I'm sorry that her mother isn't well!

Thought these few things might come in handy. The pie and the soup have already been frozen so you oughtn't to refreeze them. Whatever you do make sure the pie is *well and truly* heated before you eat it, never take chances, I say! Not with food! Maybe living is different. (Sam will explain!)

I wasn't sure if you'd prefer a chocolate or a fruit cake but my lot like this recipe best and I thought it would go further. Ella is 15 and Matt will be 13 next week, a man now, says Sam!

We also have a dog—poor Susie—she's just had a very nasty accident! It would finish Sam off if she was put to sleep, we shall have to keep our fingers crossed.

We shall keep our fingers crossed about your mother-in-law too!

And with the builders in! My goodness, have you got your hands full, I hope it's going to lead to something nice!

Well, that's all for now then, just wanted to say a very quick hello. I'm sure you and Sam will have a real old 'get-together', I look forward to hearing all about it when Sam comes home! Hope yours will be the winning team, and hope we will *all* have a real old 'get-together' soon, before too many blue moons have past!

Must close now. Much love to you and your wife and three children—*three*, gracious, however do you cope?

From your very old friend,
Junie.

P.S. Even if Sam remembers to take his camera he always forgets to use it, and I'd love to have a photograph of your family! It's the same wherever we go, Jalna the Dovecot or Kew Gardens or anywhere! It's Matt whose our budding photographer!

P.P.S. 'They used to tell us we're too young, too young to really be in love!!!' I'm sure you must remember.

In fact it was a typical Junie letter. Somehow on paper she always sounded a bit less sure of herself. At school she'd generally viewed her literary shortcomings with something of a shrug; it was only now that she tended to worry, even to agonize. (Particularly when needing to send a note to one of the teachers!) I addressed her fondly whilst sitting on the edge of the bath and restoring her smoothed-over letter to its smoothed-over envelope:

"Whatever happened to Baby June?"

And I got back the smiling, time-honoured response.

"Oh, something rather horrible!"

"Ah . . . you poor crazy mixed-up kid!"

I put the folded envelope into a back pocket of my jeans and wondered how to dispose of it. Not so much of a problem, clearly, but there was certainly going to be another, far more pressing, to do with names and ages, comestibles, photographs. What in the world was I ever going to do about that? I sat down again on the edge of the bath and told myself firmly that to every quandary there had to be an answer.

And then, just as if a severe reminder was the sole requirement, I received my answer.

I might not have to do anything!

For if John Caterham hadn't returned to Deal, so far as we knew, in over ten years (because his parents had moved away not long after he had) wasn't there now a good chance he wouldn't return at all? I could tell Junie there'd be a letter in the post as soon as his wife came back.

But letters occasionally got lost, didn't they? Or the best of intentions didn't get acted upon. (Please see above!) And after a fortnight or so Junie might think it strange we hadn't heard, might periodically refer to it over the next couple of months, might even try to have me telephone, but gradually the Caterhams would be forgotten.

And although there was obviously *some* risk involved, it really wasn't a great one. If it ever happened they did revisit Deal they surely wouldn't call on us without warning? Whereupon I'd have the opportunity to prime them; to feed them a suitably amusing story as to why I had once required an alibi.

There wasn't any need to fret. On Monday night I could improvise every last detail Junie would doubtless be eager to hear.

Moira had finished on the telephone.

I passed on the directions concerning soup and pie as though I'd only just remembered them. In fact I'd considered them expendable but this again might have seemed like a betrayal. "No, you certainly are *not* fussing!" refuted Moira, on my dear dead granny's behalf. Dear? I suppose so; but in truth a bit repressive; I wouldn't feel sorry when the time came for her ashes to be scattered afresh. But in any case I apologized for being a forgetful dunce. Moira answered, with a nod towards my pinstriped suit, blue shirt, silk chequered tie, "Oh, I forgive you. One can't be beautiful *and* brainy."

"You seem to manage it."

"Thank you."

She looked gorgeous in her dark green: more *soignée* than ever with her hair up. I had forgotten (no, to be honest, I'd never known) the thrill of being the escort of a strikingly attractive woman. They say that in appearance a potential lover will nearly always gravitate towards his equal. I considered that this evening I had more than found my equal. And although the ability to turn heads might not be your partner's most impressive feature it still felt agreeable to discover it was there.

Oh, my God, yes. It felt wonderful.

17

We returned to the flat around twelve-thirty. It still hadn't rained; we hadn't been prevented from driving with the roof down. "The luck of the Irish," she'd remarked.

"No. Nothing to do with the Irish. Sod the Irish. I make my own luck."

Despite this I was feeling nervous as we got out of the car; I imagine we both were. But the whole evening, of course, had been shot through with apprehension. Pleasurable apprehension. Which happened to be the name of a horse I'd once backed during my short-lived gambling career: *Pleasurable Apprehension*. Short-lived because I'd seldom won anything worth having and had had the sense, finally, to see the pursuit for what it was: a mug's game. Indeed, only a few weeks ago I'd had to deliver a homily to Matt on the follies of hoping to get rich quick and of relying on luck to pull you through. It had been necessary to play the heavy father, extolling the virtues of diligence in work and duty, of diligence and a down-to-earth outlook. We had just received his school report.

"In a moment," Ella had said to Matt sympathetically, very much copying his own way of putting things but probably not aware of it, "in a moment, I'll bet, he's going to throw in that bit about searching for the bluebird of happiness." We'd been sitting over supper at the time. Our only real communication, during any normal week, took place at the supper table.

"He's going to do no such thing," I retorted, in some anger. "Mind your own business, Ella. At this point the bluebird of happiness is completely irrelevant."

"Isn't it true, then?" she muttered sulkily. "Does that mean I can stop having to keep my eyes skinned every time I set foot outside our crappy old back door?"

"Don't you know yet what 'at this point' means?"

"Ella—kindly watch your language," Junie ordered. She gave a sigh. "And I do wish, Sam, you wouldn't always pick on mealtimes to start this sort of conversation. It takes me hours to prepare something which I hope we'll all enjoy and then I find I end with indigestion."

"You?" I said. "You never suffered from indigestion in your life!"

"Well, I must say! You've a short memory. Perhaps you're forgetting that I've twice been pregnant?"

"Apart from then."

She made a vaguely conciliatory gesture. "All right. That may have been true once. It certainly isn't now."

"Change of life?" asked Ella, dispassionately curious.

"At thirty-five?"

"Thirty-five and ten months?" offered Matt, slyly, understandably in favour of prolonging this or any other distraction.

"No, it is *not* the change of life!" said Junie. "The change of something, maybe, but not of that. And, anyway, it isn't ten! It's only nine-and-a-half."

She turned towards me in the same half-humorous manner: "And, Sam, I know you have this enviable talent for blocking out whatever you don't want to hear but you do always pick on mealtimes and I only wish—I really do wish—"

I shouted. I felt the rush of blood. My complexion may have gone purple.

"Have you all quite finished? Well, have you? I thought I was trying to make a serious point. Perhaps no one noticed. Does no one but me think Matt's future is important? Think it shouldn't be brushed aside with talk of people being born lucky even if they haven't got degrees? Well, I'm sick and tired of everyone ganging up on me. You can all do what you like, see if I care, I wash my hands of it! I'm off! Good riddance! Good riddance to the lot of you!"

And throwing down my napkin I'd walked out; leaving a trio of extremely startled faces. I too had felt pretty startled: once I was up and running I'd found it impossible to stop. All of it so unexpected. I'd had a pleasant day at work; been feeling quite relaxed on my return. Even when Junie had shown me the report I'd had no premonition things were going to take the course they did. None whatsoever. I later made a secret vow. Never again should I fail to see the danger signals, never again should I fail to heed their warning. Never. Never.

"What are you thinking?" asked Moira.

"Remembering a racehorse out of my guilt-ridden past."

And wondering—by no means for the first time—what Junie could have meant when she'd said, "The change of something, maybe, but not of that." And why had I never liked to ask?—telling myself that, anyhow, she'd surely have forgotten by now, even if she had actually meant *anything*.

Moira laughed. "A racehorse? Well, naturally! I'm such an idiot!"

"Its name," I said, "*Pleasurable Anticipation*."

Then suddenly I realized. *I* was the idiot! King of the idiots! Not *Apprehension* at all! *Anticipation*! Talk about getting things muddled . . .

We walked upstairs. I unlocked the second door, handed back the keys. She went ahead of me into the sitting room, switching on lamps.

"Nightcap?" she inquired.

"Please. Another whisky."

"Just help yourself." She said this over her shoulder as she made to draw the curtains. I felt surprise: had failed to notice they hadn't been drawn earlier—so much for my awareness! They were floor-length, of dark blue velvet, almost black. She paused before pulling them across. "The other night there was a glorious moon. I wish there'd been a glorious moon tonight."

I knew it was corny but forgetting about my whisky I went and stood behind her and put my arms around her waist. Then counselled her in a supposedly Austrian accent. "Oh, don't let's ask for the moon! We have the stars!"

In fact, the moment had arrived. No more procrastination. No more apprehension. Apprehension was *not*, nor ever could be, pleasurable.

And Moira leant against me with a sigh. Gave a soft laugh. "Her line," she said, "not his."

"Don't care." I could afford to be extravagant. I rested my chin on her head. My hands moved upwards to her breasts.

"And besides. Right now there aren't even that many stars."

I said: "Then we'll just have to provide a few of our own. In any case, Miss Scrumpenhouser, this is surely not a time to be pedantic."

"You're right. But remember the view of them we had last Saturday? I think you rarely see anything like that in London . . . " But she was talking only out of nervousness—which made me feel yet more loving—and I realized that what would soon be happening between us was going to match the splendour seen in any sky; excel the sunset floating on a golden sea, the moonglow falling through the Apennines, the rainbow basketing some lovely bay. In short, it was going to be beyond description. Beyond compare. Beyond anything. She turned in my arms and pressed her body against mine and lifted her face up for a lingering kiss.

And . . . oh, my God.

I came.

The man who could ram his wife more than two thousand times.

A marathon entrant who couldn't even make it to the starting post.

It could have been a catastrophe. I thought at first it was. But I was seeing it through my own eyes, not through hers. Moira was marvellous. "It's no big deal, my love. It only means you haven't been in practice. That's something we can easily put to rights."

We stood together in the bath and used the shower. I'd never embraced any woman's naked body except for Junie's—and even from seventeen years ago, when we'd been newlyweds, I could remember nothing like this. Nothing remotely like this. While I only kissed and soaped her, Moira had two orgasms. The readiness of her responses was intoxicating. By the time we'd turned off the good clean water—warm and soft and full of absolution—and gently dried each other down, my penis was again, thank God, tumescent.

When we presently got to bed (crisp white linen and a dark red duvet which had soon slipped to the floor) she asked if there were anything I fancied. I said I'd love to have her ride me; to use me as her strong-winged horse. "All the way to Banbury Cross?" she queried, and I replied, "Great Scott, no, who wants to go to Banbury Cross? I mean halfway round the world and back: over valleys and forests and above the Barrier Reef . . . "

"Good heavens! A poetical Pegasus!"

"And one who's stamping at his stable door. All ready to bear you off to Samarkand or far Cathay; to the Hanging Gardens of Babylon; or along the route that Sinbad took."

"And to think I was about to settle for a sleepy little market town near Oxford—with only a one-way ticket at that!"

Then she descended lightly onto my outstretched legs and bore down to the roots of my erection. I cupped my hands around her breasts and she glistened as she rose and fell, gasping with every downward lunge and looking more rapt and disbelieving by the instant. We came together, after possibly less than three minutes, but it felt like the first orgasm in the whole of recorded history—I mean, the one which finally broke the pleasure barrier. At last she opened her eyes and smiled at me, loving and unguarded, then sank with her breasts against my chest and I held her tightly while we lay in silence and I still felt large within her.

It was I who ended the silence. "Well, we embarked upon a voyage to Australia but hardly left the docks at Tilbury." Then—scared that she might have misconstrued my meaning—"Yet I never realized Tilbury had so very much to offer! Like, let me see now, the pyramids and the Pantheon and Durham Cathedral and . . . and we really oughtn't to leave out a palace or two and the Golden Gate Bridge."

"No," she said, "I could willingly spend the rest of my life in Tilbury." She lifted her head a short way and planted lazy kisses on the tip of my chin and at the base of my throat, teeth gently pulling at the clusters of coiled tendrils she discovered there. Then breaking my embrace she raised herself on both arms and with her red-and-gold hair draping her as if she were a mermaid from some movie, gazed down and said: "And shall I tell you how it felt? Like a thousand shooting stars splattering against a backcloth of black velvet. That's how it felt." And if her choice of simile was maybe unwittingly influenced by my prophecy in front of the window—well, so what? It was a compliment to be treasured and kept fresh forever. Not even a compliment; better than that. A remark.

Yet next time, I joyously reflected, we should get a long way past Tilbury. She'd have a thousand shooting stars exploding inside her at every second; but still we'd sail on, fly on—roll and pitch and swoop and soar. Tilbury was great but only a beginning. I dreamt of ecstasy drawn out an hour, mind-blowing, toe-curling—ecstasy verging on torment.

An hour? Well, an hour wasn't perhaps totally guaranteed, not yet . . . "But anyway," I said, "I think we're getting there."

"Sammy, you ask too much of yourself. Or you ask too much of life. I happen to think we well and truly arrived."

Well and truly. The second time I'd come across that phrase this evening.

She smiled.

"Or is it God that you expect too much of?"

We arrived again—this time far across the North Sea, even a good way into Eastern Europe—before we finally turned out the lamp and fell into exhausted sleep.

And actually I'd been chanting silently throughout: as good a way as any of trying to distract myself. Okay then . . . okay then . . . get in on this act if you'd like to, get in on this act if you'd like to! Get in on this act, get in on this act! Get in on this act if you'd like to!

What's more, it appeared to work—it really did. For, as I say, he took us into Yugoslavia. The *former* Yugoslavia. And I felt grateful.

But mine was the power. Definitely. And mine was the glory.

I didn't care so much about the kingdom. The kingdom seemed a bit abstract. I told him he could keep the kingdom.

18

I awoke to find the sun streaming in and to be given a tray containing coffee and fruit juice, boiled eggs, hot rolls, butter and honey. Moira herself looked remarkably fresh in an emerald green housecoat. She sat on the edge of the bed.

"But I can't *possibly* eat all this."

"You've got to," she said. "Got to maintain your strength."

"And what about you?"

"But I've already had mine . . . although perhaps I'll drink a little more coffee. I've been up since ten; now it's nearly twelve. Happy anniversary!" She stroked the hair on my arm, brushing it towards my wrist.

The instant effect of this was to strengthen the erection with which I'd woken.

"I love you, don't you know?"

I said it huskily.

"Thank you, Sammy. Eat your breakfast."

"But that's the real truth." It was on the tip of my tongue to start the day with my confession; this struck me as completely the right moment and gut instinct drove me on, informed me that I should never feel more calm. "Moira, there's something I must tell you."

"Yes, darling?"

But I hadn't worked it out and knew that at all costs I had to avoid hurting anyone. I couldn't bear the thought of that gentle smile being caused to disappear.

"I thought we'd be having croissants," I said. "*That's* what I must tell you."

"What a fibber you are! But never mind. We'll be having the croissants tomorrow."

"Also, I'd like to make love to you before I eat my breakfast."

"Well, you can't," she said. "Your eggs will spoil and your rolls and coffee will get cold. Besides, I might have other plans."

"Like what?"

"Like letting you make love to me *after* you've eaten your breakfast."

"So . . . ? Couldn't we find some way of reconciling those options?"

"And you hadn't forgotten, either, my mentioning a few further ideas for your delectation?"

"No, I hadn't forgotten," I answered, sadly. I'd become aware it was deflation, rather than delectation, currently taking place beneath the duvet. "But I might've hoped *you* had."

"Well, anyway," she consoled me, "maybe it's a bit late for catching a boat down to Greenwich. Or for lunching at the Zoo. Or for driving out to Richmond." However, she ignored all my punctuating nods of vigorous agreement. "But I'd also wondered if you'd like to wander around Portobello or the National Gallery or Harrods. Whether you'd like to row on the Serpentine or gaze at the crown jewels. Visit some bookshops. Be taken on a guided tour of some of the lesser-known landmarks." She sipped reproachfully at her coffee. (A car backfired. "See," I exclaimed, "there go the cannon!") "I really can't believe that in place of so many varied and interesting alternatives you only want to get laid."

"How can I convince you?"

But—for the present giving up any attempt to do this—I then ran to have a pee. I washed my hands, returned to bed and decapitated the first of my two eggs.

"What *I* can't believe is that you never . . . no, not once . . . mentioned the British Museum!" It was my turn to sound reproachful.

"Really? Would you like to go to the British Museum?"

"Not in the slightest. But I still can't believe you didn't offer me the choice." I sprinkled a modicum of salt. "And, in any case, why does it all need to be shoehorned into one weekend? You're so neurotic, Moira. What have you got against weekdays?"

Then I told her of my scheme to look for work in London.

But I soon wished I hadn't. It led to unforeseen questioning. (Which shouldn't have been unforeseen: so cotton-picking obvious.) What was going to happen to my grandmother? Was it kind—or even safe—to leave her alone in a large house for five whole days a week? And what would happen to the shop? Did I mean to sell up?

"I thought it might actually please you, the notion of our being able to spend more time together."

I didn't say: of my being able to move in here, cramped though it is, on a semi-permanent basis. This one did *not* strike me—either me or my gut instinct—as being completely the right moment.

"Of course it would please me. But mightn't it be better just to leave it for the time being? We don't really know one another yet, do we?" She said: "And Sammy. Don't you dare turn all pathetic on me!"

There was justice in this: I was aware that I'd probably been sounding aggrieved.

"Wot! Me? Pathetic?"

I drained my second cup of coffee. "Anyway. My assistant would have taken care of the shop. And as for Gran . . . well, naturally I wouldn't have left her unattended. Naturally I'd have looked for someone who . . . "

"It would have needed to be someone exceptionally congenial."

It wasn't worth discussing. (Another reason why I ought to have spoken earlier. Practically my every sentence was adding to the pile of debris that would later need to be removed. Practically my every sentence, in retrospect, might smack of a desire to deceive, a desire which simply wasn't there. I was a dolt but never mind. I wouldn't let it spoil our day.)

In any case that second cup of coffee had produced some welcome intimations.

I again handed Moira the tray. "Call of nature," I said. "That was a smashing breakfast."

"I'll go to do the washing up."

"Quite right. A woman's role."

"Do you think so? Well, I'd advise you to watch it, young man, if you have any idea what's good for you!"

In the bathroom I began to sing. Despite that brief moment of disharmony I thought even the few things which hadn't gone right yesterday were now busily correcting themselves. On Thursday night I'd slept badly but last night I'd slept so well I couldn't remember either dreaming or even turning over. Yesterday I'd been constipated; today's evacuation left me purified and clean. All was absolutely for the best, in the best of all possible worlds. And the best of all possible worlds was in Solent Road, West Hampstead.

I brushed and flossed my teeth and spent hardly five minutes under the shower. I took longer than that over shaving and splashing myself in cologne.

Moira was still in the kitchen, watering some plants on the sill. There were nets at the window. I switched off the jabber on Radio 4; got rid of the milk bottle; then drew her in close. After ten seconds or so I started to unbutton her housecoat.

"Mmm. You smell nice," she said.

"It's called My Scintillating Future."

"As distinct from Your Guilt-Ridden Past?"

I laughed. I pressed her buttocks to me and she leant back from the waist and ran her hands across my chest. "Here! What was that song I heard you singing a short time ago?" She tweaked at one of my nipples.

"Which song?"

"'If I am fancy-free and love to wander . . . '"

"Was I really singing that?"

"You were. I turned on the radio to drown you out."

"No, I think you must've misheard. I was singing, 'If I had a talking picture of you . . . ' 'If' was right. Even 'If I'. It was a fairly understandable mistake. Please don't blame yourself."

Remorsefully, she licked and soothed the red mark she had made—and which I had taken like a man, without wincing.

But not all *that* remorsefully. "Nobody could ever accuse *you* of being stuck in the sixties, could they? Or do I mean the fifties?"

"Or the twenties?" I supplied, accommodatingly.

"Yes. What on earth can one do? I suppose it must be Granny's influence. Or Kipling's."

"I don't know. Granny never instructed me to do *this*."

For, as soon as I'd spoken, I lifted her off the floor. She threw her arms about my neck and twined her legs around my bottom. She kissed me long and hard—inhaling sharply upon penetration. Between us we moved her back and forth, gently at first, then with mounting acceleration. It was murder on the biceps but nowhere else was the sensation remotely one of pain.

I needed another shower.

Moira took hers separately. "I warn you: we shan't be in any fit state to go to the theatre!"

"You wanna bet? That's another five or six hours away."

We compromised. We made love only once more before then, and that was after five o'clock, before we started getting ready. And even then it was nothing too adventurous or demanding: just the plain old missionary. To a count of under four hundred. Not good. Not bad. Incredible.

We would save the goldfingering till later.

Meanwhile we followed one of Moira's earlier suggestions. "I get the feeling that I ought to humour you," I said. So we went rowing on the lake: not the Serpentine: the one in Regent's Park. This was nearer and in addition there was somewhere nice, in Queen Mary's Garden, to have tea. (Obviously, we hadn't wanted any lunch.) The weather wasn't perfect for boating—perfect boating weather meant shirtless and a suntan rather than T-shirt and a jumper—and in some ways I'd have preferred to hire a skiff and feel that I was really showing off my paces, working hard and skimming across the surface like a skier or a bird; but all the same it was pleasant just to idle round the contours of the lake and around a central, wooded island; even—especially at those times when a watery sun tried to reproduce the brilliance I had awoken to—resting on my oars and allowing us to drift.

I said, "I enjoy rowing. I enjoy any form of physical exercise—the harder the better, really—anything that makes you feel your muscles are working. At Oxford or at Cambridge I'd have been a rowing blue."

"Do they have rowing blues at London?"

"I'm not sure. Why?"

"I was only thinking," she replied, "that if you're serious about coming to live up here why not apply to London University?" I had told her last night over dinner that I'd never been to university and how much I regretted it. "I'm sure you'd be able to get a loan and that somehow or other we could manage—one could manage—to pay it back."

Before she'd changed it, she had definitely said 'we'.

I stopped rowing. I wouldn't comment on that—I couldn't, of course—but *God!* The glory of the woman!

"That's an inspirational and magnificent idea," I answered instead.

"Better than taking on some mediocre job . . . because these days, without a degree, you're not going to find anything else. And it would certainly be a good way of fulfilling yourself."

"You know," I said, "it's extraordinary how in just one week my world has opened up. Suddenly there seem limitless ways of fulfilling myself."

"I'm glad." She was leaning over and trailing her hand in the water. "In fact," she said, "I feel it could truly be the making of you. I hope that doesn't sound patronizing."

I paused. "There's something very solid about that phrase: 'The Making of Sam Groves.' It has a ring to it. And even if it *were* patronizing (which it most emphatically is—how could you doubt it for one single instant?) let me tell you this. I know of no one I'd prefer to patronize me."

It was time to return to the boathouse; we'd had more than our full hour. As I prepared to hand Moira onto the landing stage, a father and his three children were waiting to take our places. They had with them a large shaggy-haired white dog which jumped into the boat even before the two of us had properly left it and made everybody laugh. "Jimmy can sometimes be a little overeager!" the man apologized.

"Jimmy reminded me of Susie," Moira said, as we walked away. "How is she—your little black-eyed Susan?"

As yet Moira knew nothing of the accident. I now told her what had happened; but may have kept talking of Susie as though she were my own dog, not that of our neighbours. "I still can't really forgive myself."

"Well, it wasn't exactly *your* fault!" She'd been holding my arm and now hugged it to her sympathetically.

"Wasn't it? I should've had her on the lead. Some people are such *garbage!*" Indeed, even now I couldn't credit there were those who were capable of running down a dog—rat, pigeon, hedgehog, anything—and not stopping to ascertain the state the animal was in: if only with a view to killing it if necessary. "Scum!" I added. "Bastards!"

"Hear, hear!" she said, yet seemed surprised at the pent-up rage with which I'd expressed what she agreed with. "But anyway, Sammy, you haven't a single thing to reproach yourself for. Not the least thing in the world."

"I read quite recently," I said, "about two men who gouged out a pony's eyes with an old nail."

"Dear God!"

"I think they got three months."

But happily we were interrupted. A football crossed our path and simultaneously we heard a cry: "Send it back, mister?" It broke our mood entirely. I thought, I'll show those kids a thing or two! Naturally I'd have looked a complete charlie if my kick hadn't connected but fortunately the ball went soaring in a hugely gratifying arc and covered the requisite thirty-yard distance as though it had a built-in homing device. The six or seven boys were patently impressed. "Here, mister! You want to come and join in?" I could have been strongly tempted. "Another time! But thanks, anyway!" They seemed like good kids. Totally unbidden, it crossed my mind: And I didn't have to ask *you* to get in on that one, either. Did I?

"Superman!" said Moira.

"Ah . . . What price glory?" I laughed.

"I, too, was quite impressed."

"And so you damn well should have been! Just call me Alan Shearer."

"You ought to be a father."

"Yes . . . well."

"You're as good with children as you are with dogs."

"I hoped you were going to say with women."

"Yes, even there you're not so bad. Clearly an all-rounder. All things to all people. In short—insufferable."

For a while we walked without talking. I turned my head a couple of times.

"Why *don't* you go and join in?"

"It's already after four." Actually the reason I had just glanced at my watch was because I'd briefly wondered about running across. "You know you're dying for a cup of tea. I am, too."

Besides, supposing I hadn't managed to live up to that initial impression? It was years since I'd played football.

I said: "It's one of the most underrated secrets in life—knowing when to leave the party!"

But I wasn't certain she was listening.

"Is it one of your ambitions," she asked, "ever to become a father?"

It was an awkward question and one I hadn't reckoned would come up, not carrying as it did, as I felt certain it did, the implication that Moira's childbearing days were rapidly running out and perhaps . . .

Ten years ago I'd allowed Junie to talk me into having a vasectomy. Apart from the obvious loss-of-manhood thing I'd never had a single reason to regret it. Until now.

I gave a shrug.

And thought I detected a flicker of disappointment. I hated the notion of being responsible for anyone's disappointment. Especially, of course, Moira's. I put my arm about her waist. To my relief, she then put hers around mine. It was a long time since I'd walked that way with Junie. (Junie was actually too short.)

I myself had earlier felt a flicker of disappointment . . . or, at least, of something. On the landing stage. That father with his three young children; presumably they'd all been his? He had looked lusty and attractive. I knew I had experienced envy of some kind. Or wistfulness.

Though whatever it was—and however fleeting—it had surely been uncalled-for on an afternoon like this.

"Yet I didn't finish telling you about Susie." Did that sound a bit abrupt? "It's only a week since it happened but you wouldn't believe the progress she's been making. Everyone calls it a miracle. Even the vet."

"That's wonderful." My relief was increased by the lack of any flatness in her tone. "And for you that's not just some worn-out old cliché, is it?"

I gave another shrug—as if the thrust of her remark was something anyone essentially humble ought to feel ashamed of.

"And you love that dog," she added, "as though she were your own."

19

I'd bought the goldfingering at a haberdasher's in Abbey Road, on our way to Regent's Park. I'd hardly known it could exist: a London shop that surely hadn't changed in over fifty years. Possibly much more than that? Impulsively I'd stopped the car.

There was a parking space a few yards down the road. Maybe if there hadn't been I'd simply have smiled and driven on and thought, "Oh, what the hell, some other day possibly," but the parking space *was* there and the combination of that and the haberdashery had seemed a charming gift too timely to refuse. I'd asked Moira whether she'd mind waiting.

"Not in the least. But what are you after?"

"A lifeline."

"Oh? Is that all?"

The shop had a polished mahogany counter and a wall fitted with small drawers that would have made young Arthur Kipps, or even H.G. himself, feel instantly at home. Not seeing any kind of railway overhead I still half-expected to discover, tucked away in some remote corner, a chute for change-bearing cylinders. Half-expected to be served by somebody sweet and venerable and wearing a choker.

STEPHEN BENATAR

But at least I wasn't let down in the one respect that mattered. The young woman with the unremitting sniff knew immediately which drawer to go to.

In fact, I hadn't imagined for one moment that she wouldn't. I remembered Moira had only brought me this way because she'd wanted to show me the studios where the Beatles had recorded. But I also remembered—and for the second time in far less than twenty-four hours—that apparently some people claimed there was no such thing as coincidence. Or chance.

It made me think again about *The X Files*.

The truth is out there!

When I returned to the car Moira must have seen I'd been successful. I sat in the driving seat and handed her the paper bag. Inside . . . the ball of goldfingering.

"The last they had. I'd otherwise have bought a second but I think the one should be enough."

"Oh, good, you honestly do believe so?"

"Yes. Though, by the way, I didn't realize it was called that. Did you? They also showed me a hank of wool, gold Lurex, but I thought the thread was more appropriate."

"I am likely to scream before long."

"You do repeat yourself."

"Maybe I'm driven to it. Maybe it's the kind of men I sometimes meet in Kentish seaside towns."

"I am sorry. I know you think I'm only playing games."

She said nothing—her silence was sufficiently expressive.

"And on one level, I suppose . . . yes, that *is* what I'm doing."

"What sort of games?"

"You remember the myth of Theseus and the Minotaur?"

"I know it's something I must have read about; yet you'd better remind me."

"Okay, then. But where to begin? The Minotaur had the body of a man but the head of a bull. He was a pitiful hybrid who's always received an extremely poor press. Which is obviously unfair: he was merely the victim of his own natural dictates. No more inherently evil than a crocodile. But he caused a lot of suffering."

144

"And so Theseus—Theseus, did you say?—set out to . . . To what? Kill him? Reform him? Show him the error of his ways?"

"No, that would have been sweet, wouldn't it? Really sweet. Bible lessons; cautionary tales; Just-So Stories. Aesop. But, alas, I don't think reformation was ever quite on his agenda. I'm afraid I have to tell you he was doomed from the beginning."

"Theseus?"

"No! The Minotaur!"

"Sorry. Got muddled."

"My fault. Didn't mean to snap. Any mix-up and it's me."

"At all events. Our hero slays this sad, pathetic beast?"

"Assisted by a beautiful princess who remains at the entrance to the maze. I forgot to mention that the creature lives in this maze—a melancholy place, practically impossible to get out of."

"But she couldn't have been much help if she merely remained there at the entrance. Or did you say she had long arms? Extendable? Twistable around corners?"

"No, stop it, this is serious!"

She looked contrite but I could sense she was trying to keep a straight face.

"Don't you see? It's my own slow progression I'm attempting to describe. The princess stands there clutching the thread which Theseus has attached to himself and without which he'd be lost. Utterly lost."

In one way, however, I already *was* lost: Moira's laughter couldn't be contained. Neither, suddenly, could mine.

And our giggles in that parked car reminded me of when Junie and I, not quite a week ago, had had to roll about in bed, so helpless it had almost hurt.

Moira was the first to recover. There were passers-by and for once I think she was more aware of them than I was.

She waited until no one could have overheard. "The thread! I do believe I'm beginning to see daylight. Tell me: how—or where—has he attached this thread?"

"Ah, now. Perhaps we'll have to puzzle that one out tonight?"

"Mmm. Well, I hope it's good and strong."

"Of course it is. It's golden and enchanted."

"I fear I may have got confused again. Are we talking of the thread or the thing it will be tied to? But before you answer that—you haven't told me yet the name of the beautiful princess. Was she Titian-haired and quite amazingly captivating? And did she capture all men's hearts?"

"She did! She did! Well, she certainly did mine."

"And the name . . . ?"

I had intended this to hit its mark; and hit its mark it clearly did.

"You do not mean," she gasped, "of the royal house of Scrumpen-houser!"

"The very same. Is there any other?"

"It's odd I should have known my own name."

"Yes, odd you should have realized I've been waiting for you all my life. For *you* and the excitement and the spur to good. Odd you should have known that one day you would lead me from the maze."

I put my hand on her thigh and pressed.

"That you would lead me to the light."

20

After we'd made fairly rapid love and then showered, we put on our regalia. Moira wore something silky, lavender and long; with a sash in deep lilac. I whistled at her. "Cor!"

"Like it?"

"Now I can honestly understand why this morning you had to get up two hours earlier than me." My hands were on her shoulders. "I want you to know, kid, I think you made good use of all that time."

"Thank you," she said. "But if only I'd realized what a picture *you* were going to make I think I would have taken longer."

"Course you would have! Why do you feel the need to say it?"

We were in the kitchen.

"Now stop being such an ass. Sit down, do something useful. Like open the wine, maybe—then light the candles?"

I obeyed her to the letter.

"This is only going to be a snack," she pointed out. "We'll be having our main meal after the show. On me," she added; "and no arguments—you understand? I want this to be my evening."

I decided we should have to see about that.

We ate some of Junie's soup and some of Junie's meat pie and some of Junie's fruit cake. Apart from the half-bottle of Bordeaux and the strong black coffee from Colombia, our light repast had a very homely feel to it; and I was hungrier than I'd realized, having had nothing since breakfast, save a cup of tea and a fruit scone. Now I ate a second piece of the cake—this time, though, scarcely more than a slither, and an exceedingly crumbly one at that. But as I picked the Smarties off the top—I particularly liked the coffee and the orange ones—it suddenly struck me that this was as close as I would ever get to stealing the food out of the mouths of children. At least, I hoped it was. (Whether there were three children or only one . . . ? Irrelevantly, I wondered why I'd felt obliged to supply an exact figure; was it simply a case of my never liking to do *anything* by halves?)

That second thin slice of disintegrating cake could almost have given me indigestion.

Which would have been a rich and appropriate revenge. Like Junie I never suffered from indigestion. (Except following those rare bouts of compulsive eating. But if Junie was changing, was there some fear I might be changing too? We had always been extraordinarily sympathetic.)

Moira and I left the flat later than we had meant to: it was after half-past- six. Moira had wanted to be at the theatre some fifteen minutes early, because she said she always liked to watch the audience arrive; but I myself considered privately that it might do the audience more good to watch us arrive. The latest weather forecast had again been more or less all right—well, over the short term, anyway: mainly mild and dry in the south-east—and personally it didn't worry me too much if there *were* going to be dramatic changes from around midnight; this evening was to be the high point.

"Not," I'd said to Moira, "that I can understand you having so much trust in all those dinky little weather men. You're a very gullible young woman."

"They don't usually let me down."

"How could they—in that dress? I mean . . . *you* in that dress."

"Thank you, darling. On the other hand I wish occasionally they would. I'd been thinking we might drive out into the country tomorrow—have lunch at an olde worlde pub I know, where there are tables on a lawn sloping down to the river."

"Sounds idyllic. But never mind: if we can't do that I'll take you for a ride elsewhere. To Banbury Cross and Tilbury Docks and all points west."

"East."

"Who's the pilot? Possibly I'll fly you to the Never-Never-Land, as well, where there are mermaids and fairies and lagoons—and Red Indians and pirates"—my voice had grown slowly more menacing—"and a crocodile with a great sense of timing patiently awaiting his chance . . . *to gobble you all up!*"

I pounced; and she shivered, theatrically. "Isn't that the place where all the Lost Boys go?" she inquired, innocently.

"Yes," I answered; matching innocence with innocence. "There was Nibs and Tootles. And there was Slightly. And . . . ah, yes, that's right . . . there was one called Curly, too." I nodded, reminiscently.

She looked at me in deep suspicion.

"Is it at all possible that you could be having me on?"

"Now what purpose can you ever believe there'd be in that? Begorra."

The uncertainty turned swiftly to respect. "But how on earth do you remember such very way-out things?"

"It's the downside, I suppose, of being so intellectual. Are you impressed? And I promise you it's not for nothing I have often been referred to as Old Memorybags!"

She shook her head in envious admiration.

"But anyhow," she advised, "enough of all this nonsense. I don't know why I'm laughing: I'm beginning to have some very serious doubts regarding what makes Sammy run!" She kissed my cheek. "Give me two minutes in the bathroom, then finally we're off."

I myself was fully ready—Moira had retied my tie before she'd sat down. "I'll wait by the car," I said.

Once outside, I glanced at my watch. It gave both time and date. Twenty-three minutes to seven on Saturday the third of May. It felt like a caption to write beneath a photograph.

And at twenty-three minutes to seven on Saturday the third of May there was an elderly woman standing at her front gate on the opposite side of the road talking to an elderly man on the pavement. There were two little Minnie Mouses walking gingerly towards me in white ankle socks and high-heeled shoes. There was a young man sitting on his parked motorbike while his girlfriend hurried down her path to join him. It was nice to know I would be noticed—yes, and for the first time ever in my dinner jacket in the street! An occasion. I sauntered unselfconsciously around the car, dealing casually with this and that: a scarcely visible smear on the bonnet, another on the windscreen. I propped myself against the nearside bodywork—ankles crossed—and studied my fingernails. I began to whistle. The hit tune from tonight's show.

And I *was* noticed; no doubt about that. And when Moira came swishing out of the house and I was standing there suavely holding the car door, I was still noticed; but now we both were, which made it even better. My consort had arrived. The old people opposite and the two small girls were giving us frank stares. The motorbike pair proved a little more cagey. I felt it wasn't too soon for the jungle drums to start beating out their message to alert the neighbourhood. Net curtains should be twitching; flatmates shrilly summoned to the window. By now the fashion photographers could well be on their way.

Yet, even if they weren't, they'd easily be able to catch up. We blazed a golden trail; made a royal progress. Pedestrians weren't actually lining the route but I saw many who literally came to a standstill to gaze after us. I saw the occupants of other cars, too, eyeing us with reverence. And at one set of traffic lights—again we seemed to catch so many that had just gone red—I'd swear that half the passengers on a double-decker must have rushed across to *our* side to obtain a better view.

Quite predictably, on reaching the West End, we had to proceed still more slowly and I began to be afraid we might miss the overture or even the rising of the curtain and need to find our seats in darkness. But our luck persisted, especially with regard to our parking (God, were we lucky, a turning just off Oxford Circus!), and by using the subway under Regent Street and cutting a dash into Argyll Street— apologetic, laughing, hand-in-hand—we made it to the theatre with almost as much as five minutes to spare. Perfect timing! Maybe the last lap of the journey had even added an extra lustre: the gaiety which sparkles in relief. And as we moved across the thick pile of the foyer, amid other late arrivals, then on into the auditorium, I knew that I walked with a back even straighter than usual and with a smile which in an understated way was encompassing the world. Yesterday, we had said we'd deck ourselves out *resplendently*. Today, we weren't the only ones in evening dress (this, after all, was just the third night of the run) but I saw no other couple that came close—not even within spitting distance. No potential claim-jumpers.

And then the show began. That, too, was magical. Of course. We were all in the right mood: a company of strangers forever to be linked by the forging of an evening's memory—a shipload of voyagers soon to disperse to different corners of the globe but with whom we'd merged in an unrepeatable experience. (Essentially unrepeatable. Like when I'd recently heard on the radio an audience clapping sixty years ago during a concert at Carnegie Hall: I'd been as respectful of the onceness of that applause as I was of the onceness of both Benny Goodman and Gene Krupa who'd occasioned it—two giants who had never performed together at any other time.) And how amused we all were at the absurdity of the protagonists not realizing when they were well off; at their selfish fears of growing old and missing out; at their readiness to chase rainbows and fall cataclysmically in love . . . their strivings so pathetic, our laughter so superior and benign. Added to which, the songs were jaunty and many of the lyrics gave you something to think about: i.e. live for the moment since you don't know what's to come. Likewise, be true to yourself, "and it must follow, as the night the day . . . " Not that this bit was actually written for our present entertainment, any more than was something else, "there's a special providence in the fall of a sparrow", or a further something else—though from the Bible this time, not the Bard. That was the passage in St Matthew recently learned by my son, and tested by my son's father, because Miss Martin had invented an exercise on namesakes. "Are not two sparrows sold for a farthing? and one of them shall not fall on the ground without your Father . . . Fear ye not therefore, ye are of more value than many sparrows." Now *that* would have made a wonderfully memorable lyric. Plenty of bounce! Plenty of pazazz! I couldn't understand its omission. Because if you're going to choose a title like *Half a Farthing, Sam Sparrow?* aren't you practically obligated to acknowledge your sources?

However—allowing for that one small if stupidly niggling reservation, which wasn't a huge price to pay for such a satirical, fast-paced piece of fun—the show provided an excellent evening in the theatre.

As well as the makings of an excellent evening out of it! Moira and I left the car where it was and almost floated down Regent Street, as if contained in our own iridescent little bubble—the same means of transport Glinda always seemed to rely on. The Munchkins invariably went, "Ahh . . . ," when they saw her coming in to land.

"Where shall I get it to dissolve?" I asked. "And please note I say 'dissolve'. Not 'burst'."

"Tonight I feel there's nothing that could make our bubble burst."

"No," I said, "nothing. Moira . . . ?"

"You can dissolve it at the Ritz," she said.

"The Ritz!"

"We're having dinner at the Ritz."

"My God," I remarked. (A little premature, perhaps, to inquire about my Man-of-the-Year Award?) "How much higher can we go?"

"That's something we'll just have to find out, isn't it?"

"'Up up and away in my beautiful balloon . . . '"

She said: "Wouldn't it be wonderful to go around the world in a balloon?"

I promised myself that this summer I would surprise her with a flight in a balloon. Maybe not transworld, or even transatlantic, but at least trans-Thames. That was something Junie would never have wanted: *any* kind of a balloon trip. But Matt would. Matt would! And was there any reason why he and Moira shouldn't—well, in some way—soon meet up and get to be real friends . . . and then . . . ?

"We could drift across oceans and meadows," she added, "and over mountain peaks and cities . . . "

"Do you know something? You're getting to sound a lot like me."

"My goodness, even while I was saying it, I had that thought as well! I really did. Because, in fact, going around the *world* in a balloon would be horrendous. Going around London in a balloon could be brilliant."

"I think I must have influenced you."

"I think you must have."

"Benevolent?"

"Oh undoubtedly! And, Sammy, we'd have little refreshments as we flew. Sip champagne and nibble biscuits with Stilton or—better still—with caviar."

"I've never eaten caviar."

That night we ate caviar.

We drank champagne, as well.

We lived like kings and queens, or lords and ladies. Like swash-buckling adventurers. I was Errol Flynn playing Robin Hood . . . in line for execution but still as irrepressible as ever. I wasn't sure how, or why, such a transition should have taken place: from royalty to rascal: but I suppose I must have felt there was room within me to express varying personalities—like a sailor with a wife in every port and a different face to present to each of them. That's why I knew I had it in me to become an actor. I looked about that splendid dining room for any celebrated actors and, if I'd seen one, should very likely have gone across to ask for guidance—heaven helps those who help themselves! The theatre was where I belonged. Rather than the shop, the office, or even university.

But the Ritz that night was short on celebrated actors.

It didn't matter.

"All the world's a stage . . . They have their exits and their entrances, and one man in his time plays many parts." I can't remember now if there was any run-up to this small confidence or if I even let Moira know to whom I was referring. I *can* remember, though, remarking that if *I* had written that particular speech I'd have improved on it a little. "It isn't logical. Entrances should come *before* exits—well, obviously." I saw myself, for a moment, right at the cutting edge of scholarship. "Do you love me?" I asked.

"Yes," she said. "I think I do."

"I feel I ought to tell you," I told her . . . carefully . . . "that I am not altogether very lovable."

"And I feel I ought to tell you that perhaps you're not . . . altogether . . . the best judge of that."

"Will *you* be my judge?" I then asked, earnestly.

"In this case, yes, certainly, with pleasure." She put on her white cap. "I pronounce you very lovable."

Anyone who can place a damask napkin on her head in the middle of the Ritz dining room—even for only a second or two—has to be a fairly decent judge.

I felt very safe being in the hands of such a fairly decent judge.

"But you haven't all the facts." I knew there were lots of things I ought to say—and that I'd definitely never get a better opportunity for saying them. I hoped to harvest, or harness, as many of my wandering thoughts as possible. I swallowed some more wine.

"Then give me all the facts," she invited. She gazed at me now with wholly undisguised affection. She leant her elbows on the table and put her face between her hands. "I don't know if I can reverse the verdict but I feel you'd better acquaint me with the evidence."

"Well, you see, Your Honour, it's like this."

What was it like, though? Exactly? I made a truly heroic attempt to consider what it *was* like. Exactly.

"I think it may be best if I tell you in the car."

"Coward," she said. "Procrastinator! But if it's going to take long—then, yes, you're probably right." She had glanced at her watch and made a mild grimace at what it told her.

She signalled to our waiter and drained her demitasse as he approached.

"Please! You've got to let me!" I said, fumbling for my wallet.

But her tone was suddenly imperious; and partly because of this, partly because I had a lot else on my mind, I gratefully submitted.

And, gosh, was it a time to show gratitude! I didn't see the bill but thought that very possibly it would have necessitated another interview with Hal Smart.

21

"I'm really, you see, a married man. And I've been a married man for many married years. And I've got a daughter of fifteen called Ella and a son of Matt called twelve. And my grandmother didn't even make that cake, although I told you that she did, because my grandmother is dead and no longer does the cooking. And Susie doesn't belong to any of the neighbours—she belongs to me—well, to us, that is, to me and Junie and Susie and Matt. And I love you very much and I'm very sorry that I made up stories."

And then I told her in great detail of my plans: London from Monday to Friday, Deal at the weekends ("but you'd hardly notice I was gone!"). I had the impression that all the right words were coming to me, that I spoke with unusual eloquence and was really getting through to her, letting her know all about my childhood and frustrations and mistakes. And, also, all about the compensations I had found along the way. I remember at one point I related to her the plot of *The Captain's Paradise*: how Alec Guinness, as the captain of a steamer plying between Gibraltar and Tangier, has a very domesticated kind of wife in one port and a very sensual and exotic kind in the other: the seemingly perfect situation. (In spite of its containing risks. As when the two women, each unaware of the existence of a counterpart, strike up a conversation in a store in Tangier at a moment when he himself is hurrying there to keep a rendezvous with one of them . . . ! Suspense!) Seemingly perfect, I should say, because then Celia Johnson, who's the quiet, domesticated one, starts unexpectedly to change, grows tired of always being at home and wants to go out dancing, while Yvonne de Carlo, who's the sultry one, starts wanting to stay in and cook delicious suppers . . . which also struck me as a pretty fair solution so there must have been some reason why he hadn't just adapted and why he had somehow ended up in front of a firing squad (I'm sure there hadn't been a murder) although as the film was a comedy, one naturally realized he wasn't going to get shot. I think he must have bribed somebody . . . In any case I told Moira, quite honestly, I wasn't certain about that, which led me on to reassure her that until our meeting on the beach I had never told a single lie to anyone . . . well, at least never a real whopper; there were always going to be the very small ones, weren't there, and nobody's name had ever been George Washington other than George Washington's and anyone else who'd either been named after him or coincidentally been called George when their parents had chanced to be a Mr and Mrs Washington? . . . and, anyway, I hadn't really meant to deceive her, it had just sort of grown—"O what a wangled web we weave, when first we practise to deceive!"—and it was only because I had liked the look of her so much and had wanted to make myself interesting because I had liked the look of her so much (so in a manner of speaking it was she who was to blame: she shouldn't have bewitched and enthralled me like Cleopatra enwitching and bethralling Antony) . . . It suddenly occurred to me she hadn't said a great deal throughout all of this—or indeed, perhaps, hadn't said anything at all—but this was obviously because she couldn't concentrate both on the driving and on thinking over the various convincing arguments that I'd put forward; not as well, I mean, as being expected actually to reply to all the various convincing arguments that I'd put forward.

Besides, I knew at the moment she was probably feeling angry with me (and had a perfect right to be feeling angry with me). I began to suspect that my growing awareness of there being a distance between us wasn't solely due to the fact of her concentration; and I understood this—it was natural—any woman (even the kind of woman Moira was: an angel: "there were angels dining at the Ritz") could certainly have been expected to feel angry with me.

Very angry.

Even Junie. Perhaps even Junie.

So then I began to apologize and to hope that I hadn't ruined her evening because until I had started to get everything off my chest it had been the very happiest evening of my life, the very happiest *two* evenings of my life, with the very happiest night and day dividing them. But the chest-baring had been necessary—as of course I knew she understood—although I greatly wished it hadn't. And I appreciated, too, the way that, apart from a single glass of champagne, she had stuck to only fruit juice or spring water throughout the entire evening, even at the theatre bar during the interval (although she'd also had a glass of the Bordeaux before we'd started out), which was a sacrifice which like the similar one the night before I hadn't at all taken for granted. By rights it should have been my turn tonight to make the sacrifice and I was truly a cad for not having insisted on doing so. I very much regretted that. And I was still apologizing as I followed her up the stairs to the flat; and was alarmed suddenly to find there were tears running down my face. All right, I was a beast, I knew it and I hated it, quite beastlike through and through, but I was going to make it up to her; I would eliminate the beast if it was the very last thing I did; and only weak men cried. I tried to wipe away the tears and pretended it was just a piece of grit and told her that mentioning Celia Johnson had made me think of *Brief Encounter*, about this woman with a dull but happy marriage who gets a similar bit of grit in her eye while waiting for her train and then has it removed—in the station refreshment room—by a nice-looking doctor who the following week walks into the overcrowded Kardomah where she happens to be having lunch . . . But it wasn't at all a funny film like *The Captain's Paradise* and it would depend on whether she wanted a laugh or a cry as to which I'd recommend if they chanced to be showing simultaneously, say on BBC 2 and Channel 4, and she hadn't got a video recorder.

Which she hadn't.

And neither had I.

Or neither had we.

But perhaps she'd already seen *Brief Encounter*? Perhaps it would have been surprising if she hadn't. Perhaps she'd already seen *The Captain's Paradise*? Perhaps the courteous thing would have been to find out.

Belatedly, I tried to find out.

Asked the question. But no good. I couldn't wait to hear the answer. Had to rush off to be sick.

My God but it was sudden. Yet at least I'd made it home; at least I'd made it to the loo. At least I hadn't spewed up in the car. Thank heaven for small mercies. No, thank heaven for *huge*, never-to-be-forgotten mercies. Oh, my God! Imagine! Supposing I'd spewed up in the car!

I hoped she couldn't hear me. I knew damn well she could. The tears really did fall then, while I knelt and encompassed the cool china and disgorged throatfuls of splashing brown vomit and retched and retched as though my final hour had practically arrived. It distantly occurred to me that my dinner-suited arms embracing the white lavatory bowl looked like a thick black stripe bordering an envelope of condolence.

What I obviously needed was sleep: lots and lots of sleep; and then it might come right once more. *Somehow* come right once more. But not tonight. There was no way I could take her riding round the world again tonight: either on a cockhorse or up in a balloon or even under sail, in a pirate ship, alongside Errol Flynn—this time in his role as Captain Blood. Just the thought of any kind of undulation was enough to make me heave.

And heave and heave and heave.

22

Oddly, it was again around eleven-fifty when I woke, and again I was alone in the bed. But before I realized either of these things, I'd remembered all the throwing up; remembered it with a cringing in my gut, a shrivelling in my crotch. Oh, God. Oh, God. *Oh, God!*

But that was my very last recollection: being on my knees—in my dinner jacket—with my arms around the bowl. I couldn't remember undressing, or brushing my teeth, or leaving the bathroom. Strain as I might I couldn't even recall having flushed the lavatory. I *must* have flushed the lavatory. Whatever else I had done, or had not done, during the whole course of the evening—during the whole course of my life—I must, please God, dear God, I must have flushed that lavatory.

I had been on my knees. Now I tried to will myself into a recollection of the act of getting up from them. I couldn't. *Couldn't!* Had I simply passed out? There on the bathroom floor?

Yet, here in bed, I was certainly undressed.

Except for the boxers. I flexed my feet. And except for the socks.

That was it, then. If I'd undressed myself I would never have left on my shorts or my socks. Never!

Oh, Moira.

Moira.

Where are you?

She must be in the kitchen. Drinking tea. Reading the paper. And yet . . . the depth of the silence . . . I heard the thrumming of the fridge; a far-off conversation in the street. No radio. No creakings of a wooden chair. I pushed aside the duvet; slid my legs across the bed; forced myself to find the floor.

Extreme mortification (together with a desperate desire to take at least that first step along the road to recovery and atonement), this kept my hangover to some extent at bay: kept it quivering before me at arm's length, at finger's length, while I stumbled, collided, lurched towards the kitchen. Sudden contact with daylight, even slate-coloured daylight, felt stingingly offensive.

But she wasn't in the kitchen.

I already knew she wasn't in the sitting room.

Nor was she in the bathroom.

I stooped painfully—raised both the lid and seat of the lavatory. Everything was fresh, sweet-smelling; the water tinted blue. (Well, surprise! Had I honestly expected her to leave it?) More painfully I examined the exterior of the porcelain, the fluffy rug around its base. But then I remembered that yesterday's rug had been the glowing shade of thick honey. Today's was a dull green.

My evening suit lay folded on a stool. My shirt was maybe with it but I didn't want to look.

I urinated; washed my hands; rinsed out my mouth. Made my way back to the bed. Lay down, closed my eyes, tried to think. Tried to retrieve my memory . . . gain with it some measure of reassurance.

Half an hour went by. I couldn't stay like this. I knew I had to be showered and shaved and smelling of toothpaste and *Cool Water* (My Scintillating Future!) by the time that she returned. I should be clean and penitent and dignified, not rough-skinned, sour-breathed and rheumy-eyed. No whining, no weakness. The situation wasn't lost.

Respect surely retrievable? That was the issue, the *sine qua non*. Without respect you lost everything. You lost the lot. Precious metal transmuted back to base. Second-class citizen—and, in the eyes of those who had recast you, doomed always to remain one. No appeal; no redress. You might as well be dead.

But even so. I wasn't dead yet. I could forestall this tragedy. All I needed was the willpower.

All I needed was to put the enemy to rout. My greatest enemy ... inertia. I said to myself through every stage of my ablutions: *Be positive! Broad-shouldered! Unbeatable!* At one point I was actually shouting it, in competition with a forceful jet of water. My resolve—so fragile when I'd left the bed—began to grow. My hangover began to ease.

And by the time I came out of the bathroom I felt so much better I was actually thinking I could drink a cup of tea and manage a piece of toast. Balance and sanity and hope were now starting to return in more than just a dribble.

Wearing a set of completely clean clothes—apart from my jeans and they were still in a pretty good state—I felt not merely freshened up but smart. Though that was only physical. For my spiritual cleansing I had urgent need of Moira.

Where was she?

I stood at the window in the sitting room and craned in both directions. The Morgan wasn't there. I could be sure of this—even if, last night, she hadn't been able to park it immediately below. But hardly had I turned away before there came a patter on the glass.

Well, good, I thought. At least the rain might hasten her return.

Back in the kitchen, though, I came across her note. A sheet of blue stationery beside the breadboard. On the worktop. I was surprised to think I'd overlooked it.

It read:

"Sam —have gone out for the day. Paracetemol in bathroom. Suit sponged but in need of dry-clean. Doorkey on table in hall. Please drop it through letterbox. (For downstairs door, no key required.) Thank you. Moira."

I turned it over in case there was a message on the back: "PS I love you. Everything will work out." I had even sat down before I'd turned it over; briefly speculating on what little variations might await me there.

It was the coldest note imaginable, between friends. Junie would never have written me a note like that. Forget the punctuation.

I began to analyse it. The word 'Paracetemol' leapt out at me. Her ballpoint had evidently run dry and after taking a new one she'd had to retrace the first three letters.

What also leapt out at me, associatively, were thoughts of suicide.

I put down the note and contemplated suicide.

Did so practically as a distraction.

I imagined trying actually to kill myself. Imagined giving the appearance of trying actually to kill myself. How many tablets would they find convincing? And, then again, was four o'clock or nine o'clock more likely to be the hour of her homecoming?

Yet I had heard that you should never use Paracetemol. You might initially recover but just as you were getting accustomed to being alive again—and maybe even feeling fairly thankful for it—you inescapably succumbed to liver failure; I hoped you could appreciate the irony. Aspirin, it seemed, were a whole lot kinder to the struggling liver.

But aspirin. My father had done it with aspirin. For twenty years or more I'd seen my father as a wimp: despite those rules which he'd laid down for my own manly education and presumably tried to live by himself. (Live by himself? He hadn't managed *that* for very long, had he? All of two days! And 'by himself' . . . so where had that left me?) "Sorry, Dad. Like father like son. When it came down to it, I couldn't climb to any greater heights than you!" Cruel, my lack of empathy— and cruel also, his delayed-action revenge: the influential part he'd played in making me the person I now was. (You see! Added to everything else, I'm even trying to shift the blame for that—for being the person I now am. Oh, my God, yes. How thoroughly you turned your son into a man!)

In any case, the concept of suicide, even of no more than the cry-for-help variety, was obviously untenable. Tomorrow, Junie would be expecting me home for supper—quite probably cooking something special. If I travelled the aspirin route, I could still be in some hospital at suppertime tomorrow. In no fit state even to telephone.

And from now on Junie had to be my priority. Come what may. Had to be protected. Constantly.

Unflaggingly.

But she always had been, of course. In the whole of our seventeen years this was the only time I had ever left my post. I had needed a holiday. That holiday was over.

However, the idea of suicide itself—the real thing, not merely a pitiful gesture—could suddenly sound like a holiday: some layout in a brochure showing leafy trees and sparkling water and a deckchair set in dappled shade. And simply the notion of this, coming as it did with a promise that things need never get too bad again, whether in thirty years' time with cancer, or whether just tomorrow with heartbreak, conveyed such an impression of tranquillity you were immediately tempted to get off your butt, run to the telephone and ask for details.

Oh, get thee behind me, Satan.

I did get off my butt, though, if only to put water in the kettle and to take a glance into Moira's washing machine. I suppose I must have been alerted by the small red light, which hadn't turned itself out, despite the cycle being completed.

Yes, and there it was, that honey-coloured rug, not yet dried, therefore much duller, but even so . . . wrenchingly familiar.

I switched on the radio. It was probably still tuned to Radio 4: at present a church service or some recording of a hymn: "Dear Lord and Father of mankind, forgive our foolish ways . . . " I rapidly switched off.

Went back to my chair at the table and to yet a further perusal of that graceless note.

So overwhelmingly devoid of charity. So overwhelmingly—

But then, of course, it hit me.

Hit me with the same sharpness I had just applied to switching off the radio.

I must have been blind. So blind, so insensitive. I'd missed such very obvious pointers. As soon as I saw one I saw a dozen.

Well, anyway, *five*! And, Christ, they could scarcely have been more glaring had they been handed to me in person. On Mount Sinai.

(i) The use of my name. Well, that was friendly enough. 'Dear' would have turned it into a formality and 'Dearest' or 'Darling' was currently more than I deserved—while, self-evidently, 'Sammy' carried undertones of childishness; conferred on me, almost, the status of a pupil.

(ii) She had anticipated my hangover and hinted at a remedy;

not merely hinted at but told me where to find it; could anyone deny this was considerate? In fact I didn't see what more she could have done.

(iii) And she had actually sponged my dinner suit. Frankly, up till now, I hadn't given that sufficient weight, had even taken it a bit for granted. However, by this time being a little clearer-headed and better able to read between the lines, I could begin to appreciate the meaning behind the gesture, its symbolism, its standing as an act of love. She hadn't been able to *write* 'with love' at the end of the letter but—if only subconsciously—she had incorporated that very message in her text.

And (iv) in the light of all of this, those two words above her signature acquired of course a new significance. Like I say, she hadn't managed to write 'with love' or 'my darling'—that would have been giving me back too much, too quickly—and after all, being only human and very much a woman, she had naturally wanted to make me sweat somewhat. But she *had* been able to write 'Thank you'. It was incredible I should have missed the softening of that phrase. *Thank you*. The comprehensiveness of it. Effusion. Profligacy.

And furthermore (v) she had used a sheet of top quality writing paper. If she simply hadn't cared, I now realized, she would have done what I did all the time: used either a Post-it or whatever lay at hand . . . there would always be *something*. So was that, or was it not, indicative? Was that—or was it not—a clincher?

Weren't they all clinchers?

These discoveries, all my detective work, had proved efficacious. I suddenly felt hungry; not just for a slice of dry toast but for several slices, spread with butter and marmalade. The kettle had switched itself off, yet as it returned to the boil I realized I was whistling. Already on my way back. No, in fact—already a fair distance along it, my way back. "'When you're up to your neck in hot water, be like a kettle and sing . . .'" Good old Vera Lynn! What on earth had I been getting so het up about? Nothing so terrible had taken place. Nothing irreversible. I'd got a little drunk and I'd been a little sick. That probably happened to thousands, every single day on which the sun rose.

Oh, and I had told her about Junie.

But the incidence of husbands falling for the charms of an outsider—or, in my own case, for the charms of an angel—was practically as high, in this modern age, as that of drunkenness. And if nobody was actually harmed thereby—the *one* indispensable yardstick, naturally—what was this but a means of liberating your true self, loosening the constrictions, looking deep into your psyche? Thus it became an experience which could open up a great expansive web of gleaming opportunity. For now we see through a glass, brightly. Strap on your wing*ed* sandals. Take up your mighty sword. On such a full sea are we now afloat.

Also, I'd told her I could be regarded as a free agent. During four whole days each week.

And during four whole nights each week. I hoped I had sufficiently emphasized that. Not that I believed it stood in much need of emphasis.

So we could now make a new beginning; as from this very night; a new beginning even better than the old, because it would now be completely honest—freed of all necessity to watch one's words and to keep peering carefully around corners.

I always drew as much strength from the thought of new beginnings as I did from the contemplation of old successes.

Tomorrow would be the first day of the rest of my life.

(Tomorrow, in this instance, because today was almost half gone by now and—besides—I had the feeling that perhaps I did need a bit of breathing space. I knew there was never any point in rushing things.)

And tomorrow, too, I'd really make a start on my diary: not be merely collating and editing inside my head. Anyway, thank God I *hadn't* yet made a start, not physically! In that case, I'd have had to supply details which were no longer germane, but which—once written—would have had to be granted permanency.

On top of that, tomorrow was the first bank holiday in May—and therefore the one true time to celebrate the coming of the spring. (In March, for heaven's sake, one could still get winter temperatures *and* snow!) So what better day on which to make a new beginning? Of all the three-hundred-and-sixty-five in our current year, what better day than the one immediately ahead?

And—strictly in parenthesis—this was hardly conducive, was it, to any firm belief in the randomness of things? Could the proper day for the proper start have come about purely by accident?

No. I was well aware that only published diaries carried titles but . . . *The Long and Happy Life of Samson Groves*? One up on *The Diary of a Nobody*, maybe!

He saw! And he appreciated!

And he flew!

(Like a rock?)

Tombstone inscription?

23

I decided to go home. This time, so far as Moira was concerned, I'd really play it cool. The iceman cometh. I would take her at her word—ostensible word—and by doing so cause *her* to sweat a little. There would be irony in that. She was undoubtedly an angel but even angels, potentially, could profit from periods of uncertainty.

I would telephone tomorrow.

The journey wasn't perfect. Despite my renewed optimism, it was sad to return to Victoria and remember how happy I had been there. It didn't help that the station was so much quieter than before, exhibiting a degree of Sunday-afternoon lassitude which was perhaps deepened by the long weekend, but not, I now discovered, by any means endemic just to small provincial towns. Something livelier might have supported me. Nor did it help that I'd got quite soaked whilst standing at bus stops along the Finchley Road, or constantly looking back whilst hightailing between them, and now felt chilly and bedraggled. Nor, again, that I'd found myself with nearly two hours to wait before my train left—and knew that even this would be a slow one, stopping at nearly every station. I bought a paper which I couldn't work up any interest in and sat over a cup of coffee so noxious I couldn't take more than a sip for fear of reinvigorating my queasiness . . . And this time, although in one sense I was travelling lighter than before, since I had neither cardboard box nor carrier bags (my bundled evening clothes, wrapped around the patent leather pumps, were stuffed on top of my white trousers), this time, although less encumbered, I truly couldn't believe I might be travelling towards the sunrise. And I began to wonder whether I, too, shouldn't have left some note; began to wonder whether strong manly silences could ever be worth more than correct social behaviour: a debate which was very soon obtruding between me and whatever page in the paper I had then turned to. I hated to appear ungrateful. Or as though—small-mindedly—I nursed a grievance.

It grew less obtrusive while I was reading something I'd forgotten I would find: the review of *Half a Farthing, Sam Sparrow?* In other circumstances the tenor of it might have aroused some indignation but now I didn't care that much; could even derive mild satisfaction out of the complaints of the reviewer. Along with other things, he'd panned a number of the lyrics. Called them claptrap—facile and pretentious. This struck me as mildly tautologous but I told him, and not completely beneath my breath either, that *he* had done sufficient carping for the two of us.

My dilemma over the note was vying with another doubt. The soup and the meat pie; we'd eaten no more than a sixth of each. So what would Moira do with the remainder? Suddenly I realized I didn't know her well enough to feel even remotely sure. I only knew I utterly loathed the thought of any insult to Junie or her cooking; and also utterly loathed the thought of any waste . . . which was attributable, I suppose, to my upbringing, with its constant reminders to remember all the starving little children in India. (And the most appalling waste of anything I could imagine was to throw down the drain, almost literally, that chestful of exquisite treasures from the Ritz. How *could* I have? And Moira's gift to me! How must she have felt? That dinner had cost her—well, it really made me cringe to think how much that dinner must have cost her. I wished I could have been the one to pay . . . even despite the looming presence of Hal Smart. Talk about pearls before swine! Talk about manna turned to mush!) Well, Moira might get rid of the pie and the pea soup. Yet at least I felt certain she wouldn't throw away the cake. I mean, she couldn't, simply *couldn't*. All the consideration, kindness, care which had gone into the manufacture of that cake! To bin it would have been like burying a friend, like burying him alive, still wearing his smile and his pompommed hat. In fact, I felt certain that before long we'd again be eating it together. Or I *tried* to feel certain. This entailed a frequent repetition of the statement—both in the station and aboard the train—and on a couple of occasions, as with my mantra in the shower, I even repeated it out loud—at a volume, of course, totally unmatched by my response to the theatre critic. Thankfully the carriage was empty.

At Dover Priory there was a further long delay. But count your blessings, I told myself. At least this afternoon there's no one working on the line. At least this afternoon these other passengers and I aren't waiting for some wet and trundling godforsaken bus.

There were six of us in all.

But it was easier counting my fellow passengers than counting my blessings, which were right now as mist-hidden as those bluebirds above the cliffs: those bluebirds promised to us by Vera Lynn, whose name, coincidentally, had briefly occurred to me some five hours earlier. (Now, you see, I had no problem about believing in coincidence.) Promised to us, with such patriotic fervor, about eighteen years before my birth.

The depressing thing was . . . although I still felt reluctant to readmit that word into my vocabulary . . . the depressing thing was I knew there'd been a glut in the vicinity even as recently as last Friday. Forty-eight hours ago! The sky had been awash.

I tried to convince myself that they'd be back. Already *were* back. It was only because I was so very tired all of a sudden. I couldn't see them through the gloom.

The five others on the platform were all young and laughing and together. College students? I felt that I'd have given a lot to be one of them. Out with my friends; going off somewhere nice. All bouncy and naïve and pleased to play the fool.

I finally got home at around seven. The house was dark; car not there. I'd forgotten. Junie and the children would still be at Jalna (the Dovecote). Still be celebrating Ted and Yvonne's anniversary.

169

But *this* Sunday they wouldn't have been sitting in the garden. I felt sorry about that.

Without fully understanding my intention, and without even taking off my mack, I went into the larder and started to eat. I wasn't particularly hungry but—I wanted food. I ate handfuls of Harvest Crunch and tore open a packet of biscuits. I moved to the fridge and found cooked drumsticks; devoured all four. There were three pineapple rings on a saucer and a triangle of blue cheese. I followed these with a flavourless tomato.

At last, returning to the hall, I threw my raincoat on a chair, picked up my holdall from the mat. I was walking heavily up the stairs, meaning to lie down, when something occurred to me. I was at once deflected from the thought of sleep.

I ran back to the kitchen.

Susie's basket wasn't there. It wasn't there in any part of it.

Bewilderedly, I made headlong for the dining room, stood in the centre and scrutinized the base of every wall—as though the business of locating a dog's basket, even with the light on, would require swivelling feet, untypically sharp eyesight, an attention to detail.

Nor was it beneath the table.

I half-ran, half-strode, into the sitting room . . . the TV room . . . conservatory. Kitchen again. Larder and the outside loo. Went back into the hall. Whirled round and must have caught the brolly stand. It clattered onto varnished floorboards, cannoned into Junie's piano. I raced upstairs and into every bedroom, even the couple seldom used, one smelling now of paint and boobytrapped with decorating clutter. I fell on my knees and looked beneath the beds. Looked inside the bathroom. The lavatory. Stood on a ladder and shone our torch—kept handy for emergencies—into every corner of the loft.

Giddiness shook hands with paranoia.

I headed for the telephone.

Picked up, at the other end, by Pim.

"Get Junie," I commanded. Neither greeted him nor told him who I was.

He started to mumble something but I cut across him with a question.

"Listen—is Susie there? I can't find her basket anywhere! I've searched through every room and can't find her basket anywhere! Is Susie with you? Is she there?"

He didn't answer.

"Oh, for God's sake," I was going to say, "don't you understand plain English?"

But then I heard the receiver being thrown down and instead I broke wind. That wasn't very pleasant, either, but I realized I was past minding.

After what seemed like a long time I finally heard Junie's voice in the background—along with other voices, or maybe only one other, I wasn't sure. A man's. Jake's? Oh, probably the whole family was now filing into the hallway, taking seats. But I couldn't catch the words.

"Hello!" I said. "Hello! Hello! Hello! What the hell is going on over there? Will somebody pick up the phone!"

And somebody did. Somebody female.

"And where have *you* been since last Friday?"

But it certainly wasn't Junie.

"What?"

"This is Mrs Fletcher speaking. You've been off somewhere with a woman—haven't you, Groves? And I mean to tell you how I feel about it. I'm afraid there aren't words strong enough to tell you how I feel about it. There! Did you hear me? You were never one of us. I've always known you were a mealy-mouthed hypocrite, thinking all the time you were taking everybody in, pretending to be so much better than the rest of us, pretending even butter wouldn't melt—"

"Fuck off," I said. "I want to hear about my dog."

"Oh, you do, do you? Well, your dog is dead. Your dog has been put down. Dead," she repeated.

Then she severed the connection.

24

I immediately rang back.

The line was engaged.

If they'd left the receiver off I should have to charge right over—*now*, while my adrenalin was still racing, the small supply of it I had. At least the dizziness had gone but I would need to husband that adrenalin. I was fighting for my life and I wanted all the energy there was.

Almost at our gate, I remembered that I didn't have a car. Damn it, then—a bike. But on my way to the back porch, two things happened. First, it occurred to me it might be wiser to wait until Junie and the kids came home; my own territory—no heckling from the grandstand; and second . . . the telephone rang. That might be Junie now.

It wasn't.

"Hello, Sam. This is Jake. I've been deputized."

"Deputized?"

"Yes. To let you know the lie of the land. In fact, I volunteered. I thought you'd rather have me do it than . . . well, any of the girls, let's say. You know what all these Fletchers can be like. I gather you said something slightly naughty to Mama."

"How the hell did it happen, Jake?"

"Apparently Junie tried to reach you in Lincoln. Spoke to some woman whom she didn't know and who didn't appear to know her. Or anything about her. Or anything about you, either."

"Oh, God."

"Sammy," he said, "in some ways you're an astute and erudite fellow. Yet if only you could have been a fraction more astute over the plotting of all this . . . ! You idiot. You might always have come to me if you'd wanted some sound, practical advice. Either to me or—I suspect—to Robert. But as it is, old lad, you've landed in the shit. And it's going to be a long time, too, before you manage to climb out of it in *this* neck of the woods. If indeed you ever do."

"I couldn't care less about that. It's only Junie that matters. Junie and the children. And as soon as . . . Do the children know what's happened?"

"Do the children know what's happened? Whose children are we talking of? Some that live outside the county? Sam, you really are the weirdest mix!"

"Then how do they both seem?"

"It's hard to say. Matt's been mainly very quiet. Ella . . . well, Ella's been fairly brassy. Getting it out of her system, I think is what it's called. They'll be okay. I've been trying to make them see—the family at large, I mean, not simply Ella and Matt—that this sort of thing isn't really such a big deal. And just so long as you're not aiming to go skipping off again (because if you are, old chum, your days are numbered and the end is nigh) and just so long as you're willing to dance attendance for a year or six I reckon they'll all come round in the end. All of them. Even Myrtle. Even Junie."

"*Even* Junie?"

There was a slight pause. "That's unexpected?"

I gave a non-committal grunt; contented myself with informing him tersely of the one requirement: to prise my wife loose from the five thousand tentacles of my wife's interfering mother.

"No, but it isn't that straightforward. I don't think you realize how hard she's taken this. A girl of hidden depths, is Junie."

He added: "Not that, of course, I need tell *you* that."

173

"If you want to do me a favour, Jake, you'll just get her to come home as quickly as you can."

"But that's why I rang. To say that neither she nor the children will be coming home tonight. They slept here last night, too. She's even spoken about . . . To be honest, you've *both* taken me a little by surprise."

"Spoken about what?"

"About not coming home at all. I mean—not while you're there."

"Nonsense," I said. "Only give me ten minutes alone with her. That's all it needs."

"Well, I certainly hope so, Sam."

We went on talking but not to much purpose. Tiredness redescended. I picked up the umbrella stand and went wearily to bed. Let tomorrow take care of itself, let tomorrow play any little joke that it felt like. But why had she had to take it out on Susie? Why? What harm had poor old Susie ever done her?

Already down to my underpants I ran downstairs again. Discovered that besides the basket, with its blanket and cushions, Junie appeared to have disposed of Susie's collar and lead; of her muchchewed rubber ball and bone; even of the packet of Bob Martins. The insecticidal shampoo. The brush. Large bag of biscuits. Junie had seldom fed her out of tins.

I felt inclined to search the dustbin for a souvenir. But what was the point? At least we had the snapshots. I decided I must look for snapshots—if only to keep me from further depredations on the larder. Tomorrow my thinking would need to be unclogged.

Amongst the quantities of snapshots we hadn't yet got round to sorting, I found two: two of Susie on her own. Probably taken by myself. One showed the splayed paws, the dipped trunk, the prickedup ears . . . all eager for the pitched ball. The other, the characteristic tilt of the head: someone out of camera had been telling her to stay and, almost certainly, speaking of engrossing possibilities. Both pictures smacked of melty-eyed devotion.

I studied them. I tore them savagely across.

Four pieces. Eight. I hurled them at the ceiling. Let them lie where they had fallen: carpet, coffee table, shelves.

Then I whipped off my underpants . . . but after half a minute's frenzied abuse . . . well, anyway, who was I trying to punish?

I left them where they were. Along with the remains of Susie. Trailed back up to bed.

The house felt cold, unwelcoming. This was only the second time I'd slept in it alone. That other occasion, more than fifteen years ago: Junie giving birth to Ella. (When we had both been twenty-one! Dear God. The blessing of being twenty-one!) My grandmother hadn't as yet sold up or moved in with us.

Slept in it? I may have done, that first time. But now? Despite my father I had turned into a crybaby. (To spite my father I had turned into a crybaby?) At first I brushed away the tears but then permitted them to fall unimpeded.

Those tears weren't just for me. Partly I cried for Junie, who had picked up a telephone in a fault-free world and then had it torn away from her in an earthquake. Partly I cried for Ella and Matt, who—whether loud and cynical or chiefly silent—were now having to negotiate a quicksand which the best damned dad on record had unthinkingly led them to. Partly I cried for Moira, who had booked tickets for the Palladium and a table at the Ritz, given me the keys to her Morgan and travelled with me all the way to Samarkand and back. And partly for Susie, whom also I had failed—as badly as any living creature *could* be failed.

I even cried for my parents: for the cancer in the body and the cancer in the soul and for the legacy of weakness which had disguised itself as strength. And this time I really did cry for my father. I could imagine how he must have suffered—suffered not merely during those two days prior to his suicide but during all the long, anxious months when he must have known my mother was about to die.

But in the end, of course, it was mainly for myself I cried. Cried because I no longer seemed to understand so many of the things which had once appeared so simple. Because I'd started out with such an abundance of blessings and finished up with . . . What had I finished up with? And because I didn't know how I was going to restore stability and trust . . . when trust was virtually synonymous with respect.

Or how I was going to restore even the will to try. Even the will to carry on.

25

Early next day I walked to Jalna. All my adrenalin had drained away. Also, my stomach was troubling me . . . no great surprise. In truth—through the exercise of much precarious self-control—I'd even had to stop myself from entering the kitchen. That put the kibosh on a cup of tea.

The journey took an hour and twenty minutes. It wasn't right without a dog; without the feel of all that keen companionship at the end of a leash. I arrived there shortly after ten. I had chosen not to cycle, supposing a walk might better clarify my thoughts, expel my sluggishness, provide me with some plan of argument.

Give me more time.

In all but the last I'd been mistaken.

It was Pim who came to the door. I was grateful for that; intended to apologize for my appalling brusqueness on the phone. Indeed, I experienced an uncustomary rush of warm affection—a sort of fellow feeling perhaps, as though I had never been quite fair to him; had underrated, patronized him. Had neither understood his problems nor made any attempt to.

Suffering produces strange bedfellows.

I don't think he realized he was suffering. Or cared much whether I was.

"Oh," he said, after a pause. "It's you! We didn't think you'd have the nerve to show your face."

That rush of affection dried. Wasn't there some quotation about the weak feeling they had come into their own when they chanced on anybody weaker than themselves? "Wrong, then, weren't you? I want to see Junie," I announced.

In a way it wasn't a bad beginning.

"Junie's still in bed."

"And the children, please? I'd like to see my children."

"Gone to Folkestone. With April and Robert and some of the others. To help take their mind off matters."

"In this weather?"

"There are worse things than a bit of rain."

He was starting to win points: two to my one: we weren't even level pegging.

I brushed past him. I knew which bedroom she'd be in. We had several times stayed overnight.

On the staircase I met Junie's mother. Also known as Mrs Fletcher. She drew in close to the banister and looked the other way. But my back felt her watching me intently as—with a wholly spurious reassumption of authority and decisiveness—I pushed open the door to the blue room.

And found Ted and Yvonne in there, naked, making love.

Ted jerked his head round, justifiably startled. But minimized all our blushes with aplomb. "Junie's down the landing, Sam. They've put her in the pink room."

"Thank you," I mumbled. "Sorry."

My mother-in-law was still standing halfway down the stairs. Before she turned I thought I saw the traces of a smile.

"Bitch," I told her quietly. I don't suppose she heard.

I passed three other bedrooms on that floor. It struck me as ironic that Junie should now be in the pink. Blue was evidently more suited to a man and wife together.

She was sitting up in bed, with an untouched breakfast tray in front of her—or seemingly untouched.

"Hello," I said.

She appeared to be studying a pair of kipper fillets; her expression as wooden as the tray.

"How are you, Junie?"

"I didn't hear you knock."

"No," I answered humbly—and attempted a smile. "But you should have done. I just caught Ted and Yvonne making the most of the twins being taken off their hands."

Yet it didn't cause amusement. "And ye gods! Even *then* you don't learn!"

"But I forgot to wish them happy anniversary. Ought I to return?" I paused.

"Junie, I've come to take you home."

"Have you? What a pity! Such a waste of time! Because I'm not going home."

"But why? This is silly, darling. This is all so silly."

"Well, maybe it is. Maybe you should have thought of that before."

"I know I should. So what can I do to show you that I'm sorry?"

"Oh? Sorry? *Sorry*, are you?"

"You'll never know how much, Junie. Never. But actions speak louder than words. What can I do?"

"Suffer," she said.

I still couldn't believe it. Not quite. Naturally, over the period of the twenty-odd years during which we'd been boy- and girlfriend, as well as husband and wife, we had many times quarrelled; but Junie had always appeared so . . . well, temperate . . . and her anger had chiefly revealed itself through cool detachment. Any shouting or acrimony had come almost exclusively from me. She'd been sulky, hurt, bewildered. She had never been vindictive.

I'd been standing by the closed door. Now I took a few steps forward and slumped onto an upright chair with seat upholstered in pink velvet. The chair looked fragile but I didn't care. (I hadn't very far to fall.) The room being smallish I hadn't wanted to intimidate her by getting up too close.

I suppose there were other forms of intimidation. "Why did you phone John Caterham?" I said. "Were you spying on me?"

I really hadn't meant to add that last bit, or make either sentence sound accusing.

In any case she wasn't cowed.

"All this time," she said disdainfully. "And you still don't know me, do you?"

"No, I'm sorry, it didn't come out the way I meant it." As though there were actually some way it *might* have come out as merely pleasant conversation. "Why, then?"

"Just because we hadn't said goodbye." She gave a hollow laugh. "And, believe it or not, I felt unhappy about that."

"Yes, so did I. But then you phoned me at John Caterham's simply to say goodbye?"

"And to wish you luck."

She spoke those last few words as though she found them incredible. That didn't matter. At least she was talking.

At least we both were.

"And you didn't feel Mavis could be trusted to pass on your message?"

"When were we last apart?" she said. "To me it seemed important."

"To me, too. So why couldn't you have waited in the shop? You knew I wasn't likely to be long."

"I felt silly."

We were extraordinarily alike. I remembered thinking there might have been a strain of superstition in my wish to phone her at the house.

"I tried to phone you at the house," I said.

"I know you did. I rang 1471. Missed you by about an hour." For a moment we appeared—very nearly—to be back in harmony: discussing interests that we shared. "I'd wondered what you wanted. In fact, that was a big part of it, my deciding to phone you later. That was the instant when it first occurred to me. Otherwise I mightn't have thought of it."

Dear God. Dear God.

"You could have rung back Mavis."

Anyhow, all this was way beside the point. Although being way beside the point was undoubtedly the lesser of two evils.

"And, besides," she added, "after I'd mentioned it, it wasn't only me. Was it?"

"I don't follow."

"Matt hadn't said goodbye, either."

"Matt?"

"When he left for school. And then it was him who spurred me on. Wouldn't give me a moment's peace. Straight after supper—oh, for the umpteenth time!"

Her tone had gradually become more animated.

"I told him, 'They might still be eating, darling, I expect Daddy will only just have got there,' but he wouldn't have any of it. 'Oh, come on, Mum, you said eight, it's after eight, nobody's going to mind.' He wanted to tell you something about his latest project—wanted to tell you before he told me, because he said you'd appreciate the humour more and anyway he needed your advice. And he was standing right there by the telephone, all ready to grab it, when that woman answered . . . "

Matt—Mattie—my young Matthias. *Oh, thanks, Pop. You're a good bloke.* His kiss on the back of my neck.

"And I felt such a fool," she said. "She thought I had the wrong number, thought I must be talking about completely different Caterhams. Sounded as if she thought I were being all quaint and muddleheaded."

"So what happened?" I asked.

She stared at me.

"What happened? What do you think happened? I told her I wanted the John Caterham who used to live in Deal, in Kent—because naturally it hadn't got me very far mentioning *your* name—and then of course she had to go and get him. 'My goodness, if it isn't little Junie Fletcher!' he said. 'I mean, Groves! How *are* you? Don't tell me you're still living in sun-kissed Deal, the pair of you! And how's good old Sam?' But even then I couldn't take it in; I was so *slow*, so trusting; still believed there had to be some very simple explanation. Yet then I remembered how you'd forgotten to leave me the number— and you aren't the kind who normally forgets things like that—even though the Caterhams' address wasn't transferred into our last couple of address books. And I remembered how we'd only managed to get through because Matt had soft-soaped Directory Inquiries. And then, at practically the same moment, the question came back to me, 'But how *could* he have known the name of *Treasure Island*?' . . . And I couldn't talk and I was crying and Matt had to take the receiver and he just blurted out, 'Sorry, goodbye, yes sorry, wrong number!', and they must have thought I was so strange—and rude—and must've sat there talking about it all through the rest of the evening . . . "

Reliving it, she was crying again now, and I got up a little helplessly and started to put an arm about her shoulders. But she shook it off convulsively and I found myself taking a step backward in dismay.

"It was me," I said, "whom they'd have thought strange—and stupid—and . . . and quite beyond words!"

Indeed, I felt surprised they hadn't dialled 1471 and immediately phoned back to deliver such a message. I felt if they'd been nice they would certainly have done so. John had probably been nice enough before he'd moved away from Deal, but could fifteen years have altered him? Perhaps it was the influence of an uncongenial wife; not all wives were as compliant and considerate as Junie.

"Yet now," she said, "you have the nerve to tell me I was spying on you!" She wiped her eyes and blew her nose.

"I'm sorry about that, Junie, I really am. About that and about everything! It was the first time, I swear it to you—the very first time! I truly am sorry."

"Yes, of course you are! And shall I explain why? Because you got found out!"

"Then please explain this as well: how can I try to put things right?"

"By suffering!" she said again. But this time she went still further. "By suffering like you've made me suffer! And Matt. And Ella. By suffering till it really hurts!"

And she looked me straight in the face as she said it.

I sat down again. But couldn't she see already how much I was suffering? What did I have to do? I wanted to be contrite, yes, but not self-pitying. What woman could possibly look up to any man who felt self-pity? Kipling had done more than set before me an ideal, he had handed me a lifeline: an achievable solution to every problem fate could ever throw across my path. If I'd happened on that poem just one year earlier I might not have run away and cried, face downwards in the grass, in the park, on the afternoon my mother died.

I might not have got out on that windowsill and considered the pros and cons of suicide. Or thought I was considering them.

I still remembered how I used to test myself at school: deliberately ignore my homework to invite punishment; deliberately (once) knock my wicket with the bat; deliberately (once) muff a catch I knew I could have caught—a lost opportunity which had deprived us not only of a win, but also of a draw, and thus heaped opprobrium on my head in place of adulation. Only Hal Smart had known; and not even Hal Smart had fully understood. But there'd been scores of small ways in which I'd aimed to prove I had no breaking point, that adversity could always leave me smiling. Scores? No, hundreds. Maybe thousands. At rock bottom I knew I hadn't forsworn the practice after leaving.

And how could people scoff at Kipling? Even such a brief reminder as this had the power to make me feel less battered, to give me back at least the *idea* of feeling grateful—grateful for a chance to be tested. Yes, yes! Didn't he have it all so beautifully encapsulated? *You'll be a man, my son!* Yes, even such a brief reminder as this had the power to give me back at least the *idea* of tackling each new obstacle with courage, the power to state again that every step which carried me a little further from the abyss was in itself a small victory: one more swastika notched up below the cockpit. "So, sweetheart, when *will* you be coming home?"

"Certainly not today. And I'd rather, please, you didn't call me that. You've probably been calling her that."

"Tomorrow?"

"I've given you everything," she said. "All these years I have given you everything!"

"And you'd never hear me deny it for one second!"

"Everything and everything and everything! I haven't any more to give."

She was working herself up. Fresh sobs I could have coped with; even welcomed. Hysteria was something else.

"What more?" she said. "What more could you expect?"

"Nothing, darling. Absolutely nothing."

"Sex? Was that it? I gave you all the sex you ever wanted. Did I ever say I had a headache if it wasn't true?"

At the right time we might both have smiled at that.

"No. Never." Yet I couldn't resist adding, "Though you seldom seemed to enjoy it."

"And I suppose *she* does?"

I shrugged. But it appeared she was waiting for an answer. I had to mumble it. "That isn't the same."

"Why not? Because she isn't fat, like me? Because she isn't old, like me? Because she isn't thoroughly worn out by the end of a long day spent looking after a large house, squabbling teenagers, a difficult husband?"

"As a matter of fact," I said, "you're younger than she is. Over three years." Had I really been so difficult?

"Is it that woman who came into the shop, the one who's going to buy a house down here?"

I felt nearly as surprised as when Moira had guessed I was carrying a cake.

"How could you possibly know that?"

I saw the look of satisfaction.

"In any case," I said, "I don't suppose she's thinking about it any more—about buying a house down here."

"You mean . . . she's tired of you already?"

I hesitated. Then gave a nod. If ever anything had done so, *that* symbolized a small victory. Another notch below the cockpit.

"It didn't work out," I said. "That's how I came to be home early."

"So has she discovered yet you're not that good in bed? Can't she bring herself to tell you how magnificent and strong you are, even when you feed her all the proper lines?"

"What?"

"I said, can't she bring herself to—?"

I got up and made towards the door. I was already opening it when she began to state her terms.

"If I come back, there'll have to be a number of changes." Much emphasis on the 'if'.

I wasn't going to respond. I stood there in the doorway and looked out on the landing: cream paint, red carpet, polished balustrade—all of it immaculate.

But then I thought of Matt having to take the receiver out of his mother's hands and not knowing what to say; the two of them, not knowing what to say.

"What sort of changes?" Those words weren't just reluctant. They were sullen.

And it was surprising she had even heard me.

"No more talk," she said, "of spending your weekends away from home—or of disappearing up to London for a job. No more talk of any brilliant future on the stage . . . not unless it happens to be Matt's or Ella's! And no more strutting round the house like some big he-man having to support the poor weak admiring little woman who can't—I don't know—who can't . . . "

Perhaps she was struggling to find some exalted metaphor or at least some way of avoiding anticlimax. None of it sounded like Junie. Surely she couldn't actually have been *meaning* any of those things she'd said—with the exception of that confined-to-barracks bit, obviously? It all sounded *so* unlike her that you might have wondered whether she hadn't sections of a script sellotaped to her breakfast tray, worked on by her mother and maybe one or two of her sisters, discussed and polished all day yesterday: an anniversary entertainment, perfect for wet weather. (No, why leave out *any* of her sisters or, come to that, any of her sisters' husbands? I'd already had a taste of how Pim felt. Perhaps even Jake had had a hand in it? Was there anyone, anywhere, who at some level didn't relish the downfall of a hero? Indeed, you had to look no further than Miss Martin at the school.)

"I don't understand," I answered. "What should I have done? How could I have tried any harder than I did?"

"You haven't listened to one word I've said."

"But what *have* you said? And why didn't you tell me if things weren't . . . weren't exactly as you wanted them?"

There was a short silence. When she next spoke, her voice sounded gentler. Much gentler. Practically like Junie's.

"You know, this would be easier if you'd only turn round. How can

I talk to you like that? Why don't you just close the door and come and sit down again?"

I thought about it; then did as she suggested.

"Why didn't I tell you?" she repeated, reflectively. "Because we never communicated. We got out of the habit."

"And what does that mean?" That must have been—almost—the craziest thing I'd heard this morning. Up until about ten days ago I'd always told her everything (with one very recent and self-evident exception). I'd naturally assumed it was the same with her.

"And also because . . . because I thought you couldn't help being how you were. But that was stupid. If no one tries to make us face up to ourselves . . . well, how are we ever going to change? Besides—all of this—it didn't happen overnight. Believe me, Sam, it's been a very gradual process."

What had? All of what? I sometimes wished she *had* worked harder at the County High.

But there was no doubt about it: she was softening. And for the moment I wasn't so much interested in examining the past. Nothing further back than the shock she'd received on Friday night. That was what mattered. She'd been driven to retaliate. I could even under-stand—just—how she could have let herself get back at me through Susie.

Yet, all the same, I wished I could have been clearer as to where, over the years, I'd been at fault. Apparently—if I'd understood her cor-rectly—she had felt overprotected. How could *anyone* feel overpro-tected? Unless it were some child complaining about being sent to bed too early, or about not being allowed to climb trees or to walk along high walls—yes, something like that, all right, but otherwise . . . ? I wasn't possessive or anything; wasn't proprietorial; didn't place any check on her movements. It was a woman's role to be protected. It was a man's role to protect. God in heaven! What wouldn't I have given, on occasion, to have had a sympathetic protector?

To have had a father whom I could have hugged?

"I think you ought to go," she said. "I'm feeling tired."

Her? Tired? Lying there in the type of bed the princess got—minus the pea, of course—and being waited on, and cosseted, and told she had to rest; and no doubt having it endlessly brought home to her what a victim she was and how woefully underappreciated.

Whilst I . . . I hadn't even had a cup of tea.

"Very well." I stood up. "So when will you be coming home?"

"I don't know. I'll have to think."

I hovered for an instant. Ahead of me I had an hour's walk—no, over an hour's. Our car was in the drive. I wondered if I'd be allowed to take it.

"There's something else that perhaps you ought to consider." I found I couldn't ask about the car. "I know you always gave a lot but I did things for you as well."

She yawned. "Sam, no one has ever said any different!"

"Right." I turned towards the door. Turned back again. "Do you feel, then, that it may be tomorrow? Or is it more likely to be Wednesday? Or possibly Thursday?"

"I told you! I've not made up my mind."

"The children ought to be in school."

"And do you really suppose they can't reach school from here? No, when I've decided, I'll give you a call."

"I see. This week?"

She gave a shrug.

"Next week?" I really hadn't meant to carry it through. "Sometime? Never?"

She didn't say anything. Her face resettled into its mask of sullenness and obstinacy. God, how I knew—and hated—that look of placid enmity!

"Anyway, I hear that Ella and Matt are in Folkestone. Give them a hug from me? A warm and loving hug."

"I can't imagine they'll want it. By now they know just what it's worth."

"And tell them I'm sorry."

"Why? What good do you think that'll do?"

"And please—please—come home before Matt's birthday."

"Gracious," she said. "I really can't believe this! Are you deaf?"

"All right, then. One last thing. What was it he needed my advice on? What's it all about, this latest project of his?"

"I don't feel you've got the slightest right to know!" She relented—to a degree. "Besides. When I finally remembered to ask, he only said, 'Oh, forget it, Mum. It doesn't matter.'"

"Damn."

"And, by the way, another condition. Another thing you'd have to change. Don't make it so very obvious all the time that Matt's your favourite."

I meant to argue the point but found I didn't have the energy.

Yet still I hesitated—again, with my fingers on the doorknob. How could I leave it there, this whole sad, uncertain situation? I had to make one last desperate attempt.

And forced myself to visualize nothing but the kind and gentle, openhearted Junie, the lovingly considerate wife who . . . It was a stupid thing for my stupid mind to seize on but I still had that letter folded in the pocket of my jeans, the one she'd written to accompany the food. As I stood there by the door it made me think of notes being slyly passed from desk to desk; of my being chased along the High Street clutching her school hat, laughing, brushing against infuriated, sounding-off pedestrians, contriving to remain always a few steps ahead of her despite being winded by my laughter; made me think of our first, shy, inexperienced kiss behind some bookshelves in the public library.

"Oh, this is all so silly," I repeated. "This is all so silly. Can't you see? I love you, Junie Moon!"

My back was still towards her but I heard the quick catch in her breath and felt an instant surge of gratitude.

"Oh, for fuck's sake!" she cried. "When *are* you going to grow up? Why the fuck can't you just grow up?"

But even that wasn't all.

"And damn you! Damn you! Whatever happened to my cake?"

26

Then something unexpected occurred. Walking home, I knew I didn't want her back. I knew I'd never quite trust her again. Never feel fully sure that she respected me; that she was thinking well of me.

It was as sudden and as simple and as final as that. I didn't want her back.

I wanted Matt and Ella—yes, all right, I wanted Matt in particular—but apparently I didn't want even them (or him) enough.

I started packing: two expandable suitcases, filled principally with clothes. I had a bath and a shave; washed my hair and used conditioner. I wrote out a list of do's and don'ts and dates and monetary details—"I'll let you have my address as soon as I get one"—and left it on top of the piano, weighted down by a conch which one of the children had brought home from the beach. (Yes . . . Ella: "Can you hear the sea in it, Daddy? Hold it up to your ear—no, not to your *nose*, you silly!—and listen very carefully. Can you hear it now, Daddy?" My eyes filled. What was I going to do? How was I ever going to get by?) But I didn't eat anything, was almost afraid to. Decided that I'd buy a sandwich on the train.

It was strange: for the second time in twenty-four hours I

had to drop a doorkey through a letterbox. Twice in twenty-four hours . . . when I couldn't remember, over thirty-six years, so much as one other instance. But apart from this—and the fact of my being burdened with two large suitcases—I tried to behave as if my present departure was in no way different from any of my innumerable others.

I crossed to the gate without looking at the antirrhinums which I'd helped to plant. Closed it as carefully as if Susie had still been a creature to consider. Outside it, with a similar sense of purpose, picked up my cases again, turned right and walked briskly to the main road.

But on arriving at the corner—and realizing I would never mail another letter from the pillar box which stood there—I allowed myself, mistakenly, to glance back. I remembered the cheerful kindnesses of neighbours and the hospitality of friends.

I also remembered that I'd left yesterday's underpants on the carpet in the middle of the sitting room. This could almost have induced a wan smile. "Please give me something to remember you by . . . "

And I hadn't packed my diary.

Who cared?

Grow up, she'd said. My story wasn't that important.

Anyway, I supposed she could always send it on—*would* always send it on, if I asked her very nicely. Diplomatically. Remembered to enclose the postage. But I'd never told her I had bought it—or for what purpose. I had tended not to mention my wilder moments of extravagance.

When I got to the station, I found there wouldn't be a train till two-fifteen, nearly half an hour away, so partly for the sake of having something to do I went to draw some money from Cashpoint.

Suddenly, lingering by the bank, I had an image of Hal as a teenager . . . and briefly experienced an all but overwhelming pang of longing. Of longing and regret.

Plus, a strong desire for security, which was obviously tied in with it.

To get away from such a very unexpected form of torture—to escape it just as quickly as I could, allowing for those heavy cases—I then did what I hadn't intended. I went along to *Treasure Island* and stared for several minutes through its window.

And even before I reached it I was forcing myself to think about Mavis. Poor Mavis: on Saturday, how she must have floundered! Not being able to contact Junie, having to see to everything on her own, needing to go without her lunchtime break! I wondered if she'd yet begun to realize she had signed on with an ill-starred crew serving aboard a leaky vessel. Serving under a captain who—king rat—would be the first, not last, to leave his post. Hadn't there been any albatross discernible?

I resolved to ring her at ten the following morning to offer what I could in the way of apology and to share my hope of the right buyer soon being found—one who, no question, would want to keep her on. Was there even a slim chance *Junie* might decide to run the business?

From where I stood I could see Action Man watchful on his table. Turning away, I felt almost as if here was yet another friend I was deserting.

I bought a book for my journey from a souvenir shop on the front. Commiserated with the owner on his disappointing day. My commiserations were sincere. I knew what he'd be going through.

Without any such direct knowledge, I also empathized with the hero of the paperback I had chosen: a book still fitfully holding my attention when I arrived at Victoria . . . when I arrived at West Hampstead. Mangam's wife and children had been blown up by the Mafia and he himself was on the run—although all the time preparing for the tough and arduous fight that lay ahead. *His* loss, *his* problems, spasmodically made my own seem easier to bear.

His outlook affected me, as well. I was stirred by his integrity, his persistence, and even by the set of his shoulders and his clean-cut jaw—both depicted on the somewhat lurid cover. *Exterminating Jack Mangam.* His qualities were those endorsed by Kipling. Mangam reminded me I should never lose sight of the fact that you had to accept whatever life might dump on you. More difficult—whatever life might dump on those you loved. (Even though, in this case, that happened to be death.) But Mangam had a faith and was able to convince himself his wife and children were now better off.

And if that appeared glib . . . well, at least it helped him cope with his bereavement.

Mine, too, was a little like bereavement. I tried to convince myself that such bereavement would be good for all of us: for me, my wife, my children. In fact I honestly wasn't thinking so much about me. Junie and Ella and Matt, I hoped, would grow stronger because of their experience, more self-reliant, more aware of the hitherto unfelt realities. Matt would soon become a man.

Besides . . .

'The art of living,' I told myself; told both myself and Mangam. The art of living. All things work together for good, to them that see a positive side to their tribulations.

Clearly not doing so without humour, I prayed that Moira would see it in that light. I'd been wondering what I'd do if Moira wasn't there. But the Morgan was: parked in more or less its usual place: two boys wistfully examining it. I wanted to let slip I'd driven it myself and authoritatively answer any shyly awestruck questions they might choose to put. But I imagined Moira occasionally came to her window to carry out a spot check.

Before I rang the bell I carefully pushed my cases out of sight.

Certainly she seemed surprised; it was hard to know if she were pleased. For an instant I felt she might be, because there was perhaps the start of a smile and the flicker of something joyful in her eyes; but then the eyes grew dull and when I made to kiss her she hastily averted her face . . . which put me in mind of Junie roughly eight hours before.

"I thought you had returned to Deal," she said, without expression.

"Moira, I've got to explain things."

"Why? So far as I'm concerned, there's nothing to explain."

I answered: "No, you're wrong. There's everything."

She gave a sigh. "Look, Sammy, it was fun. In many ways it was fun. We had a good time. Let's leave it at that, shall we? I don't want any explanations. And I don't feel any resentment."

"But can't I even come in?" *Mayn't.*

"No. I don't think so. What point?"

"I've left my wife," I said. "We're getting a divorce."

For a moment she appeared to be studying the two boys who were studying her motorcar. They began reluctantly to move away.

"And what do you want me to say to that? How sorry I am? How surprised I am? What?"

"I want you to ask me up. I think you owe me that much—no matter what the flaws in my behaviour. There are things I have to tell you."

She sighed again.

"All right. I can give you half an hour. But I'm expecting somebody at seven."

"What sort of somebody?" I asked it sharply and without thinking.

"That isn't any of your business!"

"No, I know it's not. I'm sorry. I meant . . . is it a man?"

"Yes . . . since you ask." But then she unbent a little; it must have been my look of pain, or at least of disillusion. "A friend. Somebody I've known for years. Not what you're thinking."

I nodded. "Thank you, that's kind. I have two cases here. May I leave them just inside the door?"

She raised an eyebrow. "So what are your plans, precisely?"

I had known what they were, of course, had known *precisely*. But naturally I couldn't tell her, not here on the doorstep. Nor, indeed, anywhere. Not now. Not in the face of such a welcome.

I had my pride. Whatever else I didn't have . . . I had the remnants of my pride.

"I'm not too sure as yet."

She didn't comment. I followed her upstairs. We sat in the sitting room—quite decorously: she on the edge of a chair, I on a corner of the couch. She got up again when she offered me a drink but after she'd handed it to me, didn't—as I'd been hoping—come to join me on the sofa.

"Good luck," I said.

"All the best."

But there wasn't any meaning to it. I remembered how she had writhed against me by that window. We'd had thirty hours of complete happiness. But nearly one-and-a-half times as many had been endured since then.

"What time did you get back last night?" As had been the case much earlier I was trying to make conversation.

"Late afternoon. Five? Six? I don't know. Why?"

STEPHEN BENATAR

I didn't ask her where she'd gone; didn't want to hear of the outing I had missed.

"Thank you for sponging down my suit."

She shrugged.

"I'm dreadfully sorry about that. All of it."

"It happens," she said.

"Never to me. Never before to me. That's what makes it so humiliating. That's what makes me so ashamed."

"Then you'd better just chalk it up to experience, hadn't you?"

"But the timing of it!"

No response.

"And then the rug and the mess and all the rest of it. Tell me—just tell me—break it to me gently: had I flushed the loo?" (*Whatever else I had done, or had not done, during the whole course of the evening . . . during the whole course of my life . . .* I remembered my exact words.)

"Yes, of course." She answered me briskly.

Oh, thank you, I said. *Thank you.*

"But how in heaven's name did you get me onto the bed?"

"You weren't out cold. You managed to cooperate. Up to a point."

"You should have left me on the floor. Or, at any rate, here on this couch."

"I slept on the couch."

"Oh."

It was a peculiar kind of reminiscence; we could almost have been talking of the weather. (No. In the past we had talked far more vigorously about *that*. In the past? All of two days ago!) I suppose I had been hoping for a sense of camaraderie to arise, even out of the ashes of such details as formed the prelude to a hangover. I suppose I had been thinking of a phrase I'd remembered only that morning while walking back from Jalna. *I take this man in sickness and in health.*

"So what was it you felt you needed to explain?"

"Mainly that I love you—and that I want to marry you."

"No," she said. "Impossible."

I had expected difficulties. I'd anticipated the necessity for a whole new period of courtship and the gradual reworking of my cause; but

194

the coldness of that word, the finality which lay behind it, had essentially pulled out the rug from under me even as I groped for the carpet tacks.

"Listen, Moira. You can't say that. We had so much going for us; we *have* so much going for us. I know you liked me—I think you loved me. You told me I was the sweetest person . . . " I veered away from that one. "You even asked me if I wanted children; you spoke about our finding money for my university fees. We seemed to feel alike about absolutely everything. And apart from all of this we had the best sex imaginable. If any two bodies were ever made for each other . . . "

I was inspired by my own words, jumped up from the sofa, moved behind her chair and roughly cupped and squeezed her breasts. Furiously she tore my hands away.

"Don't you ever *dare* do that again!" she exclaimed. "Back off or else . . . "

"Yes? Or else?"

Stunned, I went on standing there. Abruptly she got up and crossed behind the sofa. It was like a game of chess: the king and queen divided by their two lines of upholstery; obstructed, sheltered. We glared at one another. "Or else what?" I repeated. Inherently bull-headed.

"Or else you'll get my knee in your balls! Hard and crippling and delivered with delight!" It should have sounded comic but it was a statement of fact which reached out far beyond comedy.

"Unless I do it with permission?"

"Which is something you are *never* going to get."

She added, after a pause—and a good deal more calmly—"Believe that, Sam! You must. It will make it so much easier for the pair of us."

"I feel completely miserable," I said.

"I'm sorry. I truly am. But . . . Well, you did bring it on yourself, you know."

"Is that supposed to make it any better? For two pins I'd jump out of that window."

"It will pass," she answered, wearily.

There followed yet another pause. "You can sit down again," I said. "I shan't try anything. May I freshen up my glass?"

We exchanged places: Moira on the sofa, myself on the chair.

"*Didn't* you like me, then? I mean—a lot? Wasn't I someone . . . very special to you?"

She ran a finger round the base of her sherry glass. "Yes. Everything you said just now was true. Entirely true. With the exception of one sentence. You said that we had so much going for us—which I, too, thought we had. But then at once you changed the tense . . . and that's where you went wrong."

"But I don't understand. Why? I'm a free man now; or very shortly shall be. Moira, I know that I deceived you but—"

"No buts."

"Darling, I did it only out of love. I love you. I love you with all my heart."

"I'm sorry," she said.

That, too, seemed utterly final. We both sat there in silence.

"Listen, Sam. I want to tell you something." This, after perhaps a minute. "Ten years ago I was married." (It was odd: I'd totally forgotten that.) "When I met Zach I was twenty-nine, maybe old enough to have known better, but I fell in love with him in a way I'd never thought possible—possible, or even desirable. And it *wasn't* desirable: no, it was totally unsettling: although he was younger than me, he was Mr Wonderful incarnate and I was Little Miss Fairly Ordinary, gooey-eyed and quite unsure of myself, with hardly a thought that didn't revolve around this man or an opinion that couldn't be changed by him; hardly an hour—especially if we were apart—when I wasn't worrying tormentedly over some silly little thing I'd either said or hadn't said. In brief, there was no one in the world like him; never had been; never could be." She smiled. "And I had always looked upon myself as something of a feminist. Still do, as it happens."

"What was he like?" I asked, without feeling a vast amount of interest—but again the important thing at the moment was to keep our dialogue from lapsing. Her expected visitor might have been merely a pretext but I didn't want her growing mindful of the time.

"Astonishingly like you," she said. "You could easily have been brothers. I suppose that's not surprising. Don't they say we keep on falling for the same type?"

So she *had* fallen for me. Well, she'd said as much already but her reiteration of it, even if unwitting, was of comfort. And this comfort was by no means snatched away by what she told me next.

"Like you," she said, "he was kind and demonstrative and witty. Basically good-humoured and usually fine company. Everybody liked him. Fairly intelligent, fairly well-educated, practical about the house. So with all that going for him—plus his physical attractiveness—I'm not surprised, even now, that I should have thought him Mr Wonderful."

I was growing rapidly more interested. And identifying with him, in a way. "What was he like in bed?"

"Not as good as you."

Oh, did you hear *that*, Junie? The atmosphere was changing; my whole mood was changing; everything she said—well, almost everything she said—reinforced the notion I hadn't really lost her; that if I could prove master of this situation my chances of salvation were turning into certainties. I shouldn't be able to move back in this evening, I realized that, nor would it be wise even to hint at it, but by the end of the month my address could very well be Solent Road and my future thoroughly assured. Hell, no, by the end of the month? By the end of the week! And as confidence returned, all trace of tiredness disappeared.

"Was that why things went sour? Was he a homosexual at heart?"

"Oh, no. God, no. At least, I don't think so. And our sex life was . . . well, fine; I mustn't give the wrong impression. And even if it hadn't been . . . " She gave another shrug. I felt a little disappointed.

"It wouldn't have mattered?"

"Not really. Good sex is lovely but so long as I'd known that he still loved me—no—I don't think it would have mattered all that much."

"So, then. What *did* go wrong?"

She hesitated. Her answer, when it came, was nearly toneless. But it produced a similar effect to that which you'd experience if you were standing under a warm shower and the water suddenly went cold.

"He was a liar," she said.

27

"You mean," I asked, "he didn't really love you?"

"Oh, I think he loved me—after his fashion. Probably as much as he was capable of loving anybody. But after we'd been married two years I was on the top of a bus and saw him standing in a doorway kissing someone. I confronted him as soon as he came home. He denied it—absolutely; said how could I behave this way, couldn't I simply take his word for it, and hadn't I been as happy with him, then, as he had been with me? And didn't I know there were probably hundreds of fair-haired young men wandering around London in a yellow jacket and green trousers? Oh, you should have heard him! It was only after I said I'd actually got off the bus and followed the pair of them that he finally owned up. But swore it meant nothing. He'd merely slipped during a moment of weakness—we all had moments of weakness—if not, indeed, why hadn't I had it out with him right there on the spot? In any case, it was me he loved. Oh, easy to say, I answered; although in fact I think I believed him. And *then* can you guess what he came up with? He declared he could furnish me with proof. In other words—while we'd been married he'd had four other equally brief affairs and the one thing he'd learned from each of them was just how special *I* was by comparison!"

Although I kept my face from showing it—and was certainly not proud of what I felt—I was actually enjoying the stupidity of Moira's husband.

"But you said he was intelligent," I remarked quietly, with a grave, condoling look.

"I said fairly intelligent. He had a degree in mathematics. Was a qualified optician. Some of the views he held were . . . a little unthought-out; but he wasn't an idiot. What he was, perhaps, was ingenuous."

I frowned slightly.

She said, "He really supposed I'd feel so flattered by the lessons he'd learned, and so reassured about the lack of meaning to this present little escapade, I'd simply overlook the fact that he had been unfaithful; five times unfaithful. He thought I'd be impressed by his honesty—and by his resolution to confess. I'd know him for a reformed character, one who'd never lie to me again. He fully believed I'd be willing, on account of all this, merely to murmur, 'There there, my darling, come back to Momma, do!'"

"Which of course you weren't?"

"Which of course I was." She smiled. She'd clearly derived pleasure from leading me on, from causing me to form an expectation which, sooner or later, she would utterly confound. That was good. I saw it as part of a pattern. *Impossible*, she had said. Impossible would turn out, in the end, to be distinctly—gloriously—possible.

I didn't begrudge her the desire to play.

"After all," she said, "you don't fall out of love in just one evening."

This was another piece of encouragement . . . whether or not consciously given.

"And it was also very feasible," I said, "that he was being perfectly sincere, your husband? I'm sure he could have meant to reform."

I wanted to demonstrate my sense of fairness, even though I recognized the gesture to be hollow. Profoundly hollow. Hadn't I been told the ending?

"You think so, Sam?" She pursed her lips and nodded. "Yes, at the time, that's what I myself thought. But since then I've never been quite sure."

It didn't cost me much to be magnanimous. I wasn't like some—

like my father-in-law, for instance—who believed in knifing some-body already dying.

"Moira, I feel certain he must have intended to reform. He was sim-ply weak, that's all. Why won't you give him the benefit of the doubt?"

"Well, perhaps you're right." She gave in gracefully and although I realized it wasn't what you might call a *major* victory I felt dispropor-tionately elated. I, too, was a shaper of opinions. Without even asking, I helped myself to a further shot of whisky.

"Nevertheless," she continued, "I know you'll understand how ter-ribly it shook me to find out, *only six weeks later*, that he was still lying? That he had yet another woman? Or maybe the same one; but by then it didn't seem to matter."

"But what I *can't* understand," I assured her, "nor ever will, is how he could just chuck away something so incredibly precious."

"Then join the club," she suggested bitterly. "Because once again you're perfectly right—it *was* precious, the way I felt about him; every-thing I thought we had between us; those two years of—apparently—almost perfect happiness. Good heavens, did we have some great times! Good heavens, did I love him! And good heavens—wouldn't I have done practically anything he asked!"

Believe it or not, I sat there feeling jealous. Feeling jealous of this man who had so totally fucked up; this man who had a *truly* self-destructive streak—my predecessor, who must now be passing the rest of his life in limbo. *And why did I do it, Lord, oh why in the name of hell did I ever do it?* That's what I knew he must be asking. The never-ending question.

Feeling jealous of a soul in torment.

So much for magnanimity.

"But all the same," she said, in a voice from which the bitterness had swiftly evaporated, "I suppose you can sympathize. In a way. He was a liar; a pathological liar. Lied about everything. Simply couldn't help himself. At least," she pulled a wry expression, "such was the view of the psychiatrist."

"He went to a psychiatrist?"

"No, I did." (Again! Complete reversal of an expectation!) "But a good deal later. After we'd split up. And after I'd spent most of my leisure time—and some of my working time as well—just sitting about like a zombie. I asked my doctor for some pills. He sent me on for counselling."

"Oh, God, how desperate you must have felt!" I yearned to sit beside her, take her hand, but didn't yet know if I should risk it. Instead, I tried to inject into my voice, my eyes, my body language, all the compassion of which I was capable. "What a nightmare! To be married to someone who couldn't help but lie, yet who went on remaining so altogether plausible! You can't ever have been sure of anything! I can't imagine how you coped!"

"Well, as I say . . . finally I didn't. I went to pieces."

"For how long?"

"Six months . . . About six months."

"But by then you were over him?"

"Over him? I suppose so. Though you can't go through a thing like that without its changing you. And, naturally, I don't mean for the better."

"Perhaps you ought to let others be the judge of that?"

Inevitably, this sentence set up echoes and I really wished I hadn't used it. She only shook her head, however, and offered no rejoinder.

But following another instant of quiet she did what I'd been hoping she wouldn't. She looked at her watch.

"Oh, gracious, Sam! It's time for you to leave!"

"Of course."

I made to get up, but then, as if seeming to notice there was still some Scotch in my tumbler, sat back to finish it.

"Yet you can't let one bad experience disillusion you forever." I suddenly remembered something. "Though it's little wonder," I added, "that you described yourself as cynical, that evening on the beach!"

"Yes—and little wonder I should now describe myself as justified!"

"What?"

"Oh, you fool! You *fool!*" It was as if the forcefulness of 'fool' had brought her flying to her feet; but it was also as if the action's abruptness had absorbed not augmented her vehemence. "Yet perhaps it wasn't your fault," she said, "any more than it was Zach's."

I was astounded. I was so astounded that for a moment I actually wondered if I had understood her properly.

"But I'm not . . . ! I am not Zach! I am not a pathological liar!"

I could only hope that my incredulity would work in my defence.

"It was the one time," I cried, "absolutely the one and only time! I swear it, Moira! You have to believe that!"

"Oh, you fool," she repeated; but in a tone far less impassioned, a tone almost loving—yes, things were even *now* going to work out. "I took to you immediately. For the first time in years I found myself aroused. Not simply by your looks, by something that went deeper, I tried to tell you in the car, some suggestion of values these days largely disappearing . . . ? Anyhow, after we'd all met on the beach and had decided to go for that drink—and you had charmed the barmaid into bringing Susie a bowl of watered beer, even a bag of crisps she wouldn't let us pay for—well, by then I was already . . . yes, already . . . For the first time since Zach!—and when I'd never believed that it could happen to me again! You were kind and old-fashioned and dependable. And fun. I kept Liz up for a couple of hours after we got home, talking almost exclusively about you. I hardly slept that night. I was so full of dreams."

"I hardly slept that night, either."

"It was history repeating itself. The same old maelstrom. The same old burgeoning belief that there was no other man on earth like the one I'd just met."

"And I had the same feeling—exactly the same! I had already fallen in love, too! In the shop. On the beach. I had to act so quickly. I hadn't time to think. What else could I have done?"

"You could have told us the truth, for heaven's sake! You could have told us the truth!" Vehemence again but equally short-lived. "Hinted that you were trapped in a bad marriage; that you and your wife were incompatible; brought out all the old clichés . . . which are clichés only because—so often—that's the way life is. You could have told us in the pub, or told me on the phone, given me the facts, allowed me to make up my own mind as to whether or not there could be any sort of future for us . . . "

"I was *going* to tell you in the pub. I really was. I'd decided about that right from the beginning. I was even going to tell you before we got to the pub."

"Is that right?" she said, totally unconvinced.

"God's honour! God's honour! I know that mayn't sound like very much since I'm not . . . " I stopped, awkwardly.

"Not what?" she asked.

"But I was so scared I'd lose you. Can't you understand that? And then after you'd phoned—you gave me such a glimpse of paradise, I couldn't jeopardize the whole weekend, I . . . But, truly, I was going to tell you before I left London, I was going to make a very full confession, I . . . " Another sharp halt. "But hell, Moira, I *did* tell you, didn't I? I *did* make a very full confession. That's what this is all about, isn't it?" My voice rose, vindicated and triumphant. "What better proof could you possibly ask for?"

"You were drunk," she said. "In vino veritas."

"But that doesn't make one *jot* of difference. All it did was hasten the process."

"Because you knew it could only be a question of time before I found you out."

It seemed to me she was shifting her ground. (My goddess was shifting her ground!)

"Exactly! How could I ever have hoped to keep anything so fundamental under wraps?"

"Maybe Zach had been your mentor?"

"Forget Zach! I am *not* Zach! I am nothing *like* Zach!"

"Besides . . . " In place of conceding my advantage she simply altered the direction of her serve. "I used to love *The Waltons*," she said. "This must have been my punishment. I fell for someone who was so good to his granny and whose granny was so good to him . . . "

"No, you didn't," I replied, angrily. "What on earth had you heard about my granny when you walked out of *Treasure Island* on that first morning?"

She merely repeated, "It's time for you to go." And she waited until I, too, was on my feet. "Incidentally, you had better take that cake with you. I couldn't give it to the dustmen and I don't think Oxfam would be interested."

Another last-ditch attempt. (I was clearly being pretty fair in my treatment of both wife and mistress.) "Then won't you even believe it was the happiest period of my life: those moments which I spent with you last Friday night and Saturday?"

"I don't suppose your wife would be precisely over the moon to hear that."

"No, listen. There's a difference. I was only nineteen when we married. I knew nothing about anything. Certainly not about love. I may have thought I did but . . . " Suddenly I went to her and took her by the shoulders. "I'm not sure how much of this is getting through."

"Not very much, I'm afraid. I feel sorry for you, Sam, but I don't imagine I could ever trust you again. I'm sorry if that's blunt."

She made an attempt to pull free but my fingers had strengthened their hold. "You have *got* to trust me!" I declared. "I feel desperate. Desperate! I don't know what I'm going to do."

Somehow she broke away. "Now, no more caveman stuff—you promised! I'll go and fetch the cake."

"I couldn't carry it. I've two cases to carry already."

At least she didn't press the point. "Where will you be heading?"

"God alone knows!" The bleakness of my tone may have been *slightly* exaggerated but not a lot. "It doesn't matter. Earl's Court? South Ken? Aren't those the two big names in Bedsitter Land?"

"Or else there's Kilburn," she said. "Which is a good deal closer, only down the road, similarly cheap and grotty . . . maybe even more so." She glanced at her watch again. "Although after seven in the evening . . . I think you may need to go into a hotel."

"No, I'll try Kilburn. Cheap and grotty fits in perfectly with how I feel."

"Are you being deliberately pathetic?"

"Pathetic? That's a bit of a far cry, isn't it, from strong, vulnerable, innocent?" *That* is what she had tried to tell me in the car. "But anyhow . . . "

I turned my head away. It was true that in the first place I had been making something of a bid for sympathy. But the dampness which filled my eyes just then was genuine and I didn't want her to see it.

"Oh, Sammy," she sighed. It was the last thing she should have done . . . I mean, depending on your point of view. Quite suddenly, I was shaking, so racked with sobs that at first I couldn't draw breath. She stepped forward and took me in her arms and perhaps for as long as a minute I cried myself out while holding onto her.

"Please take a chance on me. You've simply no idea how much I love you."

Then the doorbell rang.

28

She remained downstairs for several minutes. I could hear the sound of two voices, Moira's and a man's, but nothing at all of what was said. When she came back, she seemed relaxed.

"I didn't tell you earlier but that in fact was Zach. I still see him occasionally, either here or at a restaurant. I can't help feeling fond of him."

She added: "Come into the kitchen and I'll scramble you some eggs."

"Did he mind being sent away?"

"A little . . . but I couldn't believe this was the time for you to meet."

"May I go and wash my face?"

"Of course."

"I didn't mean to do that to you."

"I know."

"I always used to feel contempt for men who cried."

"You're just a sexist pig!" But she gave me the sort of smile I hadn't seen since Saturday.

While we were eating, she said: "What did you mean, Sam, when you told me swearing on God's name mightn't sound like very much, since you weren't—since you weren't what? A person who believed in God?"

I hesitated, looked down at the tablecloth. Fully recognized that my answer could be crucially important; practically a matter of life and death.

The supreme irony. I almost prayed again. This time for guidance.

I said: "I know I led you to believe that I was someone who had faith in God. I . . . Well, that was also . . . "

"What?"

I'd been about to say: "A lie—I think perhaps the last." I would have added: "Except, no, one further sin of omission: I never told you that I've had a vasectomy."

I'd had it all planned out. I'd meant to impress her with my honesty. (Like Zach? *He thought I'd be impressed by his honesty, by his resolution to confess.*) Had I remembered just in time?

Or was it something else that stopped me? A reluctance to admit to yet one more breach of trust; a reluctance to shed yet one more of those qualities which originally she'd found attractive?—it seemed that, as it was, there was so little of me left, so piteously little. Where had he gone to—that fellow, Samson Groves? (Ha! *Samson* Groves! So had he had a crew cut at the same time as his manicure? Was he now a skinhead?)

I looked up from the tablecloth. Nervously. "I don't know."

"You don't know? You don't know what?"

I almost said, *Anything.* "I don't know whether or not I believe."

"But why did you encourage me to think you did—and that you were so very *sure*? You already knew that I didn't believe."

I said: "Like everything else, it grew." (Or happened, rather; had there been the time for growth?) "I suppose I felt that you had certain hopes; and I couldn't bear to disappoint them. I suppose I thought if that was what you were looking for—certainties, encouragement for a belief—then that was what I'd try to give. Somehow. Perhaps in this way if no other I was even being a little selfless . . . " I shook my head, however. "No. Not selfless in any way at all. It was purely a means to an end. I wanted you so much."

"Wanted?" she said.

But it transpired that—unexpectedly coy—it was merely my tense which she was querying and suddenly I realized that it *was* going to work out. Oh, it was, it was! The inquisition was over. Against all the odds: I had come through.

"Wanted. Want. Shall want. For ever and ever and always, amen! All the gerunds and gerundives and participles thrown in. Oh, darling, I shall change, I shall change! I'm not basically a liar, never have been, but I'm still a lot of things I know I shouldn't be. Vain, selfish, sexist, stupid, greedy"—I saw Matt using his tablemat as a reporter's notepad—"arrogant at times, intolerant—lacking in compassion and imagination—mean, calculating, unstable . . . "

She put her hand up, swiftly, with a laugh.

"Whoa! Stop! This is *not* the way to sell yourself."

I wondered for a moment if indeed I had overstepped the mark. "But I do have a couple of fairly nice points, as well. And all I need, deep down, is the love of a good woman."

She dispelled these latest doubts . . . not by kissing me nor by the use of any reassuring phrase or endearment but simply by going to a cupboard and getting out the large iced cake with its haze of cottage garden colours. "I think that, for afters, we ought to have a slice of Granny's cake."

"Junie's cake." But then—again not sure whether I had said the right thing—I told her that Susie had been put down.

"Why?"

"Because Junie . . . " Then I paused and made a fresh start. "Because I suppose I should never have tried hanging on to her after the accident."

Loyalty had been another of my father's gods.

"Oh, Sammy, I am sorry. That must have been so . . . How did the children take it?"

I realized I hadn't thought very much about how the children had taken it.

"They were both pretty upset. Naturally."

Then I said: "But in a way Susie was more my dog than theirs."

"I can believe it."

I wondered for how long she would have to go through life assuring me she could believe it. I wondered for how long I would have to go through life asking myself whether or not she could believe it.

"How do they feel about your leaving home?"

"Badly." For the moment, though, I didn't want to think about that. Just those two syllables had been quite hard.

"But, tell me, isn't there any least chance of a reconciliation? I mean, if it weren't for me, if I hadn't happened to walk into your shop looking for a present last weekend . . . ?"

"No. None," I said. "None whatsoever."

"Not even for the sake of Matthew and Ella?"

"No."

"Tell me about Junie. Just a little." She smiled. "She's obviously a good cook."

This, I knew, was going to be difficult. I realized that someday I would need to loosen up but, for the time being, talk about Junie seemed better avoided. "Oh . . . we met and married and were much too young. We had no yardsticks and . . . and we didn't appreciate that people changed; or that one of us could change and not the other. There ought to be a law: no one can marry under twenty-five."

And I hoped that, for the present, this disposed of Junie. Yet when I thought of her being made to look foolish in front of a former schoolfriend—and, worse, in front of a former schoolfriend's wife—I had immediately to add: "But, yes, that's right. She is a good cook. And a good mother. A *very* good mother. And there've obviously been times when we've had a lot of fun. I'm not saying that she didn't try to make things work. I'm not saying that at all."

But, whilst owning up to this, I had to make myself think back ten hours. The steely set of her face. That mask of sullen enmity. I must really hold onto those. Anyway, I must hold onto them for tonight and tomorrow and probably the next few weeks. *So has she discovered yet you're not that good in bed?*

She had been hurt, of course. She had been very badly hurt.

Can't she bring herself to tell you how magnificent and strong you are, not even when you feed her all the proper lines?

I wished that at that moment we hadn't been sitting there eating her cake.

"The very last lie," I said, "or at least the very last omission. I've had a vasectomy. One gets no guarantee that these can be reversed."

She simply pulled a face. I wasn't sure if this chiefly expressed sympathy for me—or concern for herself—and I didn't like to ask.

It was after half-past-eight when we cleared away the supper things.

"Momentous question," I said. "Grave repercussions for the future. Do you mainly prefer to wash or dry?"

"No, I'll see to that. To tell you the truth I'm getting a little worried. That you mayn't be able to find a room, even in a hotel. I mean, of course, the smaller, cheaper sort of hotel."

My face wouldn't have done too well for the diplomatic corps.

"Sammy, I really need to have a chance to think! I'm not going to let you spend the night here."

Which wasn't (I supposed) wholly unreasonable.

"And anyway," she said, "Zach's coming back at nine."

"Will *he* be spending the night here?"

Oh, how to win friends and influence history . . . without even thinking about it!

"No, he will not! Certainly he won't! All we do is talk. He phones me when he's feeling down . . . and when I sent him away I couldn't say I wouldn't see him *at all* tonight. Especially since at the time of his phone call this afternoon . . . "

"What?"

"Well, it was *me* who needed cheering up. He did everything he could to help."

Oh, yes, and I could easily imagine how! No doubt by telling her she would very soon get over me and that I really wasn't worth feeling all depressed about. How much *detail* would she have given him?

"Then he obviously hasn't remarried?"

"No."

"But do you still fancy him?"

"Sam, I would advise you to leave it right there."

"After all, you said he looked a lot like me."

I wasn't being aggressive. I was being rational. Pulling at the skin through my open collar with a thoughtful, almost academic air. It would be interesting to hear the answer.

She wouldn't give me any answer.

"Then I've a good mind to stay and . . . "

"And *what*?"

"Tell Mr Zach-Whatever-His-Bloody-Name-Is exactly where he gets off!" I agree that didn't sound, perhaps, so entirely academic. Or rational.

"Oh God," she said.

"Because when he says he's feeling down how can you be sure that's really what he is feeling? How can you be sure he isn't feeling randy?"

"Oh, how can I be sure of anything?"

Mercifully, her exasperation was the very corrective I needed. I gave myself some hard knocks on the temple with the heel of one palm.

"I'm not normally like this. I swear I'm not. It's been a really tough couple of days."

She smiled, albeit thinly.

"Forgive me?"

She nodded.

"No. I want to hear you say it."

"Sammy, I forgive you."

I still looked deep into her eyes, searching for that absolution, that state of grace which I would so much need if I were going to have any real sleep that night, whether in bedsit or small hotel. Despite her gentle words—her tired but gentle words—I wasn't totally convinced that absolution had been conferred. Not unequivocally conferred.

What was conferred, beyond question, was painstaking advice on how to get to Kilburn.

"May I leave one of my suitcases?"

She had to consider this.

"Yes, you may. But when do you suppose you'll be wanting it?"

"Why? Does it matter?"

"Not really. It's just that . . . "

"What?"

"I'd rather we didn't see each other for a while. Let's say—a week."

"A week!"

"You see, I want to be as certain as I can be of the way I feel."

"Then . . . not until next Monday?"

STEPHEN BENATAR

"Don't sound like that! It really isn't so long! And you'll have plenty to be getting on with."

"Oh, yes? Like what?"

"Like finding your bearings. Making arrangements. Looking for work." She paused. "Like getting things sorted inside your own head."

"Thank you but I don't think I have to get things sorted out inside my own head. *I* know what's good for me. *I* know what I want. Unlike *some*," I added—but only in a mutter, as I went downstairs to fetch the suitcase which I wasn't going to take.

"Obviously, you've got all your wash things in the one you'll be keeping? Socks? Shirts? Underwear?"

"It sounds like the end of the school holidays. When I was about five."

"Well, don't forget to wash behind your ears!" She smiled. "Soap? Towel?"

I hadn't thought of bringing either. She supplied me with both.

"Pocket money?"

"Piss off."

She laughed.

"But I *will* take the cake," I decided. Guard against night starvation; give me succour through the long dark hours. Make bloody sure that bloody Zach—Zachary?—Zachariah?—what sort of poncy name was that: him in his yellow jacket and green corduroys!—that bloody Zach wasn't going to be comfortably tucking into it five minutes after I had finished, less comfortably, doing the same. Junie hadn't made that cake for any cheap philandering fantasist.

"Sensible," she said.

I wondered also about asking for the meat pie and the soup; partly for purposes of economy.

But for some reason I couldn't bring myself to do it. Neither cars in driveways nor meat pies in refrigerators. (Possibly.)

Moira left the cake in her own tin; added a couple of plates, a mug and some cutlery. A tea towel, Jiffy Cloth, screws of coffee, Coffee-Mate and sugar. A few tea bags. She tied the tin with the same hairy string which Junie had put around the box but neither the knot nor the loop was nearly as secure as the original. Inevitably this raised a point: how well was she going to make out, then, stationed at the entrance to a maze?

"You should've used that golden thread," I told her. "So long as you meant to keep a firm hold on it while it unravelled. I'm journeying this night into the darkest reaches of the heart of Kilburn."

"But you led me to infer," she commented, drily, "that you had in mind something a little more interesting around which to tie that."

I smiled. We were back in the Abbey Road. We were once more on track for happiness. Safely on track.

"I do believe you're teasing me, Pandora."

"Pandora again? I thought my name was Ariadne."

"Tonight I'm all at sea. Ariadne is the land girl, Pandora's the self-sacrificing angel who swims out to the ship. Two sides of the same coin. You're both beautiful. Both bringers of release and of salvation."

"Oh, good," she observed. "Almost the perfect setup you've got there. Almost—dare one say it?—a Captain's paradise."

But before I'd had much opportunity to react, either clumsily or with grace (and I'd always wanted life to imitate the movies), she went on, "Now, go and bring up your other case, so we can pack the mug and plates, etc. I don't want you and Zach first meeting on the stairs."

"Why not?" I wondered if she'd told him I was there. "Afraid he'll think he's seen his doppelganger and imagine only death can follow as a consequence?"

"Idiot!" As she said it she reached up and briefly kissed my lips. But twisted away the moment I tried to hold her with my free hand. "Sammy?"

I'd already started down the stairs.

"Just in case," she said, "you find yourself starting to slip into the doldrums and feel you must either talk to somebody or bust . . . Well, I'm usually here from around six and our embargo needn't stretch to the telephone."

"Right, then."

"And Sammy?"

"What?"

"Oh, nothing!"

"Go on. Say it."

"No, it isn't unpleasant. Could maybe sound a tad sentimental, that's all."

"Well, you know me! A sucker for sentiment."

"I was only going to mention that . . . however this turns out . . . whatever we decide . . . "

"Yes?"

"Well, that we're always going to remain good friends, aren't we? We're always going to have a bit of a thing for one another—right? That's all. I wanted to make sure you understood that."

Then she blew me a last kiss, withdrew into her flat, and quickly closed the door.

29

Despite the continuing drizzle, I stood on a corner out of sight of Moira's window and kept cave. Finally I saw him. His umbrella partly screened his face but there wasn't any doubt that it was him. He all but cannoned into me. "Sorry," he said. "Sorry," I said. Ships that pass in the night, exchanging a brief toot. Golden boys that pass in the rain, smiling an apology. Little trace of tarnishing. After a moment I saw him glance back. Something of sympathy flashed between us. Something containing a charge that was almost—!

Christ, no! Not true!

But the closer I got to Kilburn the greyer everything became. Scarcely to be wondered at: the time was now approaching ten. As I stood near the underground station and scanned the notices on a newsagent's board—to which some passers-by had drawn my attention—it occurred to me she hadn't said, Come back if you can't find anywhere; or Give me a ring to let me know you've got something.

It occurred to me she hadn't asked what was likely to happen to *Treasure Island*. Nor had she refloated—or, for all I knew, even remembered—that bolstering notion of my applying to university.

There was a private hotel advertised in Admiral Road. There was also a scrappy piece of paper offering in red crayon a single room, not large but clean, in a quiet house in the same street.

Any nationality. Thirty-five pounds a week. Three spelling mistakes in just four lines.

The woman who came to the door was small and wizened. Lumpy, too, because she had on several layers of clothing, including a jumper, cardigan and overcoat. The overcoat was only partially buttoned. There was a grey woollen scarf—long, like a student's—wrapped around her head and tied beneath her chin. She wore fingerless grey mittens.

But I didn't see those mittens, nor the broken nails nearby, until I'd told her why I was there, twice apologized for having come so late (this had been my day for apologizing to everyone for everything) and until she'd at last decided to remove the chain. A welcome contrast: the hall was pleasantly heated. Well-carpeted and furnished, too—although the light was pretty dim. The landlady was Polish. She'd lived in this country for seventeen years and said she had the toothache and had been just about to go to bed. Also that her husband lived in the basement; her own bedroom was the coldest room in the house; and the summer wasn't going to get here till July. Her English was as weird as her apparel but she was amiable enough. While I waited in the doorway of her fuggy, cluttered, cat-infested room she collected a key and a rent book and an After Eight, which she pulled out of its envelope and held hospitably towards my mouth, appearing like a slightly unconventional representation of Eve. I couldn't really fancy the offering but didn't have the heart to shake my head.

She led me slowly up three flights of stairs, breathing heavily and pausing on each landing. During our initial stop she asked about my home. *Home?* She hadn't heard of Deal but when I told her it was on the sea, and was the spot where Julius Caesar had first landed in Britain, she puzzlingly supposed it was also the place from which Sir Walter Raleigh had set off for El Dorado. I felt vaguely surprised she should have known the English appellations for either the man or the destination but she then informed me—and with an air of clearing up any mystification on this or any other topic—that she had a daughter married to a drunken docker in Limehouse.

On the next landing she pointed out the bathroom—with its enormous, maybe prehistoric geyser—and the separate lavatory, which, even from a distance, smelled as though the drunken docker might recently have used it to be a drunken docker in.

It brought back certain memories.

The vacant room was one of two on the top floor. My prospective neighbour was playing glee songs at a volume that belied the advertised kwiet (glee songs, I ask you!) and on this landing the yet dimmer bulb had no shade and the paintwork and carpet looked grubbily neglected. But certainly the room itself, after the old woman had fumbled with its heavy key, appeared relatively clean. Nor was it as small as I'd imagined, although the crude wallpaper, repeatedly emblazoned with three plucky galleons proudly conveying their master towards his glorious discovery of the New World, did nothing to open things up. It seemed instead to make a mockery of the gimcrack wardrobe, table, bed, chair—cooker, fridge, sink: a mockery of everything. But in fact the room was about the right size. A refuge. Sanctuary. The proper place to lick one's wounds.

I gave the woman forty pounds. Told her I'd collect the change tomorrow; also the rent book, which she'd been going to fill in then and there. But all I wanted was to close my door. Close my door upon the world. A world still irredeemably flat, despite the reminder—so frequently repeated—of my illustrious, pioneering roommate.

She showed me where the meters were and showed me the little trick required to light the gas fire. My bed was made up but she explained about the laundering of the sheets and pillowcases. Hoover and dustpan, she said, were kept in a cupboard in the hall—I must remember to look into it, explore, when I came down in the morning. I didn't mention I'd be staying for only one week: *The Passing of the Third Floor Back*: at last, you see, I get to play the title role.

But I didn't mention that, either.

The moment she'd gone I took off my raincoat—and discovered there weren't any hangers, nor any coat hook on the door. I was about to call after her; then found I couldn't face it. I removed my splattered shoes. Remembered I hadn't brought my shoetrees, nor even my shoe-cleaning materials, and felt the instant rush of tears.

Crybaby! Crybaby!

I set my suitcase on the bed; but as soon as I'd done so decided I couldn't face that either—the unpacking.

Oh, God! What was I meant to do? What *was* I meant to do?

No polish; no shoetrees; probably a score of other things I had forgotten. All equally essential. And I couldn't afford to replace them.

I was missing my wife and family. That's what it all came down to. Missing them like hell.

But I knew I couldn't go back. I knew this with a certainty that underlay the ache, the emptiness, the gnawing sense of loss: underlay my feeling of impending doom, my conviction that nothing would ever work for me again. Underlay and overlay and wrapped it all around.

I was going to be on my own. Forever.

Unloved. Uncherished.

Ill-equipped to deal with even the ordinary details of everyday existence. Afraid of them, almost. Crybabily afraid.

And it stuck like a sickness in my throat and a pressure on my stomach: the ever-present yet recurring knowledge that I had truly burned my boats.

Just bits of debris scattered on the water. With nothing useful I could salvage.

Nothing

I'd left the cake tin on the table. Listlessly I started to untie the string. Caught sight of my reflection in the window. Was distracted; even startled—for one split second imagined I had seen a stranger. Recalled my reference to a doppelganger.

Yet this man couldn't be that. Not sinister enough. As I moved towards him I had the laughable illusion he looked much nicer than I did. Somehow kinder, more compassionate. More trustworthy.

Wiser. More humorous.

More everything, in fact, that you would ever wish to be.

I saw him as the Ghost of Potential Unfulfilled. But not a frightening ghost—far friendlier than any who'd appeared to Scrooge. I didn't feel that he was there to judge me . . . rather, to welcome me, take me in his arms, encourage me to bond, show me how to proceed.

Therefore I remained by the window. It was now so dark I

NEW WORLD IN THE MORNING

wouldn't normally have seen much, apart from that welcoming newcomer. But someone on the ground floor had their light on: probably my landlady: her room was at the back and I retained an impression of its having tall windows and of the curtains being undrawn. Even so, I really couldn't make out much: merely a patch of scrubby grass with a birdbath at its centre . . . which instantly made me think of my grandmother's garden; made me think, as well, of the night I had climbed out on the windowsill that overlooked it.

This window, too, had sash cords.

This window, too, had a bottom half which proved intractable.

But, just as before, I finally managed—having moved the table well out of the way—to jerk down the top half. To jerk it down completely.

And, just as before, I was then able to straddle it.

At my grandmother's house there had been concrete where I would have fallen. It was the same here.

I was soon fully on the outside. For support I hooked my elbows over the double thickness of wood and glass. The sill creaked; but in spite of its deteriorating paintwork—and, no doubt, galloping dry rot—seemed firm enough to bear my weight.

Presently the light went off downstairs; the grass and birdbath disappeared. The forty watts from my own room scarcely supplied illumination. No moon; no stars. Now left with all but nothing.

Nothing.

I braced myself. Sought to reinforce my dissipating courage.

In just three seconds—five?—everything could be done with. Splat! Like being caught in the full force of an explosion. Nothing.

I really didn't mind.

Nothing?

And if I myself didn't mind—then who on earth should?

I thought about the landlady, my funny little Polish landlady, who had presumably just settled down to sleep.

I thought about the effect of a body falling right outside her room. The ground-shaking thud, or squelch; the shock it must produce; the mess and horror left behind.

Remembered she was suffering from the toothache.

Wondered if it were possible she might already—doped—be drifting off towards oblivion.

Then how could I do this to her?

Could I do this to her?

Yes. Yes, I could. I felt deeply sorry for her—her in the coldest room in the house, with a toothache, and a husband who lived in the basement—but, yes, yes, I *could*. Had to. I had passed the point of no return.

Besides, I thought. It's an ill wind . . . and every cloud has a . . . Once she had recovered from that initial trauma, that first horrendous impact, mightn't the self-destruction of a golden boy make the rest of her own life seem marginally more bearable?

The passing of the third-floor back.

Eponymous hero.

Which reminded me: I'd never got around to finishing that paperback. Damn. I'd have liked to, even though I naturally realized how it was going to end: justice would be done, reparation made, personal growth assured. On earth as it is in heaven. Amen.

Exterminating Jack Bradley. The title was a good one but misleading. I knew only too well that even without his hugely missed family a happy ending lay in store for that particular eponymous hero. Lucky guy.

But, no, I'd got it wrong, hadn't I? The book wasn't called *Exterminating Jack Bradley.* It was called *Exterminating Jack Mangam.* Mr Bradley had been the old man I'd met on that other train journey, the old man I'd meant someday to take Junie and the kids to visit, the one who was chiefly waiting, so he'd said, to see his wife again. Jack, I only hope you make it, I told him now . . . and as soon as possible, if that's really what you want. (And who amongst our fellow passengers would ever have thought that, of the two of us, I should be the first to go? Indeed, just three-and-a-bit days later!) Though not, Jack, as the result of being exterminated. As the result of something a whole lot gentler and more merciful. Please.

Please, God.

Then, believe it or not, I smiled. Poised on a ledge in rainy darkness, some forty or fifty feet above my own apparently less than gentle fate, I honestly did smile. Ascribe it to hysteria or insanity. Or to whatever you will.

"Exterminate! Exterminate!"

And for an instant I was back with my children and we were all watching reruns of *Dr Who*. Junie was there as well—in the TV room, I mean—but I was the one who was afterwards being chased throughout the house and having to clutch his chest or belly as theatrically as any well-intentioned corpse could manage . . . though finally being called on "to remain dead next time, darling, if you would. Supper's ready. Hands have to be washed!" All this, to promote the triumphant malevolence of a pair of ecstatically rule-breaking Daleks—amidst the lickings and excitement of a white-haired, tail-wagging, black-eyed pup.

"Exterminate the brute! Exterminate the brute!"

It seemed like yesterday.

Yesterday . . . I was a big man yesterday but Lord you ought to see me now.

Now I was a little boy lost.

A lost boy.

A lost boy without the prospect of an awfully big adventure? Well, we'd have to reserve judgment on that one, clearly. It wouldn't be long before we had the answer. Or before *I* did, at any rate.

But I wished I could have measured up to that man who'd been looking through the window. Was there any chance, when the judging began, he might agree to represent me?

Or would he have been subpoenaed by the prosecution? Their star witness? *Samuel Groves, if only you had looked ahead! This is the man you had it in you to become!*

There'd been a trial scene in that show two nights ago.

A Broadway musical, yes, but since the writers—or producers or angels or whatever—had chosen to name it as they had, you *would* have thought, wouldn't you, that there'd be at least *some* glancing reference?

And you would also have thought—wouldn't you?—that at nearly midnight my neighbour wouldn't have chosen to turn up the volume of his gleeful choristers? After all, tomorrow was another day (right, Scarlett?) and people had to rise and shine.

Now *there* was a coincidence.

For what had he decided in his wisdom ought to be my swan song?

" . . . Gentlemen songsters off on a spree,
Doomed from here to eternity!
Lord have mercy on such as we . . .
Baa, baa, baa!"

But surely there was too much relish in it—reaffirmation—vigour. Even freshness. It sounded more like a dawn chorus. Its style might have been better suited to a song from the sixties whose words I couldn't remember but whose title declared it rigorously opposed to any thought of doom, even doom in conjunction with a spree.

New World in the Morning.

That in turn reminded me of a novel I had read in childhood, one set on the eve of the American Civil War, by Robert Hardy Andrews. (Old Memorybags!) *Great Day in the Morning.*

Scarlett would have approved. *New World in the Morning! Great Day in the Morning!* Tomorrow was—oh, irrefutably—another day. Scarlett had been determined to make good and, whatever her failings, most people over the past sixty years or so had eventually come to admire her.

Were things any worse for me than they had been for her?

I was only thirty-six. Not all roads lead to Tara but all roads lead out of Kilburn. And I had conceivably half a century in which to explore a variety of them. I mean—if I decided not to jump.

And conceivably half a century in which to meet many of my fellow travellers. Potentially, there were thousands out there who could learn to love me, both for what I was and for what I might become; thousands whom I could learn to love back, equally.

Wasn't it even possible that, one of these days, Matt and Ella would forgive me . . . allow me to grow close again?

Also, I could get another dog. A stray who, like myself, would be looking only for a fresh start and who'd want to make the very best out of whatever came her way. Or his.

Yes, a fresh start, a new world, a great day . . . in the morning.

And besides, of course, there was something else I really ought to think about.

Would there be any sea in heaven?